THE CRIMSON PATCH

Other books by Phoebe Atwood Taylor available from
    Foul Play Press

The Cape Cod Mystery
The Mystery of the Cape Cod Tavern
Sandbar Sinister

THE
CRIMSON
PATCH

An Asey Mayo Mystery

PHOEBE ATWOOD TAYLOR

A FOUL PLAY PRESS BOOK
The Countryman Press
Woodstock, Vermont

FOR ALICE

ISBN 0-88150-064-X
This edition is published in 1986 by Foul Play Press,
    a division of The Countryman Press, Woodstock,
    Vermont 05091.
Printed in the United States of America at Capital City Press

CHAPTER ONE

MR. MYLES WITHERALL, strolling blandly down Summer Street on his way to the South Station, would have been considerably taken aback to be told that he would never reach it.

For one thing, he had only three blocks to go. For another, he had fully forty minutes in which to traverse them. And finally, it was a part of his plans to go there, and his plans rarely misfired. The day just spent in Boston was a happy tribute to his methodical mind. In something less than five hours he had replenished his summer wardrobe and bought for his niece Betsey Damon a birthday present, two cashmere sweaters she had long and audibly desired. He had lunched at the City Club with some of his elderly colleagues from Allingham's, where he had been office manager before his retirement. He'd viewed the new etchings at Blaine's, looked up a quotation at the Athenaeum, and called on a friend in the hospital. And he still had forty minutes in which to catch his train.

And then, on a corner, he saw the bus.

It was not so much the color, an uncommonly vivid purple, that caught his eye, as the sign perched on the radiator. Myles read it twice, and then stopped and allowed his mind to dwell on it.

"Cape Cod—75c."

It was, he noted, a clean little bus. The windows and the nickel plating shone, the paint was bright and polished, the tires were good. And the train fare, moreover, was an uncompromising, unvarying four dollars.

The young man in a smart blue uniform, who had

been gazing on him speculatively, began to edge nearer. This spruce old gent with the white moustache and pince nez was definitely class. Get him, and he'd draw a dozen like him.

"Going to the Cape, sir?" he touched his cap politely.

"I am. Er—you advertise an unusually low price. Is this a regular line? Er—authorized?"

Miles didn't like to appear either unappreciative or skeptical of the bus, neither did he want to let himself in for any bargain trip without some investigation. As a saving, three dollars and a quarter was small. But so was the pension of a retired office manager.

"It's my own bus." The young man spoke with a touch of pride. "I'm taking it down to Provincetown to see my girl for the week-end, and I thought to myself I might make gas money. I got three folks coming back at five. Glad to have you."

"Would you stop at Skaket?"

The young fellow consulted a map stuck above the windshield.

"Ought to pass through there around nine-thirty tonight. Probably an hour earlier, really, but I wouldn't want to get your hopes up. You could do an errand before we left, or sit in the bus."

Myles fumbled for his wallet. The young fellow was polite and competent appearing, and besides, the ingrained New England habit of thrift was getting the better of him. And there was something adventurous about a bus, too. Something that appealed to him. He remembered moving pictures and stories and books, all about bus travel. It was romantic and exciting and unexpected, like the Deadwood Stage. Things happened.

He passed over a dollar bill.

"Save it," the driver said, "till we get there. I—oh—get in and take a seat, won't you? Any seat."

He hurried across the sidewalk and disappeared up an alley, and Myles climbed into the bus.

A few minutes later another driver emerged from the alley and climbed in behind the wheel. He was older, nowhere near as ruddy and healthy looking as the other, and a badly fitting visored cap was his only formal effort toward a uniform. After placing a package carefully wrapped in brown paper in the baggage rack, he spoke to Myles.

"All set, brother?"

"Set? Oh, you mean—but where's the young man? The other driver?"

"My kid brother? He got a call. Got to take a tour for a line he subs on. Tough."

The glib answer satisfied Myles, inexperienced in the habits of bus drivers. Then he had another thought.

"But the others!" he said anxiously as the man turned the ignition switch. "The others! He said there were some others coming, too!"

"Pick 'em up on the next corner."

Myles started to protest, but his words were completely drowned out by the roar of the engine starting.

At the corner the driver hesitated briefly, called back something indistinguishable to Myles, and continued. He wove the purple bus in and out of the heavy Friday afternoon traffic as though he were proceeding along a super highway on a motorcycle. Myles clutched the seat ahead, far more uneasy about the lurching and jerking of the speeding vehicle than about its abrupt departure and sudden shift of drivers. He had never ridden on a bus before in all his life, but he had no idea it would be anything like that.

Not until Plymouth was reached an hour and a half later did the driver slow down or pay any attention to Myles, by then almost too exhausted from his jolting to care.

"Get out, brother. Ten minute stop."

Myles shook his head wearily.

"Thank you, I think I prefer to sit and rest."

He wanted very much to tell the man just exactly what he thought of him and his driving, and bus travel in general, but he refrained. Myles was a fair and reasonable man. In spite of a buzzing head and a throat sore from dust and exhaust fumes, he had to admit to himself that he was getting his seventy-five cents worth in distance covered.

"Better get some fresh air, brother."

"Thank you," Myles said firmly, "no."

It never for a moment occured to him that there might be some motive behind the man's suggestion. His niece Betsey Damon and her husband Steve often went into gales of laughter over what they called his naïve credulity, but what seemed to him only a polite acceptance of people and events.

"Thank you," he said again, since the driver was still looking at him, "I'll stay here."

He was almost asleep when the man returned and called back to him.

"Where was it you was going, brother?"

"Skaket."

"Let's see." He consulted the map above the windshield. "That's where the police barracks is, huh?"

"They're this side, I think, in Pochet."

The driver nodded, and the bus resumed its rapid lurching. After a few miles of dozing, Myles fell asleep. When he awoke in the gathering dusk, the bus was stopped and the driver was standing beside the hood, peering vaguely into the engine.

"Guess we're licked," he announced ruefully as Myles clambered out. "My brother, he knows this engine like he knows his own hand, but I got to have help. I'm going up to that house over there and phone a garage."

Myles looked in the direction in which he pointed. "Is that a house? I can't see with these glasses." He yawned. "Where are we? This—yes, of course. East Pochet."

"I don't know just where, but we're goin' to be here a good long time. That house's got a phone. See the wires?"

Myles couldn't, but he nodded. If the fellow saw them, they must be there.

"Well, I'm goin' there. Tell you what I'd do, brother. If you want to get to Skaket tonight, you better thumb."

"Thumb?" Myles repeated. "Better what?"

"Hitch hike. Thumb a ride. No tellin' when you'll get there if you wait for this to be fixed."

"Well—well, all right." Myles brought out his wallet, but the man waved it aside.

"That's okay, brother. You didn't get where you wanted to get. I'll start for the house, and you just hail cars till one picks you up. So long."

He made his way through the scrub oaks that lined the road in the general direction of the shack. Myles, tired and hungry and more than a little bewildered, stood uncertainly beside the bus. The moving pictures and the stories about this sort of travel, he thought unhappily, were partly right. It wasn't romantic, and it wasn't adventurous, but it was certainly unexpected.

He drew back against the fender as a car whizzed past. He could never bring himself to thumb a ride, even though that driver seemed to look on it as the most natural thing in the world. No one he knew ever thought of picking up strangers from the roadside; it stood to reason that he himself didn't care to be picked up by the sort of motorist who might. He would walk the eight miles to Skaket.

An open roadster that had just passed was backing slowly up to him. Myles flattened himself against the fender.

"I say!" It was a woman's voice that called out to him above the noise of a car radio. A Boston announcer whose dulcet tones Myles instantly recognized was talking rapidly about the brutal murder of a mechanic—

The radio was snapped off.

"I say," the woman called again. "Are you by any chance Betsey Damon's uncle?"

It was not the young, flippant voice which Myles had half fearfully expected. It was low, older, well-bred— and the 'a' was fully as broad as his own.

He stepped foward, peering through the dusk.

"I'm Myles Witherall." Yes, she was a lean-faced, undeniably middle-aged woman in tweeds. Pleasant, he thought, and reliable looking, like his cousin Kate in Newton Center.

"I thought you were. Stranded? Hop in. My name's Sage. I run the Sage Shop in Pochet, and I've met your niece. She bought some pewter from me."

"I—" Myles hesitated. "I—really, it's awfully good of you. I was going to walk. This has been a most amazing—"

"Walk? Nonsense. Come along."

"Wait—Betsey's present," Myles said. "I've got to get that from the rack."

Two minutes later they whizzed off in the roadster.

As its tail lights passed over the crest of a hill, the driver of the bus emerged from the bushes. Climbing in behind the wheel, he studied the map above the windshield, backed up some twenty yards, and swung off on an overgrown, rutted lane.

Within a quarter of a mile he found the pond that was little more than a pin point on the map. Leaving the engine running, he got out of the bus and walked to the water's edge. Experimental poking with a willow switch seemed to please him, for he whistled as he returned to the bus and removed the map and his brown-paper wrapped package. Then, slowly, he swung the bus till its front wheels were in the water, pointing towards the middle of the pond.

Fifteen minutes later, as he put on his shoes and socks, there was no trace whatsoever of the bus. He had taken a long chance on the name of that pond, but once again his luck held.

"Good old Bottomless Pond," he said to himself, picking up the bundle, and tucking the map into his pocket. "Good old Bottomless—"

He stopped short, fingering the package, and then with a savage cry, he tore off the brown paper wrapping. Then he started on a dead run for the main road.

The third car he hailed stopped for him.

"Goin' far?"

"Skaket." The former bus driver spoke through clenched teeth.

"Nice town," the other commented. "Kind of pretty, but not so up an' comin' as some of the others. Know folks there, do you?"

"Just one guy. Just one. Step on it, brother!"

CHAPTER TWO

MEANWHILE in the brief run from East Pochet to Pochet Center, Myles, after mentally pawing over pigeon holes, finally placed his benefactress as Miss Angelica Sage of the Marlborough Street Sages. Promptly he brought to light any number of mutual friends and acquaintances and at least three cousins in common.

"And I rather think," he went on, "that it was your maternal grandfather who owned the building next to my grandfather on India Street in the old days. I—"

"Doubtless," Miss Sage agreed. "Now, Mr. Witherall, that we've run through the preliminaries, will you tell me how in the name of common sense you happened to be clinging to the fender of that pirate bus?"

"Pirate?" Myles said blankly. "Pirate? Oh, was that the matter with it! How—do you mind telling me how you distinguish a pirate bus?"

Miss Sage explained patiently that she meant an independent bus. "Not one of a regular line."

"Oh, I see. I thought you referred to the trip. It was rather amazing, in a way." Myles was not accustomed to confiding his experiences to comparative strangers, but he found himself bursting to tell someone about that trip. "Amazing," he repeated, and gave her a brief resumé of the afternoon.

"Amazing?" Miss Sage looked at him. "I call it downright fishy! His brother's bus! Did he look at all like the first man?"

"Why, no. Not except in a general sort of way. But that's not unusual. Many times members of the same

12

family bear no marked resemblance to each other. My older brother—"

"Did the fellow make any attempt to get rid of you?" Miss Sage asked.

"Oh, no. No! Well, that is—he did suggest that I step out in Plymouth to get a breath of fresh air, but I was too tired."

"Hm." Miss Sage slowed the roadster down. "Don't you think, Mr. Witherall, that it might be a nice plan to call in at the police barracks and tell them about this bus and its driver?"

"The police? Oh, no!" Myles was distressed at the thought. "After all, I was a free passenger. It's not as though I paid any money for the trip. I've no call to complain. He didn't get money from me under false pretenses, or anything. Of course, the man *did* drive extraordinarily fast, but that's no reason for my calling the police now."

"No," Miss Sage said thoughtfully, "I suppose there isn't. At the same time, I think the whole thing is fishy. There's a nigger in the bus trip somewhere. I—d'you mind if I stop at my house a moment, or are you in a hurry to get home?"

Myles assured her that he was in no hurry at all.

"Betsey and Steve expect two house guests this evening, and I told them not to bother about my dinner, or me. I wonder, by the way, if you'd do me a favor? I bought Betsey two sweaters as a birthday surprise. Would you keep the package here till next week?"

"Glad to. I'll tuck it away up attic." She stopped the car in front of her diminutive, white Cape Cod house and picked the bundle up from the seat. "Snap on the radio while you're waiting. There's a lovely new murder in Boston that's monopolizing all the news flashes. I was listening to it just before I picked you up. Or maybe you don't like murders?"

"I often read detective stories," Myles admitted, "but I think I'll just sit. This has been rather an active day for me, after six months of inaction on the Cape."

A quarter of an hour passed before Miss Sage returned.

"I'm so infuriated," she announced matter-of-factly, "that I could scream. That Barr woman's gone and done it again. Old Mrs. Myrick just phoned. She was going to sell me some quilts and a Lowestoft platter of her grandmother's, and that Barr woman went and bullied her, and offered her three times what they were worth, and naturally, Barr got 'em! There ought to be a law about women like Mrs. Wadsworth Barr! I'm boiling. Look, Margaret's got dinner ready, and she's practically weeping about a soufflé. She says it'll spoil. If they're not waiting for you at the Cole place, why not eat with me? I unashamedly admit that Margaret is a magnificent cook."

Myles hesitated. He really should get along home before Betsey and Steve began worrying about him; on the other hand, he liked this brisk Miss Sage, and dinner with her would round out a day which on the whole had been very pleasant. He was fond of his niece and her husband, but the unrelieved company and conversation of a couple under twenty-seven was occasionally rather trying to a man of sixty. Miss Sage couldn't be, if his calculations were right, much over fifty, but—

"I'd be delighted to come," he said.

At the table, she brought up again the subject of Mrs. Barr.

"I simply can't believe you've not run into her. She's a Skaket mainstay. Runs the town."

"Betsey and Steve and I," Myles said, "we—well, oddly enough, we don't seem to have run into anyone. That's why these young people are coming. Betsey's lonesome. Of course Steve works at his typewriter most of the day, and now that the house has been renovated —at least as much as we can afford at the moment, Betsey hasn't much to do."

"I should think she'd want a rest, after all she's done," Miss Sage observed. "She bought some lovely stuff. I remember when she was here that she murmured something about the natives being unfriendly, but I thought it was just because you were newcomers. I told her to ignore it. People were rather standoffish to me last year when I started this shop, but they've rallied around lately."

"There's been no rallying around us," Myles said with a touch of bitterness unusual for him. "No one except prowlers and trespassers. Even the storekeepers seem loath to sell us things."

"Really? Why, that's incredible! I can't believe—are you sure the youngsters didn't say or do anything rash at first? Sometimes a small break will—"

"Steve's quiet and well-mannered, and Betsey never wears shorts to town, or smokes in public. Oh, we've gone over everything, but we can't figure it out. Perhaps it'll pass."

"I certainly hope so. At least you've the consolation of not knowing La Barr, even if you don't know anyone else. I can't get over that woman! All the money in the world, and her house full of museum pieces, and she's trying to ruin me because I wouldn't sell her a pair of earrings!"

"An unreasonable sounding—"

"Unreasonable? She hounded me night and day, even after I told her with the utmost firmness that the earrings were mine, not for sale, and family heirlooms. Finally I lost my temper." Miss Sage chuckled at the recollection. "I'm awfully afraid that nouveau riche was the least of the names I called her, and doubtless that precipitated all this mess. Why she should become so vindictive on being told the truth, I can't imagine. Look, I forgot—don't you want to phone home and tell them where you are?"

"I'd like to," Myles said, "but I can't. We have no phone. People wouldn't give permission for poles to be run across their property, either for electricity or telephone. Steve put in some sort of independent electric system, but we have no means of communication with the world. You know," Myles added, "it seems to me—why, yes! Barr *was* the name, now that I think of it. The one who refused permission for the poles."

"I'll wager it was," Miss Sage nodded with vigor. "I'll wager she was the one who refused to give you the road right of way, too. Betsey mentioned that, but I've forgotten the details."

"Our land runs to the main road, but the last mile is sheer swamp," Myles explained. "But we have therefore a legal outlet, and we have also a water outlet. We can't do much about it without going to court, and right now we're too poor to take any action. Until Steve finishes writing Rosalie Ray's autobiography—"

"Really? Rosalie, the radio star? Is he ghosting that for her?"

"He's trying to. It's to be called 'Rays of Sunshine, the Life of America's Favorite Radio Personality.' Steve says that handicaps him from the start. Anyway, until he finishes that, we've just got to row back and forth to town."

Miss Sage leaned back in her chair.

"Row, as in a boat? How awful! You really row wherever you want to go?"

"We have two skiffs," Myles explained. "One's waiting for me now on the town side of the inlet, and Steve probably has the landing marked with lanterns. It's quite simple. We're used to it."

Miss Sage shook her head.

"Maybe you think so, but if I had to swosh around in a rowboat every time I wanted a pound of butter, I should curse Mrs. Wadsworth Barr more than I do now. She is without doubt the world's most unpleasant woman."

"Steve would disagree with you," Myles told her. "He reserves that honor for Rosalie Ray. I don't blame him. His life is a violent succession of letters and telegrams. He lives in constant fear of her coming to Skaket. At a distance he can control his own temper, but if she provoked him in person with her outbursts, Steve would surely lose a job he badly needs. Really, with Rosalie, and the unfriendliness of the local people—"

"And the rowboat! Personally I'd be worn to a frazzle," Miss Sage said. "I simply cannot understand about the natives. Hasn't a single one of them been friendly?"

"One man. Lem Saddler."

"Oh, I know him. He's the one with the tame crow named Oliver. Dour souls, both of 'em, but Lem's honest. Why don't you ask him some time what the matter is? He'd know."

"I've thought about that several times," Myles said. "It's really not my business to ask, myself, but I intend to suggest it to Steve. I think Steve had best ask him—"

As a matter of fact, Steve was at that very moment doing just that very thing.

While Betsey was washing dinner dishes with Hilda Grove, who had made a scheduled arrival on the evening train, Steve wandered down to the landing to wait for Tom Fowler, who had characteristically not arrived at all, and for Myles, long overdue.

Sitting there in the darkness, Steve brooded over the town situation and the hostile attitude of the townspeople, which upset him far more than he cared to let Betsey and Myles suspect.

It wasn't just the dark looks and mutterings on Main Street. Those could be laughed off. But several times a day for the past week he had noticed people slinking around. Slinking was the word, too. They'd all melted out of sight when he'd called, leaving him only with the unpleasant feeling of being watched from a distance. Some of those he'd yelled at had been gripping cudgels, and at least one of them sported a rifle. And for the last four nights, he'd heard prowlers around the house.

He wondered how much Betsey knew, or suspected. Last night she'd gone from door to door and window to window, locking locks and hooking hooks and sticking in wedges here and there. She said she wanted to stop rattles, but as a rule Betsey never noticed noises. Myles, too, must have got the idea. In the drawer of his bedside table, where Steve had gone for a tube of salve that morning, was a revolver which Steve recognized as an old Smith and Wesson .44 Russian. His father had had one like it around the house when he was a boy. It was an elderly sort of weapon, but extremely business-like.

The underbrush crackled behind him. Twisting around, Steve saw the figure of a man outlined by the light from the house. It was Lem Saddler.

Steve whistled noiselessly and sat back to watch.

Lem, entirely unaware of his presence, stood there with folded arms, staring at the house.

He knew not only why the Damons were unpopular with a certain group in the town. He knew also that what little they had seen, or suspected seeing, was only the merest preface to what was to come. And he knew they wouldn't believe him if he told why. They couldn't do anything about it if they knew.

Lem looked at the Cole house. He had been born there fifty-two years before, though the Damons didn't know that. Old Josiah Cole, who had sold them the place last fall, was his uncle. But the Damons didn't know that either. He knew every crack and beam from attic to cellar, and he admitted to himself that the Damons had made a good job of fixing it over. The girl and the young fellow had worked like Trojans, and so had the uncle. They were all honest, decent seeming folks who paid cash for everything they bought. It was too bad.

"Well, Lem?"

Lem swung around and cleared his throat as Steve appeared beside him.

"Oh! Oh, evenin'— How do? Cooled off some since aft'noon, ain't it? Shouldn't wonder if we didn't have a real blow with maybe rain soon." Lem cleared his throat again nervously. "Sometimes," he went on, speaking with a briskness far removed from his usual drawl, "they say a calm, hot spell like we just had, p'ticularly in June—"

Steve let him run on about the weather for what seemed like hours to Lem.

"N'en the wind veers, an'—"

"Yes, indeed," Steve said, "I know. The weather's always good. Universal appeal. I often start stories with it. But let's get down to business. I'll make the bargain with you."

"The—the what?"

"Bargain." Steve's tone startled himself quite as much as it startled Lem. "I'm a hack writer. That's the sort of stuff you read, if you read. I also do ghosting. My wife's twenty-four, an orphan, and her hair's naturally blonde and wavy. She held one hundred and six jobs in the five years before we were married, which she considers a record. My father was rich, and died poor. I was brought up to know only the rudiments of work, as other people did it for me. I—"

"What you tellin' me all this for?" Lem asked.

"Because you've tried so damn hard to find out. Now Myles, he's the salt of the earth. He lost every cent he owned last year, except a pension, and he lives with us because we love him. He's still a hereditary Republican in spite of it all, and he still believes in rugged individualism and a high tariff, and he can prove it, which is more than I can do for practically anything I uphold. Now, Lem, there are the facts. Now you're going to tell me things. What's burning up the local boys? Why the prowlers? Why the nasty neighbors? Why fences? What's the idea?"

Lem bit his underlip.

"Come on, laddie. You've known from the first. Is it your work?"

"Me?" Lem asked blankly. "Me? Say, you got me all wrong!"

"Who's doing it, then? Why? Come clean."

Lem clamped his lips together stubbornly.

"Okay. If it keeps up, I'll call the cop, if this fag end of nowhere owns one."

"Bill Penny the constable, he's up in Fall River having appendicitis," Lem volunteered. "You couldn't get—"

"Listen, Lem, this is no time for local color. Any more bullets like I got greeted by today, and I leg it for the state cops. And you can do the explaining to them."

"Bullets? Honest? They ain't gone that far!"

Steve's eyes narrowed. If Lem's agitation were as sincere as it sounded, he was off on the wrong track.

"There's one, now!" Lem started through the underbrush, but Steve caught his arm.

"No, little one. You don't go yet—"

"It was a woman!" Lem said. "It wasn't one of them. It was—"

"Look, I didn't hear anyone, and I don't care if it was two dragons spitting fire. I want to—"

"Mr. Damon," Lem said, "you got to believe me. I do know in a way what's goin' on, an' believe me, I don't see what you can do about it. I think if you was to get the state cops it'd make matters worse. Usually I don't advise runnin' from trouble, but if I was you three, I'd cut an' run. I'd beat it from here fast as I could. Anywhere, so long's you get out, an' do it quick!"

"You seem to mean it," Steve said almost to himself.

"I do, an' I'm tellin' you honest. Look, I can't go into everythin', because you wouldn't take it serious. But your cops can't help this. You git. Before they's real trouble. An' if they started shootin', real trouble ain't far off."

"Go?" Steve laughed. "You know, I think the dawn's coming. Want us to go, huh? Sure, those bullets missed me awfully carefully. No one ever came into the house, no matter how they prowled. Lem, are you any relation to old Josiah Cole, or were you, before he died?"

"Well, I—"

"I get it. And the house might have been yours. Okay. Okay, Lemsey-wemsey. Next time I get shot at, I'm going to shoot back. Understand? Well, tell your pals."

"Mr. Damon, Josiah was my uncle, an' this place might of been mine, but honest, these goin's on ain't none of my business. I'll admit to comin' here to see what sort you was, but soon's I worked with you, I knew there was a mistake somewheres. Look, there's only one man I know might help, an' I'm goin' to fetch him if I can. Mr. Damon, you got to b'lieve me. If I don't get back tonight, say by midnight, you take your boat an' leave town. I'm tellin' you—hey, there's a boat comin' now."

"Myles," Steve said, "or that idiot Tom Fowler."

He threw the beam of his flashlight out over the inlet.

"Ain't neither," Lem squinted at the approaching dory. "That's my cousin Tim's boat. Woman in it. She's sayin' something. Listen! Boy, she's sayin' a lot!"

Steve listened to the string of epithets and snapped off the flash.

"My God!" he said limply. "My God!"

"Know who 'tis?"

"Know? It's the viper herself. Radio's little face-lifted bunch of personality. Rosalie Ray, the gleam of sunshine. Lem, dash up to the house and tell Betsey that the millennium's virtually here. Hey, Lem! Lem, come back here, you skunk! Don't you dash away! Lem! I need you as I never needed anyone! Where are you going?"

"If Rosalie Ray's comin' here," Lem said with finality, "that's the worst thing could of happened."

"What? Listen—come back here!"

"That's the last straw," Lem said. "That's the end."

"Lem, you blithering nut! Where are you going?"

"I'm goin' to get Asey Mayo. I seen his boat bein' put out, an' I think he's back home. Yessir, I'm goin' to get Asey Mayo. You're goin' to need him."

It came over Steve suddenly that Asey Mayo was an amateur detective whose specialty was murder.

CHAPTER THREE

THE RAIN that Lem half prophesied arrived just as Myles began his long pull home in the skiff.

By the time he finally drew alongside the landing, he was soaked to the skin, and the mixture of rain and bilge-water in the flat bottom of the tiny craft was sloshing above his ankles. He tied the boat up, blew out the flickering guide lanterns, and started slowly and laboriously up the path to the house. He felt that he really ought to run, but he was still panting from his exertions, and so wet that a few minutes more exposure to the elements would, he decided, make no difference.

As he neared the house, the sound of a woman's voice, high-pitched and angry, brought him to a halt. Instinctively he looked around in the inky blackness before he realized that the sound came from indoors. For the first time it occurred to him that an unusual number of lights were burning—four in the living room alone.

The woman yelled again, and Myles, rather in the manner of someone attempting to diagnose the author of a letter from the postmark, stood there in the pelting rain and tried to figure out who it could be. Not Betsey, certainly, for she rarely raised her voice. Her anger was of the quiet variety; in a white heat she became absolutely mute. Hilda Grove would be there, of course, but he doubted if Hilda was the type to fly into screaming rages. The only recollections he had of her from a previous meeting were endless cigarettes, pleasantly waving dark hair, and a voice that was very nearly a husky whisper.

Myles moved quietly over to the living room window, peered in, and then drew back.

In front of the fireplace stood Rosalie Ray. There was no mistaking her much publicized white hair and girlish figure. She looked no older than Betsey though she must be twice Betsey's age. Her trailing gown of scarlet left bare her arms and shoulders and most of her back, and Myles felt himself wondering for the hundredth time how women ever managed to keep such garments on.

He peeked in again. Steve, in his customary grey flannels and tweed coat, sat puffing at his pipe. Betsey and Hilda, both dressed in sweaters and skirts, were on the couch. He couldn't tell what Rosalie was saying, for she had lowered her voice, but disgust was written on every feature of Hilda's face. Steve and Betsey might have been wearing masks, so blankly immobile were their expressions. But Myles knew they were madder and more disgusted than Hilda. He could almost feel the ominous calm around Betsey.

With a motion so quick that Myles could hardly follow it, Rosalie reached up on the mantelpiece, grabbed a sheaf of manuscript and tossed it into the open fireplace. Instantly Steve, Betsey, and Hilda were on their knees by the hearth, pulling out the typewritten sheets. Rosalie, screaming at the top of her lungs, kicked at the three, beat them with her clenched fists, yanked at their hair, did everything she could think of in her frenzy to keep them from rescuing the pages.

Myles dashed around to the front door and into the room.

Without knowing exactly what he was doing, he seized Rosalie by the shoulders and shook her till her eyes blinked and her shrieking ceased.

"Vandal!" Myles said furiously. "Barbarian! You— you rude, unpleasant woman! You unmannered viper!"

With a final shake he pushed her unceremoniously into a chair. It was the first time in his life that he had ever laid hands on a woman in anger, and he found it a peculiarly satisfying experience.

"What d'you mean, trying to destroy that manuscript? It's not yours. It's Steve's until it's done! I should think you'd be thoroughly ashamed of yourself!"

Rosalie began to cry.

"Did you save it, Steve?" Myles asked.

"All but the first chapter, and I've got a carbon of it. Myles, you swell! You old marine, you! Where've you been? We were getting worried. We—you know, this has been a pretty drab evening!"

Myles sensed suddenly that the anxiety displayed by the three young people was occasioned by something or by someone other than Rosalie Ray.

"What—"

"You can dud—do what you want!" Rosalie sobbed. "Wuh—oh, you—you brute! You old brute!"

"She means you, Myles dear," Betsey said. "You're the old brute, you are. Darling, will you promise to spank her again if she forgets herself before we shovel her out in the morning?"

"Oh," Rosalie wailed, dabbling a wisp of lace handkerchief at her eyes, "oh, you may do what you want, Stephen! You may—"

"May, hell!" Steve said. "I'm going to write the foul thing for myself, in my own way. 'The Life and Times of Rosalie Ray, Extrovert and General Ear-ache.' Bets, we can buy a yacht. Sammy Birnbaum's syndicate'll eat it up."

"I'll kill you!" Rosalie stood up and faced him. "If you do that, I'll kill you! Do you hear me? I'll kill you!"

"Bang, bang, bang," Steve said cheerfully. "Three times old Damon bit the dust and chewed it reflectively. Okay, sunshine. Betsey'll write it. Posthumous works have a good sale. Sentimental touch. They know it's your last book. Or the last of yours they'll have to buy, if you want to consider that angle. Okay. So what?"

Rosalie stood by the fireplace, her arms limply by her

sides. The four faces that surveyed her were as uncompromisingly hostile as any she had ever seen in the old days on the stage. But it was worth making an effort.

"Wait," Steve said quietly, "don't ring in Figure 6B out of Delsarte. No entreating gestures. Just don't waste your time. After all, you're necessarily our guest, and I don't want to wax any ruder. Tomorrow I'll return such data as belongs to you, before you go. My wife will show you your room. Good night. Amazing as it sounds, I hope you sleep well. You need a good night's sleep."

Looking rather dazed, Rosalie followed Betsey out of the room. Steve threw himself into a chair and chewed at the stem of his pipe.

"I hope, Myles," he said, "that you like stew. Going to be a lot of stews and rice puddings around this joint for some time to come. Oh, the—you know, I don't suppose I've ever been so mad and so disappointed all at once, in all my life!"

"What brought it on?" Myles inquired.

Hilda, lighting one of her endless chain of cigarettes, grinned.

"She wanted him to omit a few frolicsome and vivid years of her youth, and say she was in a convent instead. Stevie said okay, it was her life. Then she thought it would be fun if she went to France during the war. Forking out doughnuts with a song, and pulling Papa Joffre's beard. And then she thought it would be too peachy if she got really involved—the gal who carried the message that saved the Battle of the Marne, or something. Lady carrier-pigeon idea. And Steve said—"

"I said, she could take all the liberties she wanted with her own life, but I absolutely drew the line at prostituting history. I—did you bed her down, Bets?"

Betsey nodded wearily as she sat down on the arm of Myles's chair.

"She looks a million with her makeup all blowsy

from crying. Uncle, have you been given the low-down—"

"The blankets!" Myles was suddenly contrite. "Oh, I forgot to bring home the laundry! And the blankets!"

"That's not the low-down I mean, darling. We forgot 'em, too. Rosalie's got a couple of quilts from the attic. The silk one on top, and the red patched basket number underneath, so she won't see the Cole's patch. Anyway, don't give the blankets a thought, Myles. The rest of us'll have to put rugs over us, or something. Did Steve tell you the worst? About Lem? Well, just lean back and listen, and you'll see why the Ray of sunshine's barely moved us, in one sense. Tell him, Steve."

Briefly, Steve summed up his conversation with Lem.

"And," he concluded miserably, "the old bird wasn't joking. He meant it. Myles, what'll we do? We've all heard things and seen things, and never said anything about it. Something's up. And we haven't any insurance. We couldn't even afford new window panes, if someone chose to break 'em. And pain in the neck that Rosalie is, suppose someone tossed a brick at her! After all, the wench's a national figure in the public eye even if she's a mote in ours!"

For several minutes the four of them sat there, listening to the sound of rain drops spattering disconsolately against the old house.

"The rain should stop any nonsense," Myles said in what he hoped was a reassuring tone. "Didn't Lem give you any hint of what to expect?"

"Not a hint, not a sniff. Damn it, I wish I knew what was what! If he'd only spoken up and said whether we were going to be burgled, or rushed, or—we could settle a burglar with my Colt and your gun."

"Yes," Myles agreed. "I used to shoot with the Bennett brothers in the old days. We could."

"But—you know, for two cents I'd row over and phone the police, but I can't think of any legitimate excuse for dragging them here." Steve sighed. "You can't say, please drop over for a fourth at bridge, we feel uneasy!"

"What'll we do?" Betsey asked. "We can't just sit here like bumps on logs!"

"Well," Steve said, "I've been pondering. We'll keep the lights on down here, and the four of us'll each have to take a side of the house and keep watch. We'll keep the stove going, and kettles of hot water on it. And I'll load a basket with bricks from the old chimney in the west attic. Then—"

"Why all that?" Hilda demanded.

"Oh, stones and boiling oil, like Robin Hood or Richard the Lion-hearted, or someone. Anyway, I've read about it, I'm sure."

"But why all this anyway, Steve?" Betsey asked. "What'd we ever do? What's wrong with us?"

"God knows. Maybe we dug up the Cole family graveyard, or painted the blinds the wrong shade. Oh, your guess is as good as mine! If Lem's lying, we're a pack of fools. But he wasn't. Oh," Steve shrugged, "it's utterly silly. It's foolish to go around as though we expected Indians. But we're phoneless and friendless, and we can't get help if we need it. If he hadn't mentioned Asey Mayo, I wouldn't give the business a thought. Know who Asey is, Myles?"

Myles nodded. He knew who Asey Mayo was, and he had read every word ever written in the newspapers about the Cape detective.

If Lem Saddler was acting honestly in summoning Asey, then the situation was serious and called for action, even though, as Steve said, such preparations as they could make were certainly silly. Just the same, there was something ghoulish in the idea of calling in a detective whose specialty was murder, before any murder had been committed. Even, Myles thought, if he were an amateur detective.

"Five of us in the house," Hilda said in her husky voice, "and someone says it's time to call in a detective. I don't like to say so, but shivers have been running up

and down my spine all evening. How we ever kept from
blurting everything out to Rosalie, I don't know. You
two have bragged so about settling down and becoming
honest citizens, with a house, and taxes—" she thought
of death and taxes, and went on hurriedly, "and all. See
what it gets you, children!"

Betsey sighed. "Well, let's go lock locks and do some
barricading and get things ready. I'll lose my mind if I sit
any longer. Myles—oh, man alive, you're soaked, and I
never even noticed! Go get yourself a rub-down and a
drink and change your clothes quick! You ought to be
exempt from all this, after a day in Boston, but you're
our stabilizing influence."

Myles looked down at his wet clothes and sodden
shoes; he didn't feel like a stabilizing influence, one bit.

"Perhaps—tell me, where's Tom Fowler? Didn't he
come?"

"Tom? Oh, he's probably stopped off to ask the se-
lectmen of the town if they ever thought of putting it on
a communistic basis. Or else he got some new enthusiasm before he left New York and decided not to come
at all. You can't ever tell about him. He's not a party
issue at this point, anyway. Myles, clamber up and
change, and we'll get going."

For the next half hour they wedged windows and
doors and made the downstairs portion of the house as
impregnable as they could. All the large kettles they
could find were filled with water and placed on the coal
range. Hilda pounced on a gallon jug of ammonia and
happily filled a Flit gun with it.

"My father," she explained proudly, "always used to
brag about his bicycling days, and I can't begin to tell
you how many raging dogs fled before his ammonia pistol. I think this is the best idea so far. You can pile up
all the bricks you choose, Stevie, but I think this is the
one really efficient weapon we have."

They tried hard to banter as they moved noiselessly
around, but their flippancy was more than a little
forced. Outside the wind had increased and was moan-

ing through the willows, and the rain lashed against the window panes. Even the elements, Betsey thought, were outdoing themselves in their effort to be unfriendly.

It was after one o'clock before they finally got settled upstairs; Myles was to watch the front of the house, Steve was stationed at the turn of the back hall, overlooking the rear ell, which they had decided was the most vulnerable spot. Hilda and Betsey had the sides to guard.

Sitting by his window, peering out at the puddle of light cast by the living room lamps, Myles felt more than a little foolish. It was the sort of performance that would be funny tomorrow, if nothing happened. It was the sort of performance that would be so hard to explain sensibly. To a person like Miss Angelica Sage, for example. She, he knew, would unhesitatingly have summoned the entire state police, although as Steve said, they had absolutely no reason for making any such move. And Lem had said that the police couldn't help, anyway.

Myles mulled over Lem's story again and again, and out of it there was only one incontrovertible fact which emerged: Lem's decision to call in Asey Mayo. It was like a criminal case that never seemed important till Darrow assumed the defense, or a European crisis which the papers termed a scare, until British cruisers were reported steaming to the spot. Nothing would have mattered if Lem hadn't brought in Asey Mayo.

The wind howled and the rain slatted. Myles began to count the drops as they trickled down his window, and then decided it was too much like counting sheep. He recited 'Thanatopsis' and the first three pages of the Iliad, and the Gettysburg address. Then, with a mighty mental effort, he translated the latter into Greek. But when he looked at the illuminated dial of his wrist watch, it was only two o'clock.

He thought of his strange trip down on the bus and how he had rehearsed the telling of it as he rowed across the inlet. Pity that he'd had no chance to tell it after all. Somehow with Rosalie's temper and Lem's dire prophecy, it didn't seem at all important.

Around four, Betsey slid into his room.

"It's the longest goddam night I ever knew," she whispered. "I think it's all a false alarm. I think that wretched Lem was at the bottom of everything, even if Steve felt he was telling the truth. I think he realized we'd caught on, and wanted to give us one bad night before he quit. I'm so tired I could drop in my tracks and sleep for days, and oh—Myles, what are we going to do, now that wench has messed up that book? We'll have to give her back the money she advanced, and we haven't got it, and—my God, listen!"

Someone was pounding on the front door.

Steve raced in.

"Get your gun, Myles, and—"

"Wait!" Betsey grabbed his arm. "Wait—someone's calling. Steve, it's Tom! Listen, he's singing 'Landlord got a room?'"

But Steve was in no mood to take chances. When she opened the front door a few minutes later, both he and Myles were beside her, each with a gun in hand. Hilda, in the background, gripped her Flit gun.

"Hi, Stevie, hi, Bets. Give a poor man a night's lodging—" the grin faded from Tom Fowler's face. "For the love of soup, what's up? Playing G-men and gangsters?"

"Come in!" Steve said with more relief in his voice than he knew. "And don't bellow so, guy. Rosalie Ray's sleeping off a mad, upstairs. Come in. You look like a drowned St. Bernard."

"I feel it." Tom stood on the hearth and shook the water from his clothes. "Steve, of all the god-forsaken places to get to, this takes the cake. Never in my life—"

"Wait," Steve said, "first of all, tell us if you saw anyone?"

Tom tossed his drenched suit coat on the bricks and looked pityingly at the quartet.

"See anyone? See anyone? My God, I went to six

houses in what you laughingly refer to as a village before I could even wake anyone up!"

"But you didn't see anyone around here? Good—say, how'd you get here?"

"Get? Look at those feet, boy! Look at what I used to call shoes! I walked, boy. Walked. I wallowed. I plowed through mire after mire. Flanders fields. Only I bet the poppies would have been water lilies. I encountered poison ivy. Also thorns." He kicked off his shoes and wiggled his toes experimentally, seeming surprised to find that they worked. "Laddie, the six hundred never saw anything like it en route to the jaws of death. I could write another 'Pilgrim's Progress.' "

"You're sure you didn't see anyone around?" Steve was impressed by the recital, but he had to be reassured on the prowler situation before he could become actively sympathetic.

"Look," Tom said, "let's get this straight. I don't seem to be making myself as crystal clear as usual. I didn't see a soul. Or is it a new kind of question game? I like tag, best. And say, d'you know a game called hot coffee?"

"We'll play it," Steve promised, "only first you run up, Betsey, and tell Rosalie it's just a guest. She's yowling. Tommy, how'd you land in town so late? How'd you know the way? How'd you get through the swamp in this weather?"

Tom sighed. "I wandered from door to door, banging lustily, until an honest burgher, he came daown to see what 'twas, he did. The old buzzard was very decent, though. Drew a map and lent me a flashlight. And I got here late, because the freight—"

"Tom," Hilda said, "you didn't ride a freight!"

"Should I pour money I haven't got into the laps of fat, bloated capitalists? The railroads—"

"Come along," Betsey said hastily as she returned, "and get your coffee. We'll all have some. We need it. Only don't go into the capitalistic system just now, Tommy. We've borne a lot already, today."

"You all look more washed out than I feel," Tom commented. "Was it Apaches you expected, or d'you always pack guns in this part of the country? Feud, maybe?"

Steve grinned. "We'll enlighten you later. It seems we were misled. Come dry out. We've got a nice fire in the stove, and lots of hot water—"

"You can wash in it," Betsey added with a giggle. "Tom, I never thought I'd be so glad to see you. You've given us a new slant on life. Honestly, you're sure you saw no one?"

"I refuse," Tom said firmly, "to go through all that again. Look, did I have a wire, or a message, or anything?"

"No. If you've a wire, we may find it in the postoffice next week. You know how it is with these newfangled things."

They trooped out into the kitchen.

It was incomprehensible, as they all admitted later, that no one thought to lock the front door after Tom came in. Even if they had left the kitchen door open, it was doubtful whether they would have heard the man who slid cautiously into the living room just about the time they were getting out bread and the toaster. They would never have known of his existence even then if Betsey, suddenly pushing open the swing door of the pantry that connected kitchen and dining room, had not bumped into him there in the darkness.

As she screamed, the lights went out.

"More games?" Tom inquired. "I know—"

"Keep quiet," Steve ordered calmly. "Okay, Bets? There, is that your hand I've got? All right. Now—"

"It was a man! He—"

"He's beat it out the front door. We're not going to chase him, either, and get into trouble. Myles, hold Bets's hand while I go lock the door."

He returned with a lighted candle from the living room mantel in his left hand.

"There. Who was he, Bets? Could you see?"

"I'd swung the door, and he—I couldn't tell who he was, Steve."

"Okay. Don't fret, Betsey. He won't come back unless he's a dope. It'll be light soon. Tomorrow I pant for the state cops. We've got reason to, now. At this point, go to bed—all of you. And for Pete's sakes, don't wake Rosalie again."

"Look," Tom said plaintively, "I'm just a child, but —what's it all about? What's going on? What's the Ray here for? Why—I mean, can I ask the questions for a change?"

"Rosalie came to blast the book," Steve said. "But before she blasted, we asked her to stay. She said she wanted to spend a few days on quaint old Cape Cod. She said she had an errand. Probably wanted to see a clam. Hilda'll tell you the rest. I'm going to take Bets up to bed."

After Betsey got to sleep, Steve stole downstairs again. His first task was to wrestle with the electric light system, of which he had only a vague repair knowledge. After puttering around fruitlessly with battery connections, he discovered that the motor was out of gas. He got it going, went upstairs and turned out the lights, and sat up in the living room the remainder of the night, though he denied it when Betsey appeared at eight the next morning.

"Just came down to start things, like the stove, and to take a peek at the lights. We ran too many too long, and ran out of juice. Sure I had some sleep. Didn't you see my bedclothes all rumpled?"

Betsey kissed the tip of his nose. "Yes, darling, but you've got on last night's shirt. Go shave. When d'you suppose the Queen of Sheba breakfasts? And what on? D'you dare me to give her herring and apple pie, like we had the first morning we stayed here last year, with Old Cole? Oh, Stevie, isn't she a pig! How'll we live? And what'll we do about last night, and Lem?"

"We'll get along somehow. And we're going to call the coppers about last night, that's what. Soon as Rosalie gets gone, I'll go for 'em. If I call 'em while she's here, the whole business'll be dramatized from coast to coast, with sound effects and a symphony orchestra. She ought to get her face on by noon. We'll row her over and then make for the law."

But when two o'clock came around and Rosalie had put in no appearance, Steve decided to take matters into his own hands.

"Damn it, I want to get over to the police! I don't care if members of the profession sleep around the clock! I'm going up and bang on her door and roust her out! I'm tired of tiptoeing around and whispering—what's she done for us that we should be so considerate?"

But no amount of knocking on Rosalie's door had any effect. Calling, first gently and then in what amounted to bellows, produced no results.

Steve's face began to grow white.

"Get Tom," he told Betsey. "We'll force the door."

It gave on the third lunge.

Betsey, looking over their shoulders, noticed that the best silk patchwork quilt had been tossed over the foot of the bed. The pink and blue basket quilt, with its crimson patch, was topmost.

Betsey stared at it, turned dazedly to Myles and Hilda behind her, and then stared again at the quilt.

"The patch," she said stupidly. "Steve—look! Old Josiah's red patch! It—Steve—it's spread!"

CHAPTER FOUR

STEVE walked across the room to the bed, and the others followed him slowly, rather as though they expected the floor to give way underneath their feet.

Suddenly all five started to speak at the same time, breaking the hideous silence, and then as suddenly they ceased when Myles stepped forward and placed his hand on Rosalie's forehead. Only Hilda Grove, noticing the drop of blood where he had bitten his lip, suspected what the effort must have cost his self control.

"She's dead." Myles turned and faced them. "I—I really don't know about such matters, but I think it would be best for us to lay the door in place, and leave, and call the police. I've always understood that one does nothing until they come."

"Police?" Betsey asked in a quavering voice. "Why— that is—how, I mean, can't you look to see if—if she died, or was killed? Of course she died. I mean, it couldn't be anything else. But—but shouldn't you make sure?"

Myles drew a long breath. What Betsey actually meant was for him to pull back the covers, since only Rosalie's forehead and her startling white hair were visible above the sheet, and to judge whether or not that crimson patch meant murder. There was no one of them, Myles thought, who didn't instinctively feel it was murder, but there was always the hope that it might not have been.

As his hand touched the quilt, a tiny platinum lipstick slid off on to the floor. Tom Fowler bent to pick it up, but Myles shook his head.

"I'd leave it there, if you don't mind."

He bent over the still figure on the bed, hiding it from the others. Slowly he replaced the covers and turned around. His face was as white as his moustache.

"I don't think there's any doubt but that we shall have to summon the police."

"But what—how—"

Myles had dreaded Betsey's halting question for a full minute. He couldn't just say, "She has been brutally and cruelly and horribly stabbed. She—"

"What did it?" Steve demanded.

"She has been stabbed." That at least was the truth. "Now," he took Betsey's arm, "now I think we'd better leave. Stephen, you and Tom take the boat and hurry over to town. I'll stay in the lower hall with the girls and see that nothing's disturbed. I should hesitate," he raised his voice as Steve ran down the stairs, "to make any comments of any nature to the townspeople. I— what's that?"

"Someone at the front door," Steve called up softly. "Angular middle-aged woman. Tweedy. She—"

"Oh, dear!" Betsey said. "Don't tell me our first caller has to come at—oh, let her in, Steve! I know her voice! It's that lamb of a Miss Sage from Pochet. Thank the Lord, she's just the sort who'll help us."

And the sort, Myles thought, who would probably know far better than he did just what should be done. In her soft blue tweeds and smart blue felt hat, she looked capable and buoyant, and, Myles decided with envy, as though she had undeniably enjoyed at least nine hours sleep the previous night.

"Hullo, Betsey Damon! I've been a long time getting here, but—how d'you do, Mr. Witherall? Did you survive yesterday's escapades without any ill effects?"

"You know Myles?" Betsey asked.

"Know him? I rescued him. I fed him. Haven't you heard of his adventures yesterday? You can't mean that he hasn't told you!"

"I'm afraid," Myles said apologetically, "that last

night, and today, and just now—er—I mean, yesterday has been driven from my mind."

"I can't see how anything would have driven that trip from anybody's mind," Miss Sage returned. "Anyway, I've heaps to tell you. I think I've discovered the reason for your unpopularity in town. I'm not sure, but it's on the order of what I guessed in the first place. Sit down —or let me sit down, and tell you all about it!"

Steve looked appealingly at Myles, who rose to the occasion.

"Er—much as we want to know, should you mind deferring your story for a few minutes? You see, really, I don't quite know how to break it gently, but we've just discovered that Rosalie Ray, who was our guest last night, has been killed."

Miss Sage leaned back against the doorway.

"And a strange man broke in," Betsey said, "and—"

"I begin to see," Angelica said drily, "why yesterday's trip was a drop in the bucket, Mr. Witherall. Perhaps I—"

"Don't you dare go!" Betsey said. "We need you. Oh —what'll we do? What'll happen?" She buried her head on Angelica's shoulder and sobbed.

"Send for Asey Mayo," Miss Sage said promptly, patting Betsey's head with her left hand, and pulling a pencil and pad from her pocketbook with her right. "I think he's home. Here's his number. Go call him and then the police. Steve—you are Steve, aren't you? Take my boat. It's really Jack Meredith's that I borrowed to get over here in. But take it and hustle."

She settled Betsey into an arm chair, furnished her with a handkerchief, and turned to speak to Myles.

"I think—oh, listen to that! Will you," she asked Tom, "run down to the landing and tell Steve to turn the switch before he attempts anything else?"

"Which switch?" Tom inquired. He wanted to be helpful, but he knew even less about boats than did Steve.

"Doesn't any one of you—no matter. I'll go."

The rest of them, including Betsey, followed her down to the landing, like chickens trailing a purposeful hen.

Angelica started the engine, gave Steve explicit directions about starting, stopping, and mooring, and pointed across the inlet.

"Put in at Hallett's. Don't go to the town landing. Don't let yourself get asked questions. Then—"

She snapped off the switch.

"What's the matter?" Steve asked. "What's wrong now?"

"I've occasionally doubted," Angelica observed, "the statement that the ways of God are full of providence. I now take it all back. D'you see that mahogany object careening toward here? That's Bill Porter's speed boat and no one ever uses it but Asey Mayo. That man's a demon with cars and boats. He's heading in here."

The roar of the motor ceased in mid channel, and the gleaming speed boat pointed for the landing.

Both Steve and Angelica, fearing that it was going to bump, knelt down with boat hooks to fend it off. But they needn't have taken the trouble, for the boat slid by the guard of old tires with fully an inch and a half to spare.

Steve caught the rope tossed him and made it fast, and then Asey Mayo slid out from behind the wheel and leapt up on the landing.

Myles, watching him eagerly, was amazed to find that the man actually resembled the pictures of him printed in the rotogravure sections. Tall, lean faced, blue eyed, he looked exactly as Myles had fondly imagined all Cape Codders would look, and as, to his intense disappointment, they had not.

He wore corduroys and a flannel shirt, which the papers always mentioned, but in place of the much publicized broad brimmed Stetson was a yachting cap set at a jaunty angle. Reporters never stated his age, and Myles found himself speculating. He had hopped up on the wharf with the ease and agility of a young man, but if he had been to sea in the days of sailing ships, as articles about him always said, then Asey must be as old as Myles himself. Myles frowned, not knowing that Asey's age was a topic on which his best friends battled year in and year out.

Asey removed his yachting cap and turned to Angelica.

"Aft'noon, Miss Sage. How's the antique bus'ness? Uh—which is Mr. Damon?"

Betsey poked her husband, and then as Steve seemed unable to say anything, spoke for him.

"This oaf here is Damon, Mr. Mayo. I—we—well, we're all sort of struck dumb and speechless and all, you see, because we were just setting out to get hold of you."

"You was? I'm kind of glad to hear it, because I was feelin' silly, bargin' in here. You see, I just got back from a trip, an' found a note pinned on my door from Lem Saddler, sayin' I was to come here quick's I could. He didn't give no p'ticulars, an' I didn't know how long the note'd been there, or if it was a joke, or what. But it had a urgent sound, so I come."

He waited expectantly, but no one offered any explanations. After several minutes of uncomfortable silence, Asey cleared his throat.

"P'raps you'd tell me what it was you wanted me for? That is, if you're quite sure you want me." He grinned.

"Want is a mild word," Steve said. "I'm trying to figure out the best way to tell you that Rosalie Ray's been murdered in our house and—Miss Sage, you tell him. I can't seem to sum it up—"

"I can," Betsey said before Angelica could open her mouth. "Steve pumped Lem to find out why the natives were being nasty, and Lem wouldn't tell, but said there was funny business, and then Rosalie came and flew into a rage, and before that Lem rushed off, saying she was the last straw and he was going for you, and we put water on, and got guns, and Tommy came, and a man broke in, and the—well," she wound up breathlessly, "she's dead. There! Oh, and we just found out, too."

"Perhaps," Angelica spoke quickly before Steve could launch his rebukes on Betsey, "perhaps you'd best come up to the house."

"I think," Asey agreed with masterly understatement, "that maybe perhaps I really better had."

On his way up the path he ran his eye professionally over the group. They were all at the lip-biting stage, even Miss Sage, with whose practical competence Asey had come into contact the previous summer. But they were doing their best to control themselves, and succeeding probably better than they knew, in spite of their incoherence.

He liked the old fellow with the moustache. Steve was a clean-cut kid like Bill Porter, and both girls were nice appearing. The other fellow seemed different from the rest, and from a look at his hands, Asey guessed with entire accuracy that he was a complete stranger to any sort of manual labor.

All of them were—Asey recalled a favorite phrase of his father's and smiled to himself. They were all "seemin'ly well brought up." And certainly they were in need of help.

His photographic eye went over the large front chamber where Rosalie lay, and as Myles had done, he lifted the covers briefly.

His involuntary whistle sent Betsey's spine tingling.

"Damon," he turned around. "You take my boat an' beat it up to the East Skaket wharf. You'll find a state cop up there at the four corners." He glanced at his watch. "If he ain't there, he will be soon, so wait for him. Don't pr'sent any d'tails to anyone but him. Tell him I said to call Cummings an' Gordon, an' have 'em come here. Tell him to hurry."

"Cummings and Gordon," Steve repeated obediently. "Uh—I'm afraid I don't know how to run your boat, though."

"Drives like a car. Fool proof. Hop along." He

touched the platinum lipstick on the floor with the toe of his rubber-soled shoe, and then bent over it for a second. "The rest of you can sort of catch me up with what's been goin' on. Say, anyone touched the door or anythin' in here since you forced your way in?"

"Nothing's been touched," Myles assured him. "Is anything wrong? I did knock that lipstick off the bed quite by accident, but that's all."

"Okay. Let's go downstairs."

It took fully half an hour to acquaint him with the details of what had taken place since Steve's talk with Lem the previous evening.

"There!" Betsey said. "You've got something from all of us. Is it clear? D'you understand everything?"

Asey smiled. "I get the action," he observed, "but I wouldn't say I grasped it."

"Don't tell me we've got to go through it all again!"

"Well, no," Asey said. "I b'gin to get some notion of the extent of it all, as ole Cap'n Barney Hanks said the time he fell overboard in Boston harbor. Been goin' to sea forty years, he had, but he'd never touched salt water before. But they's a lot of odds an' ends that c'nfuse me. Like what in time'd you ever do to get the town bunch down on you like Lem seemed to think?"

"That's just it," Betsey told him. "What? It's like what started the World War. I never saw such a town."

Asey nodded. Skaket was an odd little village, untouched by tourists. In his youth it had been a flourishing and important town, but when the packet lines and the fish business began to falter, the old Cape families had moved on to more promising places. He knew many wealthy and prosperous men who had started out in Skaket, but the people there now were a motley collection. There were only a few families of old Cape stock, and the rest were Portygees and half-breeds and intermediate good-for-nothings.

"Petered out," he summed it up.

"Maybe," Betsey replied, "but they seem to be able to present a united front against us, just the same."

Asey got up from his chair and paced up and down in front of the hearth.

"They talk a lot. Whatever's brewin' or brewed, they prob'ly gossiped themselves into it. I been away near six months from my home town of Wellfleet, so I'm as much in the dark as you folks. But I'll venture to say one thing, an' that's that even in Pochet no one'll know much more. Skaket keeps its dirty linen in its own back yards. I—say, I got an idea! It's sort of crazy—Mrs. Damon, I know your husband's a writer, but do you have a job? Or did you b'fore you was married?"

"I had one hundred and six," Betsey informed him, "in the five years after I left school and before I was married. Why?"

"You ever pose for pictures? You know, model?"

"I did more of that than anything else. Mostly photographic stuff for ads, but it was all very clothed and decent and respectable."

"R'member anythin' about a tobacco ad?"

Betsey shook her head. "I was never elegant enough to rate the cigarette ads, but Harry Llewellyn once used my head on a nude he was doing for Venus Cut Plug. Sort of a poor compromise with fame. I was simply furious."

Asey was grinning broadly as he turned to Miss Sage.

"I think—first, though, did you pick up any r'verberations about these kids?"

"I did, just this morning," she said. "That's why I came over here. It's been on the tip of my tongue to tell you for the last fifteen minutes, but the longer I thought about it, the sillier it seemed. And besides, I have a sneaking suspicion you've already figured it out."

They both laughed.

"See here," Betsey said, "if you know why we're in wrong, for heaven's sakes, don't keep us grinding our teeth about it any longer. Why?"

"You're a bunch of thus-an'-so nudists," Asey said promptly.

"We—us? Nudists? You mean us?"

"That's it," Asey said. "Y'see, I stopped off at the hospital to see Bill Penny on my way home. He's constable here, an' it ain't his fault the town's what it is. He's a good sort. He murmured somethin' about gettin' violent letters concernin' a bunch of models an' artists that was startin' a nudist camp here. Ever since I seen you, I been wonderin' where I seen your face b'fore. N'en I r'membered them square little tin plate ads of Venus Plug that my town was peppered with a couple years ago. Most of 'em's still here. And—"

"But you can't be serious!" Myles said. "After all, it was only Betsey's face. Though," he added sadly, "I don't suppose anyone would know. And we're not artists and models—" he stopped short. "My goodness, Betsey, do you remember my water colors? I did do some sketching when we first came, Mr. Mayo, but only so we could experiment in a small way and find out what color trimmings and blinds would look best. You couldn't call that being artists!" he concluded indignantly. "Could you?"

"Skaket could," Asey informed him. "Steve's a writer, an' says so. One sketch's enough to make you an artist. They recognize Betsey—least, her face, from the ads. Venus Plug is a sort of county favorite. Yup, it hitches up, crazy as it sounds. Rosalie Ray's comin' here would clinch it. She was an actress besides bein' on the radio. You got to r'member Skaket still b'lieves writers an' artists is kind of immoral. It ain't seen as much of 'em—that's what Lem must of been drivin' at. Say, where is Lem?"

Betsey shook her head. "I've forgotten him. He hasn't turned up today. Look, this nudist idea is too fantastic! It—but I suppose it would explain prowlers and catcalls. But not everything!"

"I've got the rest," Angelica said. "At least, I think I have, though it's my own idea entirely. Asey, did Bill Penny say who'd written those letters?"

"He did." Asey looked up over the mantel. "I'll give you three guesses, an' you'll need half a one."

"Hm. Betsey, how'd you happen to get this house from old Cole?"

Betsey explained. The summer before she and Steve had toured the Cape on bicycles, and had met Josiah.

"By the wayside, literally. He was a grand old duffer, and asked us to stay overnight with him. We fell in love with this place, and said so, and he asked us out of a clear sky if we wanted to buy it. We said sure, only we didn't have the money. He asked us how much we had, and we told him eighteen hundred, and he took us up. Just like that."

The only provision had been that Josiah was to live in his home till he died. In December Steve had received a letter saying that Captain Cole had not survived a heart attack, and in January, the Damons and Myles arrived.

"That's all. Except that Steve bullied Lem into admitting he was a relation of Cole's, and might have inherited the place if we hadn't come into the picture. Steve thought at first that all the goings on were inspired by Lem to make us leave and sell."

"Half that would work," Asey said. "Old Siah hated Lem for marrying a Portygee. But—"

"But the real point," Angelica interrupted, "was that he didn't want to sell this place to Mrs. Wadsworth Barr. That's one of the items I picked up this morning. Barr and her precious, pudgy son, Waddy, were hounding the life out of him. I'd say that since he was faced with one or the other of them coming into the possession of his family's house, he preferred to dispose of it himself to a young couple he liked, who seemed to like his house the way he did. But Lem's not a vindictive sort. He'd never move Skaket to violence. But dear Mrs. Wadsworth Barr—didn't she write Bill Penny about the nudists, Asey?"

Asey nodded.

"You know that war horse?" Angelica asked.

Asey nodded again. He knew Mrs. Barr and he knew

that she was not only vindictive, but enormously powerful and active in the affairs of Skaket.

"There you be," he said, turning to Myles and Betsey. "That's the story on that. Gossip said nudists, an' Mrs. Barr nourished the thought along, an' said it was a pity the fair name of Skaket should be d'sgraced by a lot of no good city slickers. An' she or Waddy prob'ly got some of the Main Street bums to leave off pr'tendin' to dig alphabetical ditches for the gov'ment long enough to come up here an' plague you. Hoped to drive you out. Siah Cole's dyin' an' your buyin' this house wouldn't keep her from still wantin' it an' intendin' to have it, if her mind was made up."

"But the shopkeepers," Myles said. "Could she influence them?"

"Was they nasty? Oh, yes, I r'member you said so. Sure. She informed 'em, most likely, that they lost her trade if they sold to you. An' r'member that Lucius Barr—where she got that Wadsworth business out of Lucius, I never could make out. Anyway, he left her a couple million. Poor Loosh," Asey said parenthetically, "he used to traipse around after her like a poodle tryin' to board the 'Queen Mary' at thirty knots. There's the story—what say?"

Myles glanced up at the fireplace mantel before replying.

"I really didn't say anything. I was thinking how amazing it was you should come here and settle this, with such apparent ease, after we'd brooded and brooded about it, and got nowhere."

"It'll be fun," Asey said, "to sort of put the damper on the local boys, now we guessed. D'you think the feller that slid in last night was a native?"

"No," Betsey was very definite on the point. "I did at first, but I've changed my mind. All the natives I've seen wore rubber-soled shoes. When this fellow left, he left like a cement mixer, cloppety-clop on the floors. Though he came in quietly enough."

"I see." Again Asey stared above the fireplace mantel. "I see."

"What," Angelica asked, "is the fascination that the fireplace mantel seems to hold for you and Mr. Witherall? Or is it the panel above? Both of you have kept staring at it so."

"Lookin' at Siah's whale lances. I mean lance. He was always proud of 'em. B'longed to his grandfather, ole Freeman Cole, the whaler."

"We got 'em from the woodshed," Betsey said, "and —why—there's only one there! Where—who took the other?"

"I wish for your sake," Asey said, "that I knew."

Betsey drew her breath sharply. She began to understand why Myles had turned away from the bed as he had, and why Asey had whistled, and why the crimson patch on the quilt had spread.

For the lance head was like a flat spoon, very sharp on the edges and on the point. After they had decided to use the implements for decoration, Lem had spent half a day out in the shed cleaning off the rust and polishing the shaft, and grinding the edges of the whetstone. She remembered Lem's explanation.

"They used to use these after the harpoons'd been driven in to the hitches—that means the whole length of the metal part. These lances'd be sharp as razors, an' have a six foot handle, not like the little thing you got stuck in the shank now. Anyway, they'd hurl these things in the whale while the harpoons was holdin' the critter, an' then pull 'em back by the line attached, till the whale was weak an' bleedin'. Then finally when they worked their boat long to the shoulder, they'd thrust the lance into the vitals an' churn it up an' down."

Betsey shivered. Churning that razor-like thing even in a whale wasn't very pretty to think of. She held no brief for Rosalie Ray, but no one, Betsey thought, was evil enough to die like that.

It was after four o'clock before Steve returned with two state policemen and a stocky man in civilian clothes whom Angelica recognized as Dr. Cummings. It was another hour before they came downstairs. Hamilton, one of the troopers, strode off to the speed boat at the landing.

"What's he going after in such a purposeful manner?" Hilda asked.

"He," Asey said, "is goin' to see if he can find out just what you folks got into here. He—"

"You haven't a clew? You don't know already who did it?"

"See this?" Asey pulled from his pocket the tiny lipstick that had fallen from the bed to the floor. "Hamilton's goin' after the man who owned this."

"Come off!" Steve said. "The town may call us nudists, but enough is enough! You mean the woman who owned it."

"I mean the man," Asey said.

"Wasn't it Rosalie's lipstick?" Tom asked. "For the love of soup, Asey, I assure you it isn't mine, and I know it's not Steve's or Myles's! We're the only men—look, you don't mean it belonged to Lem Saddler!"

Asey chuckled.

"Ain't Lem's, I can be sure of that. Y'see, this ain't no lipstick, though it looks like one an' it fooled me for a spell. It's a cig'rette lighter, an' it ain't Rosalie Ray's. See the nice initials?"

"W J R B—who's that?" Betsey demanded. "I'm sure I don't know any W J R B's!"

Angelica's eyes gleamed.

"Switch them, dear child, switch them. Don't you dally with crossword puzzles and things? It's W B J R, Mrs. Barr's boy Junior."

CHAPTER FIVE

"Now," ASEY said before the others had a chance to pour out their questions, "I want you, Steve. We'll go outdoors."

Under the willows in the front yard, he made brief introductions.

"Trooper Pratt an' Doc Cummin's, this is Steve Damon. Steve, they's a consid'rable number of things to be looked into an' taken care of. Goin' to be a lot of uproar an' upset."

"Tell me!" Steve said bitterly. "I suppose the Ray murder's already wafting its sordid way into the great American living room, not to speak of bars and gas stations. And the papers are probably dusting off the three foot type, like for war."

"Not yet," Asey said. "Hamilton's goin' to phone Lindsay, the police head, on his way to collect young Barr. We thought we'd ask Lindsay to keep it out of the news an' off the air till t'morrow, an' he mostly likely will. He's a good sort, an' b'sides, he's too worked up about Bat McCracken now to want more trouble to bust. He'll send men down. Say, they ain't got Bat yet, have they?" he asked the trooper.

"Lost him altogether. They think he's got out of Boston on a boat. Some guy, that Bat McCracken."

"He sounds like two Tommy guns popping," Steve commented. "Who is he? We haven't had a paper since last Sunday."

Asey chuckled. "It's one of them crazy things that turns up every now an' then. They pinched him in New York for swipin' and hockin' a kid's tricycle. He beat it

48

after killin' a cop. They followed him to Albany, by what you might call a trail of death an' destruction. He got a bank messenger there, an' held up an armored car. They thought they had him yest'day in the South Station. I was there with Lindsay—but that ain't the point. Point is, they's goin' to be an awful hue an' cry. When a sewer-digger kills his wife for burnin' the stew, no one cares. But—"

"But when America's favorite radio personality gets hers in the house of a writer on quaint old Cape Cod," Steve finished up, "that's news. You know, I don't want to appear callous, but I can't feel very sorry for her. I've been ghostwriting her life, and I can honestly say she was a rotter."

Dr. Cummings looked at him sharply. "Seen that wound? Well, rotter or not, let me tell you I'm still sick from the sight of it, and I've seen," he added professionally, "some corkers. Whale lances were made for the purpose of finishing whales, but—"

"Oh." Steve, like Betsey, remembered Lem's dissertation on lances. "My God!"

"Just so. That blade was like a razor, and she was killed instantly, but the rest of it was sheer insane rage. Hideous."

"I—I can't understand it," Steve said. "I was up, and I heard nothing. Didn't she—she must have waked up! She woke up when Tom came."

"At four, eh? Well, I doubt if she woke up later. She had taken some quack sleeping pills. Bottle was beside her on the table. I'm sure she never knew what hit her. When'd you hear this burglar, and when d'you last know for sure she was alive?"

"Betsey went up and told her the noise was just Tom coming. She was alive then. The burglar was fifteen or twenty minutes later. I couldn't say for sure."

"That's about right," the doctor said. "I'd say she was killed around five, more or less."

"Where was you, Steve?" Asey asked. "An' what about this stray gent who popped in? Your wife says he had boots on. Any footprints? Should have been, with the rain."

"I was down cellar getting the lights fixed," Steve said. "Got 'em going around five, I'd say. Then I went upstairs. I looked for prints, but I couldn't find any. Then I turned out all the lights that had been going when the current fizzled, and brooded out in the kitchen for the rest of the night. That gent—you know, Asey, I pored around last year and wrote an article on old-fashioned burglars. Seems they used to wear two pairs of thick socks and shoes a size too big. When they got in, they slipped off their shoes and padded around in stocking feet. I think that's what this gent did. Probably didn't have time to put 'em on when he beat it, and bumped 'em against the wall or something. I think he was just an old-fashioned burglar barging in."

"An' maybe," Asey said, "it was the Queen of the May. No, I don't doubt that was how he come an' went, Steve, but no career burglar of the old school'd ever barge in quite so clumsy, with you folks clearly on the lookout. Well, we'll delve into him later—got any wire? Barb wire?"

"Cole's old chicken wire is in the shed. Why?"

"You're goin' to get barricaded against the public. Pratt, roust out Tom an' Mr. Witherall an' lay out the wire like I said. Tell the women to make out a list of provisions—"

"Of what?" Steve asked.

"Food. You may not be leavin' for a while," Asey explained with ominous simplicity. "Doc, you can give the order when you run back."

"Run?" the doctor snorted. "You mean swim, don't you? My wife'll be furious. There's a baked bean supper on tonight, and I swore I'd go. I've been wondering how I—you know, I think I'll go see that woman again."

Asey grinned as the doctor walked back to the house.

"It's a cinch Mrs. Cummings eats her baked beans alone. He hates bein' dragged places. Steve, when you forced that door, did you notice anythin' funny about it or the handle?"

Steve closed his eyes and thought back. "Perfume," he said at last. "The handle smelled. Say—how about fingerprints?"

"That's just it. Some bright soul took some of her cold cream on a paper hankerchief, an' rubbed it over the lance shaft, an' the door handles, an' that lighter, an' then polished 'em up nice. Real neat an' careful, just like the nice p'rcise way he left the lance lyin' beside her in the bed. See the door key? We couldn't find it."

Steve shook his head. "I just assumed it was in the key hole. Asey, if someone cleaned up that lighter, then it was deliberately left behind, wasn't it?"

Asey shrugged.

"What about this Waddy Barr anyway?" Steve went on. "I grant that he and his mother might have tried petty, mean little things to provoke us, and scare us into leaving, but those bullets that grazed me; would they go in for that sort of thing? After all, there's the law and the police, even in Skaket."

Asey looked at him and smiled. That Mrs. Wadsworth Barr had lent the town of Skaket many thousand dollars over a period of years was common knowledge. When she cracked the whip, Skaket jumped.

"Miss Sage said that when she asked 'bout you today in Pochet, pretendin' she didn't know you, more'n one said, 'Oh, the nudists.' Nudists an' trombone players an' folks who drive Baby Austins are all sort of common game. You give the local boys a nice focal point to air their excess spirits around."

"But—"

"Wait. In any city or town, Steve, they's always a lawless bunch ready to spill over, an' nudists is a nice excuse. P'raps Mrs. Barr didn't tell 'em to go as far as they went. P'raps it was Waddy set 'em off. P'raps it was only a handful of people botherin' you. But r'member that once you give a bunch like that a start, it ain't no cinch to hold 'em back. I think that's what Lem was gettin' at. He realized if they started shootin', they wouldn't stop just b'cause you strolled out an' told 'em to. They wouldn't stop till they shot someone or hurt someone. If you'd called the p'lice, they'd of just b'gun again after the cops left, feelin' thwarted like."

Steve sighed.

"I suppose you're right, but it doesn't connect with Rosalie. What's Skaket got against her? Did the burglar kill her? Who was he? Where's Lem? Does anything connect at all in your mind? Everything's so muddled and mixed up!"

Asey admitted to a mental haze. "Closely resemblin' an encirclin' gloom. An' they's a delicate point here. But it seems to me, Steve, if anyone felt like killin' her last night, you was it."

"Don't spare my feelings," Steve said. "We're it, all right. Capital I-T. She left us with forty dollars cash and no prospects. That leads me to something else. Offhand I'm sort of vague about police methods. But if I were a copper, I'd arrest either me—well, I'd arrest me for this. I've got a motive, and hell, I was the one who ordered the lances sharpened. I was prowling around the house last night. I haven't any alibi. I can't prove what I did after Betsey went to bed, and I came downstairs again. Anyway, I'd like to hire you to help us, only I'm broke. You—well, you wouldn't consider taking this on in behalf of the Damons, would you? Like for a dollar down and a dollar a week?"

His tone was flippant enough, but Asey could feel the compelling tenseness behind it.

Asey leaned back in the wicker chair and stared at the young fellow. He was probably twenty-five or so, and he didn't look more than twenty till you noticed the smell network of lines on his forehead, and surveyed carefully the line of his jaw.

"Sorry I asked," Steve said uncomfortably. "Of course—"

"Your father was Humphrey Damon, wasn't he? I thought as much. Used to be a friend of old Cap'n

Porter. Went with him to Bermuda once on Porter's boat."

"You're not—but of course you are! I never connected Asey Mayo the detective with dad's Asey the cook-sailor-mechanic-navigator! Why, you drove the first Porter car, didn't you? The one that blew up? Why, then you're—"

He started to say rich, but broke off in time. No wonder the man brushed aside his feeble offer of money. Asey owned enough Porter stock to sink a ship, and people still bought Porters.

"That's me," Asey said, "but let's get this settled. I knew your father, so I'm a fam'ly friend. If I can help, I'll be glad to. Fam'ly friends can't go on the installment plan. Ain't proper. But Betsey didn't mention the lance, did she?"

Steve fell headlong into the trap.

"No, she just said she'd like to murder her, and— damn it, Asey! But I'd have blurted it out soon anyway. She didn't do it, Asey, you know that as well as I do. But if we have to tell the truth about everything—well, there we'll be. I'm worse off. You know, we weren't normal last night, any of us, with Rosalie going dramatic on us, right after Lem's little chat. And the more preparations we made for what we didn't know was coming, the worse it seemed to get."

"Did the Grove girl or Tom know Rosalie?"

"Hilda didn't, except from what we've said, until Rosalie barged in. Tom knows her. He knows everyone. No matter how often headlines or headliners change, Tom knows 'em all."

Asey wanted to know what Tom and Hilda did for a living.

"Tom—well, I used to think he was wonderful when we were at school. He's still amusing if you're not tired. He just babbles. He interior decorates one week and house parties the next, and lives like a lord when he gets his allowance—his father was smart enough to stick his money in a trust fund. When he's broke, he bums around. Hilda's like all girls her age. Wandered from job to job if they could get 'em. Right now she's secretary to a woman who's the head of a peace foundation."

"Havin' a vacation, huh?"

Steve chuckled. "On leave with pay. The woman got three months for assault and battery on a former husband. It puts me in mind of Ford's Peace Ship. I think it's a nifty—what—d'you see something?"

Asey had risen to his feet and was peering off into the woods behind the house.

"Expectin' any comp'ny?"

"God no, haven't we trouble enough? Why?"

"Lady in a bush over yonder," Asey announced casually. "Surveyin' the environs, she is, like she was either waitin' for someone or bein' waited for. I think—"

Almost before Steve understood what was happening, Asey was sprinting easily across the lawn. Steve tied a flapping shoe-string and set out after him.

They pounded half a mile through the underbrush until they came to the new boundary fences of Mrs. Wadsworth Barr's adjoining land, where Asey stopped.

"She's cut through, an' most likely in her car an' away by now. Anyway, I've lost her. How 'bout you?"

"Me?" Steve was panting. "I never even saw her. Well, well. Come to Cole's Acres. Burglars, murders, marauders and fleet-footed wenches to chase. Let's go home and see what's happened there. Probably the house is on fire."

Halfway back Asey crowed with pleasure, bent over and picked up a white suede pump from a thick bed of leaf mould.

"Left her callin' card, anyway. Bet she has a sore foot t'morrow, with all these prickers an' brambles. 2 AAA. Smallish lady. Know any 2 AAA's, Steve?"

"All I know is that Betsey's five for shoes, seven for gloves and nine for stockings. That took years and years, and I'm not entirely sure of it now. That's no help here."

"Not much," Asey agreed, sticking the pump into his

belt by the heel. "Anyway, this is somethin' tangible, as you might say. Lady in a bush with a shoe is more'n a gent apparently shoeless scurryin' around a house."

"Don't scoff at our burglar," Steve said. "He was real as hell. He wasn't any wind playing tricks in the chimney. I never really even saw this lass of yours—say, your boat's back. Is that Waddy out front, that plump lad in the white suit?"

"That's mother's little Waddy. He always," Asey murmured in an undertone as they approached the group in front of the house, "puts me in mind of a charlotte russe."

Asey had expected that young Mr. Wadsworth Barr would be indignant at being summoned, but he had hardly anticipated that he would be quite so highly indignant. Waddy was ready to burst.

"Oh, Mayo, eh? See here, Mayo, what's your idea in sending this man after me? What right have you to order an officer of the law to—"

"Where," Asey inquired, "is your ma?"

Both Myles and Angelica sensed from Asey's bland tones that Waddy was in for a very bad quarter of an hour.

"Wah!" Tom whispered to Steve. "What a man! If he were a cat, he'd be purring!"

"What's my mother got to do with this?" Waddy's round face was pink and his nostrils were twitching. "What—if you want to know, she's getting her lawyer, that's what! I'll have you understand you can't put anything over on us!"

"Which lawyer?" Asey asked interestedly. "Ole Pop Pardy, or Weasel Smith? Say, Hamilton, what'd Lindsay have to say?"

"He said okay. You're the boss. He's sending the bunch you want."

"Fine. Mr. Barr, if your mother's bringin' the Weasel, I'll be real glad. I ain't seen him since he got back from Charlestown jail. He ought to be able to tell you all about it."

"About what?" Waddy demanded.

"Charlestown jail, of course." Asey grinned. "Okay, Hamilton. See Mr. Barr is well taken care of, would you? We'll wait for his mother an' the Weasel. They'll want to say good-by, I shouldn't wonder. Mr. Witherall, I'd like—"

"Wait!" Waddy said. "What d'you mean, jail? Who's sending me to jail, and what for? Say, my mother—my mother'll break you in two!"

"How old are you?" Asey wanted to know.

"I'm twenty-six. My mother'll—"

"If you was six," Asey observed, "I'd think you was a fine lad. Twenty-six—pshaw! You've had your fun, Barr, an' now you can brood over it at Charlestown. You know perfectly well what you're here for. Don't bluster an' brag about what your ma'll do. You ain't goin' to be in any p'sition where her money'll help. Court'll settle you."

"I had a perfect right," Waddy said hotly. "I had every right in the world to do what I did. It's perfectly justifiable."

"What is?" Asey used his quarterdeck voice.

"Why, fencing in my land! If a gang of nudists came and squatted on the property next to yours, wouldn't you take steps to protect yourself? The land court—"

"The land court," Asey was purring again, "ain't got nothin' to do with murder, Barr. Rosalie Ray was killed in this house last night. An' your little platinum cig'rette lighter was on her bed. Tell your ma to pry you out of that!"

Waddy, who had been standing by the trestle table under the willows, moved back a step. His face was ashen. By sheer luck, as Betsey said later, the chair happened to be where he sank when his knees buckled under him.

"Murder? Murder!"

"Just so. You read about it often, an' you hear about it, but this trip you're in it. Sounds dif'rent, don't it? Where was you last night?"

Asey had to repeat the question.

"I—I went to the Pochet Playhouse, and had supper in Hyannis later, and came home and went to bed. Around two, it was. I listened to the radio before. I got," Waddy swallowed, "I got Japan."

In spite of himself, Asey laughed.

"Mother," Waddy went on, "she—"

"I know," Asey said. "Don't tell me. I bet your ma can prove it, an' so can your servants. Maybe Weasel can prove it too, huh?"

"Well," Waddy retorted, "fourteen people ought to be a sufficient number to prove where I was last night, anyway, from the time I got back last night till this morning. Plenty of people saw me at the theater. And as for that lighter, I lost it on the golf course a week ago. My mother, she—"

"Sure." Asey nodded. "Her an' the caddies an' the caddy master, an' his family, an' his wife's fifth cousins, they'll all prove it, too. Sure."

"If that lighter of mine," Waddy's face was beginning to assume its usual state of pinkness, "if that was found in this house, and connected in any manner with a murder, the only answer is that some of this bunch here was sore because mother and I wouldn't give them a right of way. They probably planted it to get us into trouble. That's the answer, all right."

Asey turned to the younger trooper. "Pratt, take a boat an' hop over an' do some phonin', will you? Call the Pochet theater an' have 'em check on his seat, an' if he was in it. Got a stub?"

Waddy fumbled in his wallet and pulled out a scraggly pink piece of cardboard.

"B Center 110."

"Okay. Where'd you eat in Hyannis? Charley's Tavern? Okay. Phone there, Pratt. Then hop over to the Barrs' an' chat with the servants, b'fore they get a chance to be told what to say."

Out of the corner of his eye, Asey watched young Mr. Wadsworth Barr.

He had been pretty scared at the mention of murder, but he had regained his composure with amazing swiftness. Now he was nearly as cocksure as he had been at first. And relieved, too.

There was no doubt in Asey's mind that the fellow had expected to be accused of something more than putting up fences and squabbling about rights of way, but murder wasn't it. Just the same there was something suspicious about his confident ability to prove his whereabouts the night before. When you came right down to it, it was seldom easy for even the most innocent bystanders to prove just exactly where they were at just such a time. But Waddy had it down pat. There had been, Asey felt, rehearsals.

"Where was you night before last?" Asey inquired gently. No harm, he thought, in proving his point.

"Er—Thursday? Why, I don't know. I—yes. I had dinner with the Blairs, and then—no. That was Wednesday. Thursday I went to a party at the Sandersons', and then to the club, I think."

"What'd you do this mornin'?"

"Oh, I knocked some tennis balls at the bat board, and—why, I didn't do much of anything that I remember, much."

Asey nodded. That was just about what he expected.

Waddy remembered Friday night with an ease bordering on glibness. The vagueness of Thursday night's actions he might claim to be due to the passage of time. Yet he couldn't remember the events of that same morning.

"Primed, ain't you?" Asey said gently. "No matter. It'll all come out in the wash. What day did you lose your lighter?"

"If it's the round one you mean, a week ago last Thursday," Waddy spoke with assurance on that point.

"Thursday?" Myles asked. "Now that was the day it rained so hard, wasn't it?"

Asey grinned. It had poured in Boston, and he had intended to ask about the weather in Skaket.

"Sure it rained," Asey said. "Always play golf in the rain, don't you, Barr? Yeah, I got a picture of you doin' it. We'll have the steward on the carpet an' the caddie master, an' find out. Now just you r'lax, Mr. Barr, an' wait for your mother an' Weasel. My, my, what fun they're goin' to have! R'move him, Hamilton. Now, I want Tom an' Miss Grove. Where's that girl? Miss Sage, where'd she go?"

Angelica didn't know.

"Didn't she come out with us?" Betsey asked. "Why, she was the one who saw Hamilton and Mr. Barr coming! She did say she was dog tired, I remember. Probably went upstairs. I'll get her."

But Hilda was not in her room, or any other room in the house. She was not in the cellar.

"An' it's a cinch," Asey said, "she ain't clingin' to the roof. Yell. She's around somewheres."

"Let me whistle," Betsey said. "That'll bring her. Good old boarding-school chirrup."

Betsey whistled until her lips gave out, but Hilda did not come.

Steve sat down disconsolately on a rush-bottom chair.

"If anything's happened to her! Look, she wouldn't be fool enough to wander out into the woods, with all this going on here! And it's a cinch she hasn't melted into air, thin or otherwise. Where is she?"

"What size shoe does she wear?" Asey asked, thinking of the white suede pump.

"Six or seven, but I can assure you," Betsey didn't understand what he was driving at, "that they aren't seven leaguers. I mean, she didn't say 'hocus-pocus' and fly away, or dissolve with a puff of white smoke!"

"With nine or ten people around—she—what'll we do?" Steve demanded.

"Hunt," Asey said succinctly. "Hunt."

It was Myles who finally found Hilda, gagged and bound, in the dark corner of the coal bin, out in the shed.

CHAPTER SIX

ONCE released, Hilda gazed unhappily down at what had formerly been a crisp, blue linen dress.

"He might," she remarked indignantly, "at least have had the common decency to throw me on the nice clean woodpile instead of the coal!"

"Are you all right?" Steve asked, feeling that it was a silly question, but somehow proper.

"If you mean, did the gent attack me with base motives, no. Get me a drink of water, will you? It's what I set out for an hour ago, and I was parched with thirst then."

"Now," Asey said after she had gulped down three glasses of water, "just what went on?"

"What happened?" Betsey demanded. "For heaven's sakes, stop guzzling and talk!"

"For the first time in my life," Hilda remarked pleasantly, "I have the center of attention. I am the cynosure, as my boss says. Don't think I'm not going to make the most of it. Betsey, that whistle always sent shivers rippling along my scalp, and I had to listen and listen to it! I ground ten feet of enamel off my teeth. And there you all passed by me at least forty thousand times!"

"Hilda," Tom said, "stop jabbering. Who did it?"

"I didn't see his face. He was back to when I caught sight of him, out by the ice box in the kitchen entry. He popped into the shed here, and like a fool I popped after him instead of howling. He grabbed me and gagged me with my own scarf before I could open my mouth. Then he tied me up and dumped me in the coal bin. Say, Bets,

60

remember the jiu jitsu Miss Stiff-neck-whoever-she-was taught us at school?"

"You mean," Betsey pursed her lips and put on a prim expression, " 'How to repulse a forward male, girls?' "

"Uh-huh. Well, it doesn't work. Anyway, the gent went back to the ice chest, and I think he swiped some food. I'm pretty sure, too, that he snuk around to the front of the house and listened to what was going on. He hurried by just before you started milling in. That coal bin has marvelous acoustical properties. Oh, he wore a pink-striped shirt, did I tell you? And dungarees."

"What?" Betsey and Steve and Myles spoke in unison.

"Pink striped shirt. Broad stripes. Dungarees and a cap that didn't fit. Know him?"

"Lem Saddler!" Betsey said.

"He never wears anything but pink striped shirts," Steve added. "Maybe it's the same one over and over again, but broad pink stripes, always! Asey, I bet you it was Lem last night. Lem all the time! The louse wanted this place for himself. Or else he's working for the Barrs."

"You didn't happen to hear a crow cawing, did you?" Angelica asked.

"A what? You don't honestly think I gave any notice to our feathered friends, do you, under the circumstances?"

Angelica smiled. "No, except that I've never seen Lem anywhere without his tame crow in the near vicinity. His name is Oliver. Once he stole the keys to my car, and I had a frightful time getting them back from a robin's nest in my elm tree. But my idea was, if Lem was around, you'd either hear or see the crow."

Hilda shook her head and admitted that there might have been a flock of crows around, for all she knew.

"Or a bevy, or a covey, or what crows are. I feel so futile! After literally letting him slip out of my fingers. I

was so sure that old thumb and forefinger business
would work! I'm maddest about that. It's given me a
sense of security for years. And I always prided myself
on having a sense of detail, but all I can remember is
pink stripes. He might have been a Rooshian, or anything."

"I'm glad you're safe," Asey said. "Now—"

"Aren't you going to search the woods for him?"
Myles asked.

"Nope," Asey said. "If 'twas Lem, you'd never get
him there, any more'n you'd get me. Not unless you had
a livin' chain surroundin' the whole area an' whacked
through it with clubs. Prob'ly not then. It ain't such
shakes as a forest, but it's native land. Now, let's get or-
ganized."

Waddy was sent home in care of the trooper, Pratt,
who had returned with the information that the playhouse and the Hyannis restaurant and the Barr servants
all corroborated Waddy's story of the night before. The
caddy master at the golf club remembered Mr. Barr had
reported the loss of a small platinum lighter that looked
like a lipstick, the week before. The professional remembered it.

"Even so," Asey said, "Pratt's goin' to play shadow
with you, an' don't try to lose him, no matter what your
ma or the Weasel has to say. When I send for you, you
come runnin'. Now, doc, go with 'em if you got to go,
an' see that someone comes back with the stuff on this
groc'ry list. Make arrangements for your ambulance to
wait by the shore, an' when some more of Lindsay's
men get here, they can settle things. Don't let this business out. You too, Waddy. Your ma can say Pratt's
there to keep you from bein' kidnapped, until the papers
come out. Pratt, you see he keeps quiet if you have to
choke him!"

Next Asey saw to the chicken-wire barricade.

"Impromptu," he said, after he, Tom, Steve, Myles,
and Hamilton finished their labors. "Kind of rickety,

but it'll do till we get somethin' better. It'll keep out
stray ladies in white pumps—"

"Who?" Tom asked.

"Stray ladies flittin' about. Dunno who. It'll keep out
Lem in his pink striped shirts, an' other complications.
An' t'morrow, when the gapers line up, they'll have to
gape from a distance."

"What do I do?" Miss Sage asked. "Stay, or go
home?"

"Stay!" Myles and Betsey said before Asey could
answer.

"May I?"

Asey nodded. Miss Sage would know many local details which he had necessarily missed during his six
month absence, and which the Damons and Myles had
no opportunity of absorbing, since they knew no one in
the town.

As they sat down to supper, four state police arrived
by way of the swamp.

Asey greeted one of them.

"Hi, Gordon. Glad—"

"You won't be glad, Asey. Guess who's being sent
along too?"

"Not Leary!" Asey said. "Not my ole pal Lieutenant
Leary!"

"That's right. Lindsay sent him because he wanted to
get him out of the McCracken hunt, I think. He told
Leary you were the boss, but you know Leary!"

Asey sighed. "Well, I s'pose it just means I ain't
never et my peck of dirt. What about McCracken? Got
him yet?"

"Got him? Say, Bat's been seen in Pittsfield, in Fall
River, in Worcester—well, they've seen him everywhere
but climbing Bunker Hill monument. I'm glad to be out
of that mess. Even after plowing through that swamp. I
wanted to cut around, but the place was plastered with
'No Trespass' signs, and the going wasn't much better
from where we started. But that swamp!"

"Isn't it a nice swamp?" Tom asked. "I met it last

night. I particularly enjoyed those hard spots that turned soft as you stepped confidently on 'em. I—"

Before Tom could launch on his memories of the swamp, Asey put the troopers to work. Later, after Rosalie's body had been taken to the doctor's waiting ambulance, Asey stationed them around the house and in the woods.

"Catch anyone if you can," he ordered, "an' shoot if you can't. Don't get fooled."

Avoiding the group in the house, Asey walked around to the chairs under the willows and settled himself for a little quiet thinking.

The coming of Leary, he admitted reluctantly to himself, was going to be a drawback. Leary was a good man. He had been a good desk lieutenant. He probably was a pip at unsnarling Boston traffic or giving the third degree to a good city gangster. But in any situation that required tact or imagination, Leary was a washout.

Asey thought of the Damons, or their guests, or Miss Sage, or Myles Witherall, being bellowed at by Leary, and the picture made him laugh shortly. At the first bellow, the whole bunch would freeze up. Partly from annoyance, and partly because they weren't used to that sort of thing. As the bellowing continued, they'd all lose their tempers, separately and en masse.

Then—Asey shook his head as he pulled out his pipe and slowly filled it. Then Steve would blurt out things, and Betsey would blurt out more things, and Myles would try to save the kids, and it would be a swell mess. Perhaps if he could switch Leary on to Waddy Barr, he might have a chance to try some unravelling.

At the same time, Asey reflected, Waddy would just throw everything back on the Damons. The Weasel would do just that, so it could be expected he would advise Waddy to. He'd say that the lighter had been found and planted by Steve. Probably, since Waddy's story checked, the lighter really had been a plant. But who had done the planting? The mysterious burglar of the night before, or Lem, or the woman with the white pumps?

Asey leaned back in the chair and stretched his feet up on the table. Overhead the willows were creaking, and through the moving branches he could see only an occasional star. The wind was shifting to the east again, and that would probably mean fog. He didn't like the idea of fog. Too many things could happen. Too many people could wander unobserved around the old Cole place.

It occurred to him that too many people were wandering around it anyway. Why? The Damons frankly admitted to being poor. They had nice silver and some good pieces of furniture, but none of them were worth the dangers involved in carting them away. It was unlikely that the man the night before was from Skaket, unless it had been Lem. Even so, why slide into a lighted house where people were obviously up and doing? Why, like this afternoon, should Lem dispose of Hilda, while the house was teeming with people, and swipe a pie and a loaf of bread, and two cans of baked beans?

Whether or not Lem had been the burglar of the night before, both the intrusions were characterized by a certain urgency, a sublime disregard of consequences, as though someone who had been extraordinarily lucky was banking on his luck to hold, and to carry him through.

And Lem Saddler, Asey knew, wasn't that sort.

"Any luck?" Angelica, cigarette in hand, sat down opposite him. "I know you don't want to be bothered, but I'm sick of indoor speculating. I thought fresh air would help. It's amazing, but everything you look at turns out to be a state trooper. Like Thurston or Fred Keating. Have you figured out anything?"

"It all r'minds me," Asey said, "of a steel engravin' that used to hang in the Wellfleet Academy when I was a kid. Said under it, 'Labyrinth of Crete.' I never understood much about it, but this is the same idea. How are the others?"

"Bearing up. I think they're just beginning to realize the enormity of the thing. I am. Tom thinks he'd make a lot of money as a correspondent in the field, so to speak, but he doubts the taste of it. Myles—did he tell you about that bus trip of his yesterday?"

"Don't talk of busses," Asey said. "Enough action is enough."

"It seems to me," Angelica retorted, "that there's no action at all. Asey, who on earth could have killed that woman? Who would have wanted to?"

Asey puffed at his pipe.

"In gen'ral," he said finally, "I'd say they was three major groups. All her ex-husbands.—'Member the old Lillian Russell wheeze about it's not a question of why men marry, but why they all marry her? Well, first off they's Rosalie's ex-husbands. Must be four or five official ones. Then there'd be the wives of the men who loved her, over the radio an' less r'mote. N'en, 'cordin' to my way of thinkin', there'd be the biggest bunch, includin' most anyone who owned a radio an' wasn't color blind in both ears. Comin' right down to earth, I'd say Betsey an' Steve an' Myles. Just as sure as shootin', Leary's goin' to land on one or another of 'em."

"But what about Lem? Or Waddy Barr?"

"Why in tophet would Lem Saddler, who's never been out of Skaket in his life, 'cept to county fairs an' to Boston once or twice, why'd he kill her? You can get funny about it, but it don't stand to reason. I can't understand this Lem part at all. An' as for Waddy, offhand I'd say he hadn't the brains or the spirit to kill anythin' more'n a fly, 'less his mother planted the idea in his head when he was a baby, an' cherished it along in cotton wool wrappin's ever since. This fog," Asey got up, changing the subject abruptly, "is comin' in fast. I'm goin' to try a little baitin', an' then I'm goin' to call on Lem. I—"

He stopped short.

"Say, you hear—listen!"

Angelica obediently listened. "Your boat."

"Yessir, someone's at it. Hear—"

"Wait!" Angelica pressed a small flashlight into his hand.

Asey took it and started off on a dead run, and Angelica stumbled down the path after him.

Before they reached the landing they could hear the engine of the speed boat turning over. By the time they got there, the boat was purring out in the inlet.

"Take my boat!" Angelica said. "Jack Meredith's— here, get in! Turn the light here for a second while I untie this—you take the wheel!"

Asey slid into the boat and Angelica followed.

"All clear," she said. "Watch the reverse. It sticks."

A minute later they were out in the current after the speed boat.

"He was headin' out to the harbor," Asey said. "Keep your light focused ahead. Maybe we can catch sight of him."

"Are you—are you sure it's not one of the troopers that took—"

"They wouldn't sneeze without bein' told," Asey said. "Sweep the shore with that flash. Either side."

The little boat bounced along the length of the long inlet, and as they reached its mouth, Asey slowed down.

" 'F he turned left, he's aground. It don't seem hardly sensible he'd turn right an' try to go out the harbor, not with the fog headin' in an' the tide so. Well, we'll run around the eel grass an' see if he come to grief. Say, ain't this craft got a search, or somethin' more powerful than that flash of yours?"

Angelica reminded him that it was Jack Meredith's boat.

"You know Jack. Holy wonder that the thing has held together this far."

"You don't mean," Asey sounded incredulous, "this is the old 'Gum Tree', because it always stuck? She don't look like it."

"Had her overhauled last summer and changed the name. Calls her 'Mae West'," Angelica observed, "but even that didn't visibly pep it up any. There's no light, no bell, no life-belts. If I turn the light on shore," she added as Asey swung to the left, "you'll get messed up in the grass, or lobster buoys, or moorings."

"We'll take the chance. Hang onto the wheel a sec while I take the flash."

He could find no trace of the speed boat.

"Can't even hear the engine," Asey said. "Wait—I can. He's over to the right. They's some boat there."

"Yacht club," Angelica said. "Don't you remember, they've moved to the new quarters here from East Pochet?"

Asey shook his head sadly. "That's what comes of takin' vacations. I forgot. Well, we'll run easy over to the harbor entrance an' see what we can see. Anyone tryin' to take that boat out this harbor without knowin' either one wouldn't get far."

"But the fog's thicker! Are you sure you can make it?"

"In this tub, easy. We'll go slow an' hug the shore. This don't draw much. Doggone, I wish I had a good search!"

They chugged across the mouth of the inlet and proceeded cautiously along toward the harbor. A cough in the engine brought a cry of alarm from Angelica.

"Asey!"

"I hear it. Shoot the light on the gas gauge. Sounds to me—"

"It's an inch below empty! Can you make it into the club? We could get gas there, if there's anyone around tonight."

The engine coughed protestingly, barked sharply and stopped.

"D'you suppose," Asey inquired with mild sarcasm, "that Mister Meredith observes the formal'ties sufficient to have an oar aboard this packin' case?"

"I doubt it," Angelica said, "though for our sakes I hope he does. I also hope your public never hears of this."

Asey laughed. "Sailor D'tective Hoist With Own P'tard. Huh. Let's have your light. They's somethin' under the floorboards that might be an oar."

It turned out to be a broken canoe paddle, too short to scull with. Asey sighed and rolled up his shirt sleeves.

"I'll take a few swipes on one side an' then shift to the other. Don't see no lights at the club, do you? Thought they had doin's there Sat'day nights."

"They do ordinarily, but they'll all have gone over to Tonset today. Races this afternoon, supper and dance tonight. They'll keep the boats there for more racing tomorrow. That's how I happened to borrow the 'Mae West'. Jack took his sail boat over. Can I help?"

"Just hold the light—oh, confound it, listen! Hear that? That *is* my boat. He dashed out to the harbor entrance, an' d'cided not to chance it. Now he's comin' back! I ain't goin' to waste time tryin' to get gas at the club or the float. All be locked if the bunch is away. I'm goin' to board the first motor boat I come to an' see what I can steal. If I can't get gas, I'll swipe a boat. Nev' mind that light for me, or for that feller. Throw the flash ahead an' see if they's any prospects."

"The 'Pixie's' dead ahead," Angelica reported. "That's no help. I don't think she's been touched this year since they put her out. That—oh, look! To the right! There's the Grew's boat, the 'Pellet.' And it looks like a can of gas in the stern! Maybe it's empty, but make for it!"

Asey paddled furiously. In less than two minutes, during which they heard the speed boat pass and swing apparently into the inlet again, Angelica had the 'Pellet's' mooring in her hand, and Asey was clambering aboard.

"Full!" he said happily. "This'll give us a mile or two."

Angelica grinned at the characteristic understatement.

"We'll dump it in our tank. I'd like to swipe this boat, but she's crawlin' with padlocks. There—help me ease this—leggo that moorin' now. We'll just fill up an' proceed—what's that?"

The powerful beam of a searchlight from the club wharf blinded him so that he nearly dropped the precious gas can overboard.

"Hey!" he shouted, making a megaphone of his hands. "Ahoy there! Lay off that light! This is Asey Mayo! I'll bring your gas back tomorrow! Can't explain now!"

"Put that can back!" The bellowed command echoed across the water.

"I'm Asey Mayo, d'you hear? Mayo! Asey Mayo!"

"It's no use to yell," Angelica said. "It's that deaf old post. That lame duffer. The caretaker."

"Who, Reub Rich? That deaf old haddock? Oh, God A'mighty! I forgot him. Well, there don't seem to be much use r'mindin' him he's my second cousin at this point. Let's have the light. We'll swipe the gas anyway an' explain later."

"Put that thar can back, you bloomin' tarnation thieves, or I'll shoot!"

"What are you going to do *now?*" Angelica was beginning to get nervous.

"Let him shoot. Way we're bobbin' around, he couldn't hit us 'cept by mistake. Come closer with that light. There. I got it. Now turn off the light an' let him pot away, if he's so inclined."

As the gasoline went sloshing into the empty tank, Reub Rich fulfilled his promise and started shooting.

"Huh," Asey said. "A mile wide. Only a twenty-two, anyway."

"Possibly a twenty-two is child's play to you," Angelica retorted, "but I can picture myself punctured vitally from a stray twenty-two just as easily as I can see myself pierced by a forty-five. Asey, do hurry! He's getting uncomfortably near!"

"Just a sec—there. I'll toss the can overboard. Now, 'fore we start up, d'you hear my boat anywhere?"

"All I hear," Angelica told him bitterly, "is the whine

of bullets around my ears, and the splatter of the incon-
sequential little things hitting the water. I thought I
heard it a minute ago, but I can't now. Asey, you'll
never get out of this boat-cluttered region without a
light! And if we snap on that flash, Reub's sure to get
us. Look, he's stopped shooting and taken up that
search again! Asey, *do* something!"

Asey grinned to himself in the darkness. Even the
sanest of women, he thought, got a little screwy about
firearms.

"Five seconds more," Angelica observed, "and I'll be
a raving maniac in a padded cell for the rest of my life!
Why don't you do something, now you've got gas?"

"I'm lettin' him light my way for me," Asey said.
"He's got a better light than we have, an' he's makin' a
nice broad arc round. Cuts through the fog like a knife.
Say, we drifted some! Give him a few feet more, an' I'll
start, an' then we'll zigzag out of this. Better grab somethin' an' be ready—hey—hey, look! Look yonder!
Gimme that flash! Yessir, there's my boat! The son of a
sea cook, he coasted in here! He was goin' to anchor an'
—hold the light!"

Asey started the boat just as Reub's flash flicked hesitantly beyond the speed boat and picked them up.

"He's got us!" Angelica cried. "He's going to shoot
some more! He can't miss this time!"

"I'll guarantee he won't, now we're movin'. We'll get
that feller—"

But the man in Asey's speed boat had also started his
engine.

"Hold the light on him!" Asey said. "Hold it—what's
the matter? Hold the light on him! Say, he's got on a
striped shirt, an'—hold the light, keep it steady! He's
havin' trouble gettin' out, an' I think—what's the matter
with that light, Miss Sage? He's the guy, I bet, that went
after Hilda, but it don't look a bit like Lem to me. Hold
—what's the matter?"

"That flashlight," Angelica said unnecessarily by
then, "seems to have gone out."

CHAPTER SEVEN

ANGELICA thought it was sheer luck, but actually it was sheer instinct that carried them safely out of the fringe of anchored boats and into the harbor current.

Asey swung the boat in the general direction of the mouth of the inlet. Squinting up to check his route by the north star, it worried him to find there wasn't any. The fog had blotted it out.

At half speed he chugged cautiously along until he felt the rudder meet the swirling eddies of the inlet, and then he slowed down till the boat's speed about balanced the current.

The hum of the speed boat had disappeared entirely.

"Now," Angelica inquired, "what?"

Asey chuckled. "I'm broodin'," he told her, "'bout your magnan'mous disposition. For a lady that's gone through what you have, it's wonderful. I know very few females that'd get de-gassed an' shot at, an' unlighted, an' still be able to speak in their natural tones."

"It's my bringing up," Angelica said. "A lady never raises her voice, a lady invariably has a clean white handkerchief, scented with—"

"I know. C'logne. Yup, Boston's a great place. You do it credit."

"What's the reason lurking behind all this blarney?"

"Well, I'm hopin' you won't make such a funny story out of all this as you might," Asey said.

"Funny? It hurts me to say so, but I don't think it's so very funny. What are you going to do now?"

"I ain't afraid of careenin' round this inlet," Asey told her, "'cause I come in too many times in worse fogs

72

an' worse boats. Pity of it is, I know that mahog'ny craft of Bill's, an' now we're lightless, I can't play cat an' mouse like I'd intended. I was goin' to tease him aground. Now we can't lure him. We can only chase him. An' chasin' that boat in this is like matchin' a model T with Malcolm Campbell's Bluebird."

"Have you considered the possibility of returning home?" Angelica asked drily. "I mean, before it's too late. I think there's always such a solid touch about home, don't you?"

Asey laughed. "Home's always a good thought, an' they ain't no place like it. But that feller in the pink striped shirt—"

"Lem, you mean."

"I ain't a bit sure of it's bein' Lem. That's why I'd sort of like to get another look at him, or see him, or somethin'."

Angelica sighed. "Are you going to ram him?"

"I think our best bet's to stay right here an' see if we got him bottled, an' then try to run him aground by scarin' him a bit if he cuts out. If we leave him entirely, he's all set to do anythin', an' Lord knows where he'd be if we went back for a light."

Angelica pointed out that the man had no lights either.

"He pers'nly may not, but that boat has. She's got more an' better lights than craft ten times her size."

"Look, Asey, what gives you the impression that man isn't Lem? He certainly wore a striped shirt. And there certainly can't be two people around with shirts like that!"

Asey agreed. "I ain't wonderin' much about the shirt, but the man that's in it."

"You mean it's someone dressed in Lem's shirt? I don't understand."

"Neither," said Asey with complete and cheerful honesty, "do I. Listen, I hear him again. He's—yes-siree, he's comin' up this way. See the glare? He's got his lights on. An' glory be, what speed! Either that feller's God, an' made this inlet in person, or else he's takin' terrible chances."

The boat shot by, far to their right.

"Makin' for shallow water again," Asey said. "P'raps if that guy ain't God A'mighty, he'll ground. We'll look into it, in a cautious way."

Angelica could feel the boat rock as they hit the wake of the speed boat. Asey picked up speed too, and Angelica, compressing her lips, took a firm hold of the seat and the guard rail. Asey might consider himself a cautious navigator, but in her opinion there was little to choose between him and the strange idiot in the striped shirt.

"K'out!" Asey yelled. "Hang on!"

For all her preparations, Angelica bounced off the seat as the boat ran aground with a jerk like hydraulic brakes under the foot of a nervous woman.

"Hurt?" Asey asked. "Thank goodness. I thought we could cut across the bar, but it seems like we couldn't."

He helped her up, and then sat back and laughed and laughed.

"I'm still not amused," Angelica said. "Oh, no, I'm not hurt, but I can't see where this is funny."

"I'm laughin'," Asey said, "b'cause—oh, I'm weak! Y'know, if this was a book, we'd of got that feller an hour ago. 'F I was the d'tective the papers claim, I wouldn't be dashin' around in this crazy fashion in a fifth-rate tub, on a foggy night, without even the apology for a light. Or gas, or oars, or anything else. Just goes to show you how life runs. Miss Sage, we're plum on the center of Skaket bar, owin' to that brain wave of mine, an' I could pract'cly guarantee that 'Mae West' ain't goin' to rise up an' see no one for some time. Tide's runnin' out."

"That fact," Angelica said, "has been indelibly stamped on my mind for some time. Are we in any particular danger?"

"Not a bit. 'Less you feel they's somethin' fatal in

bein' cold an' bored. Engine won't turn over attall, but we may drag off. I'm goin' to anchor so's we don't."

Angelica knew better than to ask why he didn't prefer being dragged off. If the boat did get free while the tide was running out, they would simply float along out the harbor and into the broad Atlantic with it, since the engine wouldn't work. The broken paddle was no asset. As long as the anchor held till the tide came in again—

"It's a lovely anchor," Asey said reassuringly. "In fact, my—my. Two anchors, an' new ropes. What came over Meredith? Well, we'll just set back an' wait. Ole pink shirt, he's done another disappearin' act. Prob'ly the fog. Get dead spots in it, an' it'll play all sorts of tricks with sounds. Many a time I've heard a fog horn to port an' had a boat loom up off the starboard bow. Funny stuff."

"Oh, awfully," Angelica said. "Awfully funny. Haha."

"Ole pink shirt," Asey ignored her irony, "he sort of puzzles me. I'd take him a lot more serious if that was a blue stripe, now. Always seemed to me to be somethin' kind of foolish about pink. Ever hear tell of the time old Deacon Simsbury's daughter got sold on what she called the vibrations of colors an' folks? She dyed all his dye-able clothes a nice ripe sort of pink, like crushed strawb'ries, an' then—"

He rolled along easily from anecdote to anecdote until Angelica found herself giggling and at last laughing in deep chortles far removed from the manner of Marlborough Street.

The more she laughed, the more relieved Asey became. He always thought Miss Sage was a sane and practical sort of woman, but you never knew just how much it took to set even that kind off. Hysteria, under the circumstances, would have been a problem, he thought.

He continued reminiscing, but his mind was not more than a quarter fixed on what he was saying. His friends claimed he could turn local color off and on as though it were something out of a faucet, and once again he thanked his lucky stars that he could. It gave you time to consider other things.

Had he been alone, he would unhesitatingly have hopped over the side of the boat and waded or swum to shore.

But you couldn't leave even the most practical and clearheaded woman in the world alone in a busted tub stuck on a sandbar at twelve o'clock of a foggy night. Not with a crazy man careening around in a stolen boat. Or even without him.

Alone, he would have made a bee line for Lem Saddler's house and Lem's Portygee wife. He had a theory he wanted to prove and prove quickly. As a side issue, he thought casually, he might also test the truth of his grandfather's often repeated statement that the Skaket flats contained quicksands. He personally had never believed it. After all, you kept away from quicksands, you didn't bother investigating.

He broke off suddenly in the middle of his story about Bijah Snow, who decided on his sixtieth birthday that he was a bird, and obstinately set out to live thereafter in trees.

"Go *on!*" Angelica said weakly. "Don't stop at—"

"Listen. Boat comin'."

"Boat, my eye! I can't hear a thing!"

"Just you listen. I hear oars—yessir. Ahoy! Ahoy there! Ahoooy!"

A feeble "Ahoy" came drifting back through the fog.

"Ahoy, you in the rowboat!" Asey called again. "Who is it?"

"Er—ahoy! Is that you, Asey?"

"It's Myles Witherall!" Angelica said. "That—what an amazing individual that man is!"

"I'll keep yelling," Asey called out. "Make for the sound, and mind the flats! Don't get aground! Whatever you do, don't get aground!"

Nearly ten minutes passed before Myles, in his battered old skiff, located Asey and Angelica.

"Ship your oars," Asey ordered as the sharpy loomed through the fog. "Ship 'em! Oh, pull in your oars! Yank in your oars, man! An'—hold it! Ease her off—my goodness, Mr. Witherall, ship your port oar an' hold her off—backwater—there! Oh—oh!"

Words failed Asey as he heard a splash that could only be made by an oar falling into the water.

"Take the other oar," he said patiently, "an' pole 'longside here. Careful! We need that oar!"

Myles, wearied by his long pull up the inlet, far more frightened than he realized, and utterly confused by Asey's staccato commands, did his best to obey. As he leaned on the oar, digging it in to the sand beneath the shallow water, it seemed to slip mysteriously from his hands.

"It—it's going!" he said weakly. "I—oh, dear!"

While he weighed the problem of keeping his balance in the boat against the advisability of holding the oar at all costs, despite a wetting, self-preservation and nature made the decision for him. Myles let go the oar.

Asey sighed.

"Take your anchor," he said gently, "an' toss it over. That's it. That's right. Now just you set quiet amidships, an' you'll bump us in a minute or two. That's right. Now—"

"The oar," Myles said. "It just—it just slipped, Asey. Down into the sand. I couldn't really do anything about it, Asey. It seemed to melt away."

"Quicksands," Asey said. "Of a sort. There. Now, I've got your boat. You clamber in with us. Easy. That's it. Now I'll draw your anchor—nope." The anchor, apparently, was going the way of the oar. "I'll cut your anchor rope, an' make your craft fast to this. Now."

"I'm really awfully sorry," Myles said breathlessly. "I didn't mean to lose those oars!"

"After what we been through t'night," Asey said, "a couple of lost oars is nothin'. Less'n the dust. Er—what brought you out?"

Myles explained at length. He had heard the boats start out, and called the troopers to investigate.

"But they wouldn't. They said you told them to do what you told them, and not to let the house remain unguarded. I wanted to row out, but Steve and Tom wouldn't let me. They said it was crazy, in the fog. So," Myles concluded simply, "I just waited until their attention was otherwise distracted, and came. I was worried. I'm—really, I'm afraid I'm not much help. I was going to row up to the mouth of the inlet, and then beach the boat and walk back, if I didn't find you. What—er—what happened to you?"

"Ours is much louder an' funnier," Asey said. "You'd hardly b'lieve it. Tell him, Miss Sage."

Briefly, Angelica summed up their evening.

"Now the only thing I know to match it is the story of your bus trip down here. Tell Asey all about it. We have time, haven't we, Asey?"

"We got time enough to hear his life story, but say, I'm pinin' to get ashore an' do some proddin' before Leary gets here—"

"Leary?" Myles said. "Lieutenant Leary? Leary has come." He spoke in the sad final tones that a distant onlooker might have used in reporting, "Well, that's the last of old Pompeii."

"Grim, huh?"

"Very."

Asey sighed. "If only I—look, how's your courage, you two?"

"You mean," Angelica said sweetly, "how should we feel about staying here alone while you scampered through quicksands to shore? Really, Asey!"

"I'll just slip into the skiff an' crab along in with my busted paddle. I could scare up someone to take us home, too, or get a tow."

Myles and Angelica said nothing. Both of them felt that there wasn't much they could say.

"You're safe enough," Asey went on, pulling the skiff

alongside. "Our anchor's okay. Honest, you'll be all right. I'll be back in an hour or so, prob'ly."

"Oh, don't hurry on our account," Angelica remarked acidly. "Just scurry along, and if you attend my funeral, I hope you succumb, yourself. From pure embarrassment."

Asey chuckled as he pushed off. The tide would turn before long, and even if they floated off with it, or the anchors didn't hold, they could float only up the inlet. He feared no catastrophe, anyway. Miss Sage could handle a boat with anyone. The two of them could make out.

Kneeling on the floorboards of the flat-bottomed skiff, Asey used his broken paddle as though he were in a canoe. It took all his strength to cut across the current, and he heaved a mighty sigh of relief at the appearance of the eel grass that meant he was nearing shore.

Once in shallow water, he clambered out and pulled the boat high up on the pebbly beach. A pile of lobster pots nearly tripped him; he lighted a match and scrutinized the buoy markings. L.S. He wasn't more than a hundred yards from Lem's little box-like house.

He stumbled around the beach grass till he found a path, and followed it straight to the back door. As he raised his hand to knock, the door opened. Lem's wife, Lina, stood there, clutching a scant, flannel wrapper around her ample figure.

"Lem, you better—why, Asey Mayo! I thought you was that man of mine! I—you want Lem?"

"I do. Know where he is?"

"Come in," Lina said. "Come in the kitchen. Wait— I'll light the other lamp. That Lem! He better wait till I get my hands on him! Not home since supper time yest'day! He goes off to the Damons', an' that's the end of him, the no good loafer! I told him last time. I said, next time you go to Pochet an' get drunk, I give you plenty. I do, too. See?" She pointed to the kitchen table, on which a businesslike rolling pin, a razor strop and an ugly looking stiletto ominously reposed.

Asey laughed. "Nice friendly little r'ception you got planned. Say, what'd Lem have on? What was he wearin'?"

"Like always, a pink striped shirt an' dungarees an' his cap. You seen that bum?"

"Sorry, I ain't. Lina, they had some trouble over at the Damons'." He told her about the murder.

"Rosalie Ray?" Lina said in horror. "You don't mean Rosalie Ray, the radio one? Oh, I loved her. She was swell. I always listen to her. So does Lem. He thinks she's the best one he ever heard. He sent a box top for her picture. She's been killed? Gee, that's awful, ain't it? She was a wonderful woman, too. So thin, an' all. Lem'll feel bad. Ain't it terrible?"

Asey nodded and leaned back in his chair.

If Betsey Damon or the Grove girl, or Miss Sage had spoken like that, he would have become suspicious at once, knowing full well they didn't mean it. Lina—well, there was no doubting her sincerity. She thought Rosalie Ray was wonderful, and now that Rosalie Ray was dead, Lina cried. It never occurred to her to involve Lem in the murder in any way. She accepted the fact of his absence, and she accepted the news of Rosalie's death, but to her they bore not the remotest connection.

"Say, who's been raisin' hell over to the Damons, anyway?" Asey inquired. "Whyn't Lem do somethin' about it?"

"It's them no-good cousins of mine, them young Barradios," Lina told him honestly. "Them an' the Mallon boy. Lem didn't find out how much they done till Friday. There's been a lot of talk about the Damons since the day they come, even though Lem said they was all right. Anyway, Lem got so mad Friday he went to old Tony. You know old Tony? Well, he told Tony to make 'em stop. Tony didn't know about it till then, either. He said he'd fix the kids. He promised. You know Tony. If he says he'll stop anything, he'll stop it quick. The Mallon boy wouldn't dare without them."

"Who hired 'em, Waddy Barr?"

Lina nodded. "He got a grudge against the Damons, an' he was mad they got Cole's land. He's the reason for all the badness in this town. They was all good boys —at least, they wasn't all bad, until Waddy started on 'em. It all begun when he run liquor."

"Huh?" Asey opened his eyes wide. "I thought I knew all the—huh. Running' for Glynn, was he? What for? Ain't he got money enough of his own?"

"He don't have no money," Lina explained, "'cept what his ma gives him. Five or six years ago, she got mad an' didn't give him none for a long while. That was when he started, an' he's still at it."

"Say," Asey asked, "can I take Lem's truck? I want to see your cousins. An' could I borrow your knife, too? I'll r'turn everythin' in good order real soon."

"Sure, you take 'em. You see that no good bum Lem, an' you bring him home! What I'm goin' to do to him!"

"I bet you do him brown," Asey said. "Say, you sure Lem's off on a binge?"

Lina pointed in the direction of the stove.

"See there, that crazy bird of his? That fool crow? He always comes home when that bum gets drunk. Lem don't feed him then. He comes here to get fed. He been here all day, fussin' around."

"Where's the Barradios live now?"

"Up the road to Jose's old place. If you find Lem—"

"I'll drag him home by the hair," Asey promised. "Night, an' thanks."

As he drew Lem's old truck up in front of the Barradios' tumbledown shack, another car lurched crazily out of the fog ahead and slowed to a stop. Three figures piled out of it, and in the glow of the headlights, Asey recognized the two Barradio boys and Mike Mallon. They were, he decided, just about two-thirds sober.

"Hi, Lem ol' boy, do—Mayo?" Ramon's voice changed. "What you want, huh?"

"You three." Asey slid out from behind the wheel and walked up to them.

"What for, huh? What we done? We ain't done noth-in'—hey, ouch! What you got there? You—"

"Get indoors, all of you," Asey said, flicking the borrowed stiletto casually into the air, and as casually catching it. "Quick. I'm in a hurry. Git."

"Honest, Asey, we meant to report that. It was only a bump. It didn't hurt the car none. We'll report it in the mornin', only Mike didn't have no license, see?"

"Okay. Git."

The three boys seemed anxious to precede him into the kitchen. Old Tony, their grandfather, sat at the table playing solitaire by the light of a kerosene lamp. He looked up, nodded at Asey, and returned to his game.

"Honest," Mike said, "we didn't—how'd you know it was us?"

"Set down," Asey said, still fingering the knife. "An' listen to me. I don't care a picayune about your drunken drivin'. I want to know what you done around the Damon house last night. I want to know it quick."

"We wasn't there," Ramon said promptly.

"Waddy Barr says you was."

"Then he's a dirty double crossin'—"

"Uh—huh. Where was you last night, then?"

"Here." Old Tony smiled briefly at Asey. "I beat the hell out of them three last night."

"What'd Waddy want 'em to do?"

"Set fire to the woods," Ramon said. "Lem heard Frank an' Mike an' me talkin', an' told Tony. He—"

"Show him your back," Tony ordered. "I say, show him! Quick!"

He started to rise from his chair, and Ramon quickly pulled off his coat and shirt. Asey looked at the ugly welts and unhealed sores, and nodded.

"Bull whip, Tony?"

"That's right." Tony resumed his seat and put a red queen on a black king. "That Barr, he thinks he's so big. Next time he come here, I whip him too. I don't know before what goes on. I know now. You—" he

jerked his head toward Ramon, "you tell him everything, see?"

Ramon looked from the immobile face of his grandfather to Asey's stiletto, and shrugged.

Waddy, he said, had hired them to bother the Damons. And they had done so, Asey gathered, as effi-
ciently as they could. Friday they were to have set a
fire.

"But Tony got wise to you first. Okay. Who fired the
shots at Damon?"

"Waddy."

"Does he know you're through with this business?"

"He thinks we're goin' to set the fire tonight."

"Hm." At least, Waddy's prepared alibi for Friday
night was explained. "Barr still runnin' liquor, huh?"

"That, an' other stuff. I—that's why we had to go for
the Damons," Ramon said.

"I get it. Dope for Glynn, an' Waddy had you comin'
an' goin'. Where's he keep his boat, here in the inlet?
You might as well tell me. Oh, I don't want you kids!"
Asey said impatiently. "I want Barr. Stop jitterin'!"

"On this side of the inlet," Mike said. "Like yours,
sort of. That's why Waddy wanted to get these people
out. He used their place when ole Cole was there. He
went to bed at sunset an' never knew a thing."

"Why's Mrs. Barr want the place? Same reason?"

"No! She don't know about Waddy. She just wants it.
She told Waddy she'd give him five grand to get the Damons out an' scared so she could get the house."

Asey nodded. "So with them b'hind you, you didn't
care what you said about the Damons, huh?"

"Well, he was a writer, an' she was a model, an' the
ole feller was an artist," Mike said, as though that justi-
fied everything. "We said they was nudists. Mrs. Barr
thought that up."

"She did, huh? Now, what about that woman?" Asey
was guessing wildly. "That small girl you seen around?"

The three exchanged grins.

"On Friday?" Ramon said. "Yesterday? We seen her,

all right. In the aft'noon. Early. She was a pip. We chased her, but she beat it."

"Who was she? Did Waddy see her? Did he know her?"

"I don't know who she was, an' I don't think Waddy seen her as close as we did. We didn't know her, but Mike says he seen her somewheres before, he thinks."

"Okay," Asey said. "Now, about Lem. Any of you seen him since last evenin'? No? Any of you been near the Cole place since Tony beat you up? Swear it?"

They nodded in unison.

"Prove it?"

"I can," Tony said. "They didn't leave here from the time I beat them till nine tonight. They couldn't."

"Fine. Now, you kids, listen to me. I don't want you for your drunken drivin' tonight, nor for your rum runnin' nor your dope runnin' for Waddy an' Glynn. If you an' Tony can prove where you was last night, I don't want you for the murder that happened there then." He paused for a moment and let that sink in. "They's some things I do want, though. I want you to find out who the woman you chased is, an' I want you to find Lem. I want you to start findin' right now. Don't tell me you can't. You got to."

Tony smiled. "They will," he said.

"One more piece of monkey business," Asey went on, "or the sniff of one, an' I'll see you get yours for everythin', beginnin' with the dope an' workin' back. You'll get the bull whip, an' then Lindsay. See? Got it? Fine. I'll be at Cole's. Tell the troopers who you are when you come. They'll be waitin' for you. Now, find me a lantern an' a couple flashlights, an' a pair of oars an' some rowlocks."

The three fell over themselves in their dash for the door.

Half an hour later Asey returned Lem's truck and Lina's stiletto, and then, shouldering his borrowed oars and swinging his borrowed lantern, he made his way down to the shore.

Pulling out into the inlet with the short wrist strokes of a Banks fisherman, he called only twice before Myles answered. After manoeuvering around, he drew up beside the motor boat.

"We're afloat," Angelica said cheerfully, "but I think the propeller's broken, or something. I can't start her. Did you have fun?"

"Loads," Asey said. "Very enlightenin', as the feller said when he tossed the match into the oil well."

"What now?"

"What? Oh, you'n Myles crowd into this pea pod. We'll leave 'Mae West' to be collected tomorrow. We'll just skim home. No trouble with the tide comin' in."

Even so it was nearly dawn before they reached the landing at the Cole place. Angelica, holding the flashlight, yelled so loudly as they came alongside that Asey rested on his oars and turned his head.

"Asey, d'you see what I see? Myles, do you see it too?"

"For the love of Pete!" Asey said blankly.

His mahogany speed boat was neatly tied up to the wharf.

CHAPTER EIGHT

"BUT FINGERPRINTS!" Angelica said the next noon, as she poured out Asey's third cup of coffee. "There *must* have been prints somewhere on that boat! Coffee, Myles, or another egg?"

"Both," Myles told her. "But there weren't any prints anywhere. The—er—gentleman erased them."

"Really?" Angelica turned to Asey, who nodded over the brim of his cup.

"Yup. He took some waste an' an oil can an' done a nice job. Thorough. That's that."

"Whoever he is," Angelica remarked, "he doesn't seem anxious to be known."

"Yup. An' when anyone goes that far, you can be reas'nbly sure he's got somethin' that could be found out if he did get known. I—deary me!"

He shook his head as the hum of voices, dominated by Leary's harsh tones, rose higher in the next room.

"Can't you," Myles asked politely, "do anything about that?"

"About Leary? Guess not. As that crowd outside behind the chicken wires increases, so'll Leary. Let him run on. He's enjoyin' it. Wheee!"

Tom Fowler's voice mounted above Leary's, and stayed there on a sharp staccato. The trio in the kitchen could not distinguish his words, but his meaning was evident.

"Leary's gettin' it all back now," Asey said. "Huh. Didn't know Tom could get that worked up. He never—"

"What about Leary?" Angelica asked. "Has he decided anything?"

"Wa—el," Asey drawled, "I wouldn't say he'd done much more'n get awful confused. Can't see why."

"I suppose you're not confused at all?"

"I was, but it's sort of clearin' up. When you come right down to it, Rosalie Ray come here an' got stabbed. That's all."

"All? What about the prowlers?"

"And Lem, and all?" Myles added.

"Prowlers is settled, an' they won't prowl no more. Pink shirt ain't Lem. Oh, no. Didn't I tell you? Lem's off on a drunk. Feller swiped his shirt, I guess. I sort of gathered that when Lem's drunk, he's drunk all over. Like the pig that died in clover. Nope, it boils down to she was killed, an' they's a feller come here for somethin' who's sort of complicatin' matters."

"Sort of," Angelica said. "Just sort of. What for, and why couldn't he have killed Rosalie?"

"If he come here to kill her," Asey returned, "why'n't he do it an' go? Why hang around? I got a feelin' Hilda was right in her hunch—that he heard us out in front yest'day, when we was talkin' to Waddy. Wouldn't be a mite surprised if he hadn't got wise to the murder for the first time then. N'en he tried to grab my boat an' run, but couldn't make it on account of the fog. I—oh, h'lo, Leary, how they comin'?"

Before Leary could answer, Tom and Hilda and Betsey and Steve, entering the kitchen behind him, began to talk all at once.

"If you don't do something about this man—"

"If he thinks one of us did it, why doesn't he break down and arrest us?"

"I simply will *not* be bullied!"

"Asey, for the love of God, can't you tie a can on this lad?"

"Now, now," Asey said soothingly, "that ain't cooperatin'. Is it, Leary?"

"I never saw a bunch to beat 'em," Leary said in disgust. "Touchy!"

"Seen the r'porters?" Asey asked. "No? Well, you better run right out. I chased 'em away once an' said they was to wait for you."

Leary hesitated. "Don't you—"

"I don't want to see 'em. That's your job. I think you ought to see 'em."

Leary looked at the group in the kitchen and then looked yearningly at the door.

"I suppose," he began, "we better keep the boys— here's Hamilton, Asey."

"Comin' for you," Asey told him. "Yup, you better go. Reporters out there, Ham?"

"Fifty thousand. They all want—"

"Leary. Yessiree. Leary, you hustle right along!"

"They happened to want you," Hamilton said after Leary hastily departed. "Asey, here's some stuff from Lindsay. Just come through."

"Okay, Ham. Keep him out there, will you, as long as you can? Thanks."

Asey scrutinized the envelope and thrust it into his pocket.

"Can't you do something about things?" Tom asked. "What about Barr? Why don't you do something? Isn't there anything to work with at all? Wh—where are you going?"

"Goin' to b'gin doin' things I set out to do last night b'fore I was so rudely took on a boat trip," Asey said. "An' what I was settin' out to do earlier b'fore Waddy come. Don't take Leary so hard, Tom. Kid him along. Steve, c'mere."

Steve followed him into the little book-lined study that led off from the living room.

"I want all the stuff you've got on Rosalie," Asey shut the door, "an' all you wrote about her, an' all she wrote you. That's all. Thanks. You can run along."

"You want—"

"Peace an' quiet. Scoot."

He settled himself in an easy chair and read through the hundred odd pages that Steve had written of Rosalie's life. Occasionally he muttered to himself and once in a while he laughed outright. When he finished, he leaned back and lighted his pipe thoughtfully. Rosalie had led a full life.

As he began on the pile of clipped notes and typewritten index cards, Leary stomped in without knocking and plumped himself down on the leather chair.

"Say, Asey, this is tough! Clem O'Mara says—"

Stifling his snort of annoyance, Asey looked up.

"What d'you care about that fool columnist? Look, how'd Rosalie get here?"

"What? Why, she come to see Damon, didn't she?"

"But how? How'd she get to town?"

Leary looked surprised. "Don't you know? Didn't she come by train? Does it matter?"

"I got somethin' here," Asey pointed to the papers, "that makes me feel it's awful important. You better look into it. Tell the boys you got a lead, an' let 'em string along up town with you. They'll eat it up. Oh, what you think about the Damons, by the way?"

Primarily, Leary felt flattered that Asey should ask him.

"Oh, I don't know. Too easy, don't you think?"

"Somethin' in that," Asey kept a straight face. "I thought so. Okay. You find out how she got here."

Leary bustled out, and Asey grinned to himself as he continued reading the notes. He didn't really think that Rosalie's choice of transportation was so vital, but it might be, and if ferreting out the details would keep Leary and the reporters busy and happy, that was just so much to the good.

The last two items among the notes made Asey sit up.

One was a brief letter from Tom Fowler to Steve. Asey read it through twice.

"Dear Damon—Well, I pulled it on her at Jerry's party, and she had apoplexy. Said who told me she had a daughter, and to go to hell. No one around here seems to know anything about the daughter, except one or two recall her having had one by some early husband. I tried sleuthing, but no soap. Why brood about it? If she didn't bring it up, and flew into a temper when you mentioned it, just let it ride, why not? Let sleeping daughters die, and all. I'll try again before I see you at the Cape, but apparently you've landed on the only thing the Ray won't publicize. For God's sakes why not try your hand at pulp confessions or mysteries, and leave ghosting to hardier souls with fool proof stomachs? Tell Bets I love her dear and will bring her many socks to darn. They say it is spring but I haven't been above sixty-third street in months. I wish I would bring myself to leave this city of insufficient sleep. Yrs, Tom."

The last item was in Steve's handwriting, a sheet of yellow manila paper with the heading "Husbands, etc."

"1. Barney McCullough. Pass gently over. Longshoreman, bartender and general liability. Q:did she ever divorce him?

"2. Potter Van Altimus. Lasted four mos. Brickbat divorce with good headlines. Net $100,000. Society angle, taught her to use forks, dress, talk. 'I would of been happy with Pottsy, but his family was a bunch of cheap skates.'

"3. Pierre La Roc. Bohemian interval. 'We loved each other. He was a great artist.' Conveniently passed out of TB year after marriage. Paris. Q:why Paris?

"4. Ike Goldman. 1 yr. to Reno. She crashed Hollywood on him.

"5. Richard Grove. Seems to have been gent, but she had marriage annulled and he killed himself soon after. Barely mentioned. See if he was R. Grove, auth. Whaling Ships old New England, Romance of Whaling, etc., tho Rosalie says he was sort of an engineer or something."

Asey whistled. Grove, huh, and Hilda's name was Grove? And Grove wrote about whaling, and Rosalie had been killed with a whale lance.

He glanced briefly over the remainder of the sheet, headed "Sweetie Pies" by the cynical Steve. It read like a "Who's Who," and by no means confined itself to the United States.

Asey grinned, wondering how much the reporters would pay for the privilege of reading those names.

" 'Just a lot of nice men,' " Asey read Steve's footnote, " 'that I met traveling.' "

As he thrust the two papers into his pocket, he came upon the envelope from Lindsay. In it was a report on the Damons, Myles, Hilda and Tom. He read it through thoughtfully, and then strolled to the window.

He smiled involuntarily as he ran a finger over the frame. Whoever put that screen on was going to have some job getting it off next fall. The Damons had sloshed paint around as lavishly as most amateurs, and that frame was almost cemented in.

From where he stood he could not see the mob milling around the barricade at the rear of the house, but he could clearly hear its buzzing hum. The sound increased, and Asey heard a door slam. Apparently someone had come out of the back door, and the onlookers were having a field day.

Probably Leary. Asey shrugged and looked across the inlet with its sparkling little waves. There were half a dozen boat loads of curiosity seekers out there, and only the presence of a trooper at the landing kept them as far off as midstream. He sighed and looked back at the woods and the Damon's pitiful attempt at a lawn, and a small flower bed best described as meager. They had put a new rope on the old well sweep, he noticed, and—

"It's a hell of a pass when you can't put out a dish

towel," Betsey's voice was wrathful, "without having
mobs of camera men pop out of bushes like—like—"

"Jack in the boxes," Hilda helped her out. "Or is it
Jacks in the box? Anyway, cheer up. Maybe you'll get a
movie offer. Oh, Bets, look out in the inlet! More of
'em! We might just as well go indoors and prepare to
camp there for weeks and weeks. No more ultry violet
rays—oh, dear, there I go, bringing up rays again!"

As they passed by the window and around the corner
of the house, Asey heard a clinking sound that puzzled
him for a minute. Not pebbles. That bunch in the boats
wasn't near enough for that. Not—a slow smile spread
over his face.

"Now who," he murmured, "would of thought that?
Huh. I'll look into—"

He turned around as Leary again burst unceremoniously into the room, followed by Hamilton, another
trooper, and a bewildered and entirely strange couple.

"Asey, say, that was a lead all right! Look—these
two was hers!"

"Who was whose?"

"Ray's. See, she drove down in a limousine. You
ought to see it! Chrome, with a yellow stripe, and
streamlined to beat hell!"

"I don't doubt it a bit, but who're these folks?"

"We're her maid and chauffeur," the woman announced excitedly. "I'm the maid. I've been her maid
since 'Mimi's Garter,' and Charley's been with her since
the 'Kiss of Love.' And—"

"And they know all about her jewels," Leary interrupted, "and the diamond!"

"Look," Asey said patiently, "slow up, will you?
You," he nodded to the woman, "you tell it."

By degrees he got the story.

Charley had driven Rosalie and the maid, whose
name was Gerty, to Skaket on Friday. Due to the inac-
cessibility of the Damon house and the dearth of hotels
in Skaket, Charley and Gerty had gone on to Provincetown, with instructions to wait there until they were sent

for. But the Sunday morning papers had brought them rushing at top speed to the Cole place.

"Think," Leary said, "if Ham hadn't decided to stop 'em for speeding, God knows when we'd got 'em. That limousine—"

"Yup. What about the jewels?"

Rosalie carried with her, it seemed, a jewel case whose size was no indication of the value of its contents.

"She loved jewels," Gerty said, "and she had beautiful ones. She bought some, and people were always giving them to her."

"But a diamond and sapphire bracelet," Asey murmured softly, "lasts forever. What say, Leary? Oh, I was just quotin' a lady named Lee. No, you don't know her. Now—"

"But the jewels!" Gerty said. "They're gone, aren't they?"

Her face lengthened as Asey shook his head, and Leary looked as though he wanted to break down and weep.

"They're here? God," Leary said, "and I give that to the papers! Say, are the jewels all there, for sure?"

"The box wasn't locked, but it was as full as any reas'nble body'd wish. We locked it up inside her biggest bag. S'pose, though, you come up an' take a look at it, Gerty."

After Gerty recovered from a fit of weeping at the sight of Rosalie's possessions, she blew her nose in a determined fashion and set to work going through the jewel case, item by item.

"That was the Count, that ring, and this was that smooth Spaniard at Cannes, and this was the Hungarian at Palma, and—"

"Look," Asey said, "couldn't you just take inventory without goin' into the matter? Not that it ain't int'restin', but we ain't got all week. Is anythin' missin'?"

Gerty nodded. "Her diamond ain't here. It's the Lewis diamond, you know. She used to wear it in a sort of lavalière, but now she just wears it as a pin. It's gone. I *told* you," she added with a touch of pride, "I told you. I said to Charley we oughtn't to of let her take that jewel case. I didn't want her to. I wanted to take it and put it in the hotel safe where we was going, but she was stubborn and wouldn't. That's it, all right. Someone killed her for that."

Gerty sat back as though for herself, at least, the problem of Rosalie's death was forever settled. Leary began to look more at ease.

"Then it's all right for the papers. Say, is the Lewis diamond worth a lot, Asey?"

"Diamonds ain't a specialty of mine, but I seem to r'call the name. Corral the rest of the bunch, will you?"

Steve remembered the diamond pin.

"I do, too," Betsey said. "She had it clasped in a fold of her dress. Casually, as you might wear a five-and-ten pin. Sure it isn't still in the dress?"

"I looked," Gerty said. "It's not. I knew that was it. I felt it!"

"It's just not possible," Steve said. "Good God, would a woman wear the Lewis diamond outright, in a forsaken spot like this? I didn't think it was real. I thought you only wore things like that at court presentations or—or, well, places! Why," he made a helpless gesture, "I was so sure it was a fake, a piece of—what's the name, Bets?"

"Costume jewelry."

"Yes. I brayed around to Bets I thought sham diamonds were just her speed, and a lot of wisecracks went on about people who wore that gaudy stuff! Asey, I can't believe it was real!"

"Let me tell you," Gerty was bristling, "none of Miss Ray's jewelry was sham, let me tell you that! That was as real as the crown jewels of England!"

"She have it on when she went up to bed?" Asey asked.

"I wouldn't know, I suppose so. Hilda, you or Bets remember? Myles, how about you?"

"With all the tempest that was going on," Myles said, "I couldn't remember. I can't seem to remember it anyway. I shook her. It might have come off then."

"If it dropped off," Angelica said, "perhaps the burglar got it."

"I don't think so," Steve said. "We were all in front of the fireplace during that little scene, and if it had dropped off, it would have been in plain sight. And we roamed around that room plenty after she went to bed. We couldn't have missed anything as large as that. I remember it at dinner. That's when it began to annoy me. I don't really remember it later, but I was too mad to think of diamonds. Oh, lord, this is just another thing!"

"I s'pose," Asey asked Gerty, "you can prove your whereabouts Friday night?"

"I? Me? Sure. Well," she amended, "up to a certain point, that is."

"You see," Charley the chauffeur came to her aid. "You see, we been sort of on the go, lately. It was our first night off for a long time. We sort of—well, we sort of celebrated. We had a party. But the desk clerk would remember, all right."

Gerty had difficulty controlling her giggles.

"Charley give him a black eye," she explained. "When we come in, he done it. Charley thought he winked at me. You remember what time that was, Charley?"

"Five or six or so. The clerk'll know, all right."

"We'll look into it," Asey said. "Tell me, who give this diamond to Rosalie? She think a lot of it?"

"Why, she liked it best. It was the most valuable," Gerty explained simply. "Of course there was the sentimental value too. Her husband gave it to her."

"Which?" Asey asked.

"Well, I never knew him, but she always seemed to like him. He was the one that killed himself. Just from love of her, they say."

"That so?" Asey seemed to be staring at the top of the dressing table, but Myles, looking up, saw that his eyes were glued to the mirror above. From where he stood—yes, Asey was watching Hilda, who was entirely unconscious of his scrutiny.

"Yes, I guess he was a nice man, all right. His name was Grove. She always wanted this diamond and he bought it for her. After they were married—well, I don't exactly know what happened, but the marriage was annulled, and he killed himself out of love of her."

"But she kept the diamond?"

Hilda's face, Asey thought, couldn't get any whiter.

"He gave it to her, why not?" Gerty said. "If someone gives you—"

"Say," Leary, who had been striding impatiently around the room, touched his foot against the door. "What about that door, Asey? What about that key? And the light? Don't you have any idea who's got that key, or who took it? Don't you know where it is?"

"Key?" Asey said. "Oh, that door key. Sure, I know where it is. I was goin' for it when you bust in with these two."

"Well, for—where? Where is it?"

Asey watched Hilda's shoulders slump.

"In the bucket," he said. "In the bucket of the well sweep."

CHAPTER NINE

"IN THE bucket of the well sweep!" Leary snorted. "In the—Asey, are you nuts? In the bucket of the well sweep! The bucket! The bucket of the—"

"Wouldn't it be more fun," Angelica suggested acidly, "to investigate the bucket of the well sweep instead of playing parrot about it? If Asey says the key is there, I personally imagine that it is."

Leary swung on his heel and started out of the room.

"You know," Asey suggested, "I'd bring the bucket with the key, 'f I was you."

"Huh? What for?"

"Fingerprints, maybe," Asey said.

Hilda turned to Tom. "I want a cigarette. Didn't you take my case? Thanks. Now, Asey, suppose you and I go off into seclusion somewhere and have a nice long talk. I—"

"Is this quite the time," Tom asked, while Betsey and Steve and the others stared at her uncomprehendingly, "for a tête-à-tête? I mean, probably the story of your life is fascinating, cram full of thrills and heart throbs, but wouldn't it be just as well not to monopolize the head man now? Isn't it carrying—"

Leary dashed back into the room, bucket in hand.

"It's there! Can you beat it? It *was* there! What'll I do with it, Asey?"

"You could," Asey told him gently, "stand an' hold it, if you wanted. I'd s'gest you call Brady off the barricade an' have him get to work on it. Wait. Take care of this couple. Put 'em up in town somewhere, an' have someone take charge of 'em. An' mind you," he said to

Gerty, "reporters is fun, but you keep your thoughts to
yourself. Say all you want to about Rosalie, but omit
this business. See? Fine. C'mon, Hilda."

Down in Steve's study, Hilda stubbed out her cigarette and lighted another.

"I wonder," she said, "where I begin?"

"The b'ginnin's always good," Asey told her. "Like
where you found the key an' who you think put it
there."

Hilda smiled. "Two leaps ahead of me, aren't you? I
found it in my bureau drawer this morning. I've no idea
who put it there, or when it was put there. It's a drawer
I haven't touched since I stuck some things in it when I
unpacked. I suppose I should have brought it directly to
you, but I was scared stiff. I didn't know what to do
with it. I thought when I got the chance I'd toss it in the
water. I was going down to the shore this afternoon, in
spite of the trooper at the landing, but there were too
many people watching. I flipped it into the well. Just my
luck it hit the bucket! Betsey was too mad with the
camera men to notice, but I suppose you happened to
be at the window then. Look, that key *was* planted. You
may not believe me, but it was. I'm too scared not to
tell the truth. I couldn't lie if I wanted to."

"Scared because of your father, huh?"

Hilda nodded. "I—well, you probably know it all."

"Did Steve know?"

"Oddly enough, though I've heard him talk about Rosalie's husbands, and Betsey wrote me reams about
them, I don't think it entered the head of either of them
to connect Richard Grove with me. To them I'm just an
orphan. There's something awfully final about being an
orphan."

"Were you, by any chance, Rosalie's daughter?"

"I? My God, no! Look, don't you know the story? I
thought you did. I'm not her daughter. I never saw her
in the flesh till she came Friday. If she'd thought, I suppose she'd have doped out who I was. I look like father.
But I don't think she even heard my name when I was

introduced. She was too furious with the man who rowed her over, and with Steve, and the house. Just general annoyance and her digestive system, all coming to a head at once."

Asey pulled Lindsay's report out of his pocket.

"In here, they can't find much record of you. Where you was born, or anythin'. Want to go into it, an' all about your father?"

"I was born in Chile twenty-five years ago," Hilda said. "Father was working there, and Mother wouldn't stay alone in New York, and so she came. We lived there till I was five. Then we went back to New York, and Father met Rosalie Ray at a bawdy banquet." Hilda leaned back in her chair and looked at Asey. "I don't quite know how to explain it, even now. He just went haywire over her. Forgot Mother, forgot me, forgot his business, and his friends, and everything else. He spent every cent on her. Mother couldn't pry enough from him to keep herself and me. So we went to Boston, and a cousin of hers took us in."

"Was your father a wealthy man?" Asey asked.

"No, but he looked it, if you know what I mean. He loved to spend money. Rosalie thought that was a nice idea, too. She wanted the Lewis diamond. Some jeweler had got a lot of reporters going on it about then. So Father got her the Lewis diamond. If she'd wanted the Kohinoor, Father probably would have thrown that in, too."

"Where'd he get the money for it all?"

"That comes in later, Asey. Mother read in the papers about the diamond, and then read that Father had married Rosalie. That finished her. She'd always stood up for him and said he'd come to his senses, and come back, and everything would be all right again. But the marriage sort of settled that. Father hadn't bothered to get a divorce, and Mother wouldn't have, I think, even if she'd had the money."

"Thus all parties was placed," Asey said, "in a dif'cult p'sition."

Hilda nodded. "Naturally Mother wondered where the money came from to buy the stone. So did Father's firm. They did a little quiet checking up, and found out. I guess about that time Rosalie caught on, too. To lots of things. She had the marriage annulled, and when the firm's detectives came to get Father, they found he'd killed himself. Mother died two months later, and as for me, I was farmed out from cousin to cousin, all over New England. Dad's people were New Englanders too, and they chipped in. People can laugh all they want to about this stern and rock-bound coast, but I've considerable respect for the clan spirit."

"Sea cap'ns, your father's folks?" Asey asked. "Whalers, maybe?"

"Yes. Why—oh. You know those books he wrote? I suppose," she got up and walked restlessly around the little room, "I suppose of all the people in this house, I'm the only one who really knew what a whale lance was used for. I know those books almost by heart. I used to read them and read them. They seemed—well, the only decent heritage I had from the Groves."

"I wonder what you felt," Asey might have been talking to himself, "that night she ramped around, with that diamond on."

Hilda admitted that they weren't very pretty thoughts.

"That stone—well, perhaps if it hadn't been for that, Father might have come to his senses. Things would have been different. I didn't realize that till I was in school. All of it happened when I was such a kid. Still, I don't think I was as resentful about Rosalie and her diamond Friday night as I was plain mad at the dirty deal she was handing Steve and Betsey. Those kids have had their share of rotten luck, and they don't deserve any more."

Asey looked at Hilda with something akin to admiration in his eyes.

"You," he said, "should be an authority on bum luck."

"Oh, I don't know. I wasn't a playboy booted into a breadline, like Steve. I've always some loyal clan member to fall back on if jobs give out entirely. Betsey never had. Not that Myles and the rest of her relatives didn't help her, but they weren't the kind who sent roast chickens in laundry cases, if you know what I mean. Asey, your pal Leary is going to have a dress parade with me. Practically a carnival. I'm not psychic, but I feel it coming."

"I'm kind of afraid so, if he gets the whole yarn."

"D'you believe me when I say that I didn't know she was coming, didn't kill her, didn't honestly ever think of killing her, for all the bitter thoughts I may have had from time to time? I'll admit to the key-throwing business. That was sheer panic. No one wants to be dragged into a thing like this. Not when people could make such a story out of it. I suppose the saga of Richard Grove still sits in the newspaper files, waiting for some bright lad to drag it up."

Asey puffed at his pipe. "I'm sort of sure they will."

"I feel it. I'm positive. But the point is, do you believe me? I can't prove anything about Friday from quarter of five on. No more than the others can. We were all too exhausted by the time we got to bed to think anything, let alone prove anything. Steve must have made superhuman efforts to stay up. I couldn't have. Why, by the way, haven't you gone into the time elements there?"

Asey shrugged. "S'pose I did? You was all done up. You couldn't be sure of anything. None of you woke up. If somethin' incrim'nated any of you five in the house, the rest'd all lie manful about it. Hilda, didn't you ever even want to kill Rosalie?"

"Death doesn't pay scores." Hilda lighted another cigarette. "D'you think it does? You can mutter all you want about eyes for eyes and teeth for teeth, but had I ever thought it my job to get back at her for what she did to Father, I think I should have tried to make her suffer about something to the same degree my mother did. I shouldn't have killed her. I should simply have made her wish she were comfortably dead. Besides, if Father hadn't wanted to be led on, he wouldn't have been. You can't blame Rosalie exclusively."

"Even if you hadn't told me of your New England upbringing'," Asey told her, "I'd of guessed it from that. I do believe you. Tell me, what about Tom? You know him before you come here?"

"Dear me, yes. He knew Steve and I knew Betsey, and we practically married them off, between us."

"He knew Rosalie?"

"He knows everyone," Hilda said. "Everyone. From traffic cops and elevator men and janitors to Park Avenue and all the way back. He's the happy-go-lucky sort people phone when they feel drab, or want a fourth for bridge, or anything. I've heard tell he does ferreting for a keyhole columnist, but I don't know. He could. He knows all of God's children and all their business. But I'd count him out of this affair, from the start. He's got too many irons in the fire to burn himself. He dabbles. He couldn't get intense enough about anything to commit murder. I don't know, but you always think of him patting dogs, and winding up toys for youngsters, and helping old ladies across streets. That's the sort of person he is."

"S'pose," Asey said, "you send him in here."

"Right. Does Hilda get the works?"

Asey grinned. "Wasn't you holdin' that key by your handkerchief? I thought so. No prints. Well, then. Hilda minds her p's an' q's, an' the next clew comes to Asey, an' not to the ole oaken bucket. Send Tom—hey, what'm I gettin' embraced for?"

"Why? Because," Hilda's eyes were moist, "if parents could be picked, I'd throw bombs to get you. Okay. I'll send Tom in."

Asey smiled as the door closed behind her. Ordinarily he took little stock in the younger generation. But the young folks in this mess seemed to be measuring up. He emptied the overflowing ash tray as Tom knocked and entered.

"Next! Asey, what is this strange power of yours for reducing females to tears of joy? Every now and then Bets says 'Asey!' and weeps happily, and even the Sage gets misty about you. They say it's because you're so *good,* as though all other men were a bunch of dirty crooks in comparison."

"Just my fatal charm," Asey said. "Is it tobacco you're wantin' for that pipe? Catch."

Tom caught the pouch. "I hope someone remembers to get cigarettes. The supply is weakening, what with Hilda chimneying around. What've I done, Asey? Or what can I do for you?"

"Dunno. S'pose you b'gin with the story of your life. Oh, not all of it. Just the high spots."

"Well," Tom settled himself in the leather chair and dangled his legs over an arm, "I'm not much, Asey. I'm the sort of man that women give pep talks to. You know, why don't you get a nice job and make something of yourself, or stick to something long enough to get somewhere? That sort of thing. Fellows like Steve call me Good Old Tom, like Good Old Fido. Always depend on Good Old Tommy for a laugh. They think I was born to take their sisters out."

"Were you?" Asey asked.

"Not a bit," Tom said cheerfully. "The infinite trust which mankind invariably puts in me is probably the reason I'm such a good-natured bum. Nobody thinks of thwarting me. It would be on a par with peppermint stick swiping. So I have no competition. No stimulus for self-advancement. Good Old Tommy will sleep it off."

Asey rubbed his chin reflectively. "It's a pip of an act," he said at last. "I s'pose you sort of b'gun it as a pose, an' took it up as a pol'cy. If I had a sister, I wouldn't let you out of sight with her. I—what say?"

Tom took his pipe out of his mouth. "Just an exclamation of wonder, Asey! No wonder you get the women!"

"Yup. Now, snap out of this an' tell me about Ros'lie's daughter."

"Rosalie's daughter," Tom removed his legs from the arm of the chair, "is getting me down. Steve asked me about her. Matter of fact, I think I brought the subject up. I'd heard about the girl somewhere. I tried to get the lowdown on her, but no soap. If she exists, she's covered herself up nicely. Or Rosalie saw to it she was."

"Whose child is it, or was it?"

Tom shrugged. "Officially La Roc's, I believe. He died of T.B. Very likely if he was the father, the child died of it too. I wouldn't know. No one does. Ray blew me sky high when I asked her outright. Got me fired from a swell job on a morning radio program, to boot. Of course her name was never mentioned, but it got around that she didn't care for me. People were afraid of that temper of hers. She could be more ruthlessly nasty than any other woman I ever knew."

"How'd you get here Friday night, through that swamp?"

"With a borrowed flashlight and a map some worthy citizen gave me. He lived near the station. I said I'd return the flash—maybe one of your men could?"

"What was his name?"

"I wouldn't know, but he wore a beard. I—"

Leary marched in.

"Say, can you beat it? Brady says there's no marks on that key!"

"Well?"

"Well? Asey, what're we going to do?"

"Just what we did before we found it," Asey told him.

"How'd you know it was there in the bucket?"

"Guessed. I'd of tossed it down the well, myself."

"Who put it there? Did that girl put it there? If she didn't put it there, who did? Who—"

"Who," Tom said, "is the aunt of the gardener's boy? Is the aunt of the gardener's boy fond of cabbage? Leary, you sound like a French primer!"

"I bet *you* put it there," Leary said. "I been thinking about you!"

"That's nice of you," Tom said. "Lieutenant Leary, thinking only of me. Very few people take the trouble, as I've just been telling Asey. They—"

"Look," Asey tried to stop Tom before Leary blew up, "has three local boys shown up askin' for me yet? Will you tell your men to let me know the minute they do? An' say, I wish you'd get a full report on that couple, Ros'lie's two. You do that sort of thing a lot better'n I do. Thanks."

"I begin to see your method," Tom said after Leary left. "Honest soft soap. What about Waddy Barr? I may be doing him a grave injustice, but I think he's pretty nasty."

"He is," Asey said, "an' the chances of workin' him into this is nil. But I'm goin' to try awful hard, an' I have a sneakin' feelin' that if we try long enough, little Waddy may blow up."

"Crack?"

"He's too soft to crack." Asey laughed. "I can see where we have fun with his mama. I'm kind of wonderin' where she is. I expected her long ago. She ought to show up most any minute. I'm lookin' forward to that."

Tom raised his eyebrows. "I thought she was on the battleship order, not a one to be incited or aroused."

"She's more of a super-d'rigible," Asey said. "As for 'rousin' her, well, didn't you ever blow up a b'loon for the sheer joy of havin' it bust? Wait'll she comes, an' you'll see what I mean. If I could puncture her, I might get Waddy meltin'."

True to his prediction, Mrs. Wadsworth Barr arrived that afternoon around three o'clock. She came in a massive motor boat whose beam, as Angelica tersely suggested, matched Mrs. Barr's to an inch.

"Pig-headed windbag!" she continued. "Asey, if you can prick her self-complacence, I'll remember you in my will. She's got Weasel with her! Oh, give it to both of 'em, good and plenty!"

"Vengeance," Asey reminded her with a grin, "is the Lord's, but as ole Cap'n Scull used to say, it does seem like as if you should ought to give heaven a helpin' hand once in a while. Ever hear of Veeny Scull, Miss Sage? He was the one that fought tooth'n nail against the 'malgamatin' of the first an' second Meth'dist churches. He said—"

"She's knocking!" Angelica interrupted.

"I know. He said, 'It's agin' reason an' it's agin' common sense, an' agin' all princ'ples of lawr an' order an' justice—' "

"That front door," Steve said, "is not as strong as it might be. Just a suggestion."

"Let her bang on," Asey said. "An' when the final vote was three hundred an' sixty-nine to one, Veeny got up in his pew an' said, says he, 'It's still agin' reason an' common sense, an' all the princ'ples of lawr an' order an' justice, but it sort of appears that it's the Lord's will just the same.' I'll go."

Mrs. Barr swept into the Damons' living room rather, as Steve said later, like a large, determined icy blast. Weasel Smith, her lawyer, hovered behind her as though he had been blown in by mistake.

"This is a disgrace," Mrs. Barr announced. "This whole affair is a blot on the escutcheon of Skaket. I should think Josiah Cole would turn in his grave. I knew what would happen. I told him so."

Asey saw his opportunity and seized it.

"Leary!" he went to the door and called. "Leary, hey, Leary, here's the person we been lookin' for. C'mere, Mrs. Barr. C'mere, Leary. Mrs. Barr, meet Lieutenant Leary. Leary, she says she knew all this would happen."

"You did, huh?" Leary asked truculently. "Well, just you tell me the whole story, see?"

"I know nothing whatever of *this* affair. I—"

"Don't let her kid you," Asey said. "She just told us she knew what would happen. Weasel, ain't that so?"

Mr. Smith looked at Asey, and then looked at Mrs. Barr. He was in a spot, and he knew it.

"Why, she—"

"I said nothing of the kind! I said, I told Josiah Cole I knew what would happen."

"Then what on earth," Angelica had caught the faint flicker of Asey's eyebrows, "what on earth makes you say you didn't say it? Really, Mrs. Barr, if you had any knowledge of this horrible business, I consider it most reprehensible of you not to have taken the matter up with the proper authorities."

"P'ticularly," Asey said, "since you wrote Bill Penny up to the hosp'tal that you suspected there'd be some trouble over here, an' that he should ought to do somethin' about the Damon fam'ly an' their goin's on."

"And you built your old fences," Betsey chimed in, eager to add her bit, "to make sure nothing happened on your land. Of course you knew. It's disgraceful!"

"Yup," Asey said. "You felt b'forehand that Skaket's 'scutcheon was goin' to be peppered with blots. Whyn't you do somethin'?"

"Why?" Leary thundered in his best third-degree voice. "If you had any idea, let me tell you—"

At some length Leary proceeded to tell her just what should have been done to avert the tragedy, what would happen to her because she had taken no steps, and what he thought of women like her in general.

Myles, Steve, and Betsey listened with glowing faces. Hilda was grinning. Tom chuckled quietly. Angelica had reached the stage where the white, eau de cologne-scented handkerchief had to be applied to her eyes.

Asey alone kept a straight face, feeding an occasional word or suggestion to Leary when he showed signs of running down. Weasel Smith shrank into his chair; he had always thought himself a master at that sort of thing, but he recognized a past master.

Mrs. Barr's frigid indignation gave way to blank

amazement, then worked through startled wonder to a more or less complete deflation. She was gulping when Leary finally stopped, but no words came.

"There," Asey said. "See? Leary, you know what I think? I think you'd ought to let the r'porters know. You take her out an' tell 'em about it. Local Woman Anticipates Slaying. Prom'nent Res'dent—er—Foretold Débâcle. No, make that Golgotha. That's right, Mrs. Barr. You go with the lieutenant."

"Not," Steve remarked after the two had gone, "not even a zephyr. Oh, Asey, how did you ever think of matching that couple?"

"It was downright cruel," Angelica said weakly. "Oh, I don't suppose anyone ever bellowed back at her before in all her life. My, that was magnificent!"

Asey turned to the lawyer. "Well, Weasel, now that's over, what'd she come for? What you two been hatchin' up b'tween yourselves?"

Weasel passed him a sheaf of papers. "Waddy," he explained. "Where he was Friday. Affidavits."

Asey flicked through them.

"Just thought of everything, didn't you, Weasel? Huh. 'Mr. Barr returned home at one-fifty-five a.m., driving his grey roadster. After listening to the radio for a period not exceeding thirty minutes, Mr. Barr retired an' to the best of the undersigned's knowledge an' information, did not again leave the house. Deponent—' Yes, that's fine, Weasel. Anythin' more?"

"She—she really didn't know anything about the murder," Mr. Smith said timidly. "She just meant, she knew no good would come of Cole's selling the place to these people."

"No, did she?" Asey said. "My, my, how we wronged her! Didn't we, Weasel! I tell you what. You hop out after her an' Leary, an' you just tell the r'porters she's bein' wronged."

"But—"

"I know it's my job to tell 'em, but they like new slants. You go, Weasel. Tell 'em about Charlestown, too. Go quick, b'fore Leary's wronged her too hearty. That's it!"

Mr. Smith left with hasty reluctance. He wanted to be rid of Asey, but he did not look forward to the interview he expected from Mrs. Barr.

"What about the affidavits?" Tom asked.

"Take 'em or leave 'em. It'd be very hard to try an' prove in court that Waddy Barr wasn't sleepin' sound an' dreamin' dreams 'round five Friday mornin'. I know why he was plannin' to be sure of where he was Friday."

"Why?" Betsey asked.

"Oh, 'mong other things, he expected this place to be set on fire. Didn't I tell you? Even so, he took a lot of trouble. I sort of wonder about it all, still."

"You mean you actually found out who Waddy hired to harass Steve and Bets?" Tom demanded.

"Sure. But just the samey, this is so doggone ironclad. One af'davit wouldn't of bothered me. All this bunch of 'em, carryin' him from dinner to bed, when all the al'bi he needs is from bedtime on—what's up, Ham?" he broke off as the trooper entered. "Mrs. Barr excited again? Exudin'?"

"It's this." Hamilton passed a letter to Asey. "Mrs. Barr slipped it to me while Leary was busy with the reporters. Had a bill wrapped around it. Here."

Asey whistled. "A century note, huh?" He read the inscription on the envelope and frowned. "She make any comments about it?"

"Only that Waddy wanted it to get to Tom Fowler quick as possible, without you seeing it."

CHAPTER TEN

"Tom!" Betsy's wide open mouth reminded Angelica of the nest of robins outside her south window. "Tommy Fowler—did you know that pig of a Waddy Barr? Do you?"

"He knows everybody," Hilda nodded to Asey. "Didn't I tell you?"

"Tom, I think you're a skunk! I—why didn't you say so yesterday? I'm raging! I—"

"No need to rage at me," Tom told her with a grin. "I never laid eye on him till yesterday—after all, Bets, where's your wit? Granted that I know a lot of odd folk, did any of 'em ever resemble that pudgy, stodgy, overfed cream puff? Can't you give me any credit at all? Asey, open the letter and read it. I haven't the remotest idea why Barr should pen me little missives. I'm sure I never gave the little pill any encouragement. This correspondence is entirely his thought. Read it to the assembled multitudes. My conscience is clear."

Asey looked searchingly at him for a moment, and then slit the envelope with his forefinger.

"Huh," he said, after glancing over the single sheet of cream-colored notepaper. "Crest, even. Where d'you suppose she thought up a crest for old Loosh Barr? It's an anvil with a sword. S'pose she was the sword an' Loosh the anvil. Maybe it's because ole Zachary Barr, Loosh's grandfather, was a blacksmith, but 'twas salt codfish balls in cans that made 'em all rich. Should think a can opener would of been better—"

"Read it," Tom said. "After all, it's my letter."

" 'Dear Fowler,' " Asey read, " 'will you do your best

to convince Mayo that whatever I may have done in an effort to dislodge the Damons, I am entirely guiltless of any connection whatsoever with the events of Friday night and the murder?—' Y'know," Asey broke off, "Weasel must of wrote that for him. Waddy couldn't of thought up a sentence like that to save his life."

"What's the rest?" Tom asked.

"That's all. He's sincerely yours, Wadsworth Barr. For the love of Pete! What got into him?"

"I told you," Tom sighed, "my trusting face is responsible for a lot of things. Probably the lad looked over this assembled crew and instinctively recognized me as a Good Old Tom, someone to depend on. He wanted to come clean. Couldn't exactly appeal to Bets and Steve, under the circumstances. Couldn't ask a strange lady like Hilda, or someone like Miss Sage, who obviously hated the sight of him. Myles—well, Myles is a kindly trusting soul, too, but I've the advantage of being a contemporary. He thought—well, I wouldn't go so far as to say that he *thought,* exactly, but it came over him that I was a man in a thousand, someone under whose honest exterior beat a heart of purest ray serene. Beaten gold. Platinum. An eighteen jewel movement—"

"At the sound of the musical note," Hilda interrupted, "I shall bash you one. Dry up!"

"No, I've been appealed to," Tom said, "and my better nature is on the loose. Asey, don't send little Waddy to jail. Please. Think of his mother. Think of him in sailor suits—God, mustn't he have been a ghastly sight? And don't you think, since the letter was addressed to me, that I ought to have a cut out of the hundred? Then I could buy some cigarettes and stop bumming Hilda's. Now personally—"

"How long," Asey appealed to Steve, "can he keep this sort of thing up?"

"Indefinitely," Steve said. "He thinks it's smart."

"Now, now," Tom said, "now, now. I'm barely started. I want to—"

"Come 'long with me," Asey interrupted. "No—on second thought, Miss Sage, you come 'long with me. Hamilton, distract Brother Leary for a while, will you? I'm goin' to town. My car ready?"

"The doc saw to that. It's in Henderson's barn."

"Fine. Come 'long, Miss Sage. Better take a coat. Ham, tell Leary I got an idea an' I'm chasin' it, an' to look after things till I get back."

"What about Mrs. Barr?"

"Let Leary play with her. If she asks you about the note, say you got it to Tom. If—"

"If she gives you any more presents," Tom said, "I hereby demand an agent's commission. I might make carfare home. I might even rate a pullman. I—"

"Yah," Hilda jeered. "What about the capitalistic railroads? Yah-yah. Parlor pink."

"I'll make a speech to the engineer," Tom said, "and clearly point out to the brakeman that as a member of the working class—"

"So long," Asey said. "You might help amuse Leary after this crowd boots you out."

"Only Waddy Barr," Tom said in tones of grief, "really understands me. Bets, can I eat worms in your garden? No one loves me—"

Asey took Hamilton's arm as they went out the front door behind Angelica.

"Just keep an eye on Tom, will you? An' say, got that flashlight of his? I'll take it."

Apparently unaware of the sensation he was causing among the newspapermen and the curiosity-seekers behind the barricade, Asey strolled down to the landing with Miss Sage.

"Mind bein' in the rotogravure? It won't look like you, so don't worry. We'll hop over the inlet in the boat an' then pick up my car. I got some odds an' ends to look into."

Angelica tried to match his poise, but she couldn't help glancing occasionally at the skiff-loads of people out in midstream as Asey and the trooper on guard at the landing fiddled with the moorings.

"I don't mind much, but my family will." She yanked her hat brim down over her eyes and thrust up the collar of her tweed coat. "Is it Waddy or Tom you're looking into?"

"Both. Hop in."

He shot the boat out into the inlet, deftly circled around their curious audience, and sped across to the opposite shore. The tall figure of Joe Henderson uncoiled itself from a rocking-chair on the end of his wharf.

"Hi," he said, "okay—I got her. Been waitin' for you a long time. Doc said you'd probably be in a hurry when you come. Car's in the barn. I'll look after this craft for you."

"Thank you kindly," Asey said. "Just keep folks off her, an' you don't know where we went. See you later."

"May I ask," Angelica inquired as they walked up the path to Henderson's barn, "just why I—er—got the call on this expedition?"

"Always nice to have a witness," Asey said. "You—"

"I get it. I neither distract nor allure, and I love to know what's going on. But why not Myles? He was itching to come."

"Myles," Asey said, "is a nice feller, but that ca'm p'liteness of his sort of wears me down. He's so trustfully acceptin'."

"Pooh!" Angelica said. "Asey, I wish you'd listen to the story of his bus trip Friday. Really, it was amazing! You wouldn't make cracks about Myles if you—"

"When this business is over," Asey opened the barn doors and wedged them back with stones, "I promise to set down some evenin' and let myself be told a blow by blow d'scription of that bus trip. It ain't that I ain't yearnin' an' burnin' to hear all about ev'ry jounce, but right now the story'd distract me. How d'you like m'new car?"

Angelica surveyed the long, shining, open roadster

with an admiration only slightly tinged with qualms. The manner in which Asey drove was legend.

"It's a beauty! Brand new?"

"Bill Porter wished it on me two weeks ago. It's next year's model—"

"But the mileage is four thousand!"

"I played with her at the plant track. She's a nice car," Asey said appreciatively, "easy to handle an' fast as any human'd want to travel this side of heaven, but I dunno." He shut Angelica's door and climbed in behind the wheel. "There don't seem to be fun with cars no more. Just a question of how soon you want to be where. In the ole days, it was more of a prop'sition— like how near you could get to the place you hoped to get to, b'fore it'd be too late to get there on time by catchin' a train."

"Where are you going?" Angelica asked as they swung out on the tarred road. "Weesit?"

"I want Doc Cummings to play with this note of Waddy's an' see if they's more to it than meets the eye. I don't get this business one bit. I put Waddy down as a fool—"

"He is," Angelica said firmly.

"Maybe. What you think of Tom?"

She hesitated. "I can't exactly explain. But he's no fool even though he likes to pretend as much."

"Just so. Y'know, a clever person who pretends to be stupid is always sort of rated higher than he is. Most any crack he gets off is lots smarter seemin' than if he was just himself. Ord'nary man that juggled words like Tom wouldn't be a bit funny, but when he leans back, an' half closes his eyes, an' looks sleepy, an' then banters away at top speed, he's almost amusin'."

"That's probably why he knows everyone," Angelica said thoughtfully. "He's really as bright as most people he meets, if not brighter, but he makes them think he's way beneath them, and people like to feel above other people—I'm getting awfully involved here."

"P'raps, but you're right. An' it makes Tom feel

swell, 'cause he knows at heart he's twice as bright as anyone else. They laugh at him free and hearty, an' he laughs back up his sleeve, an' a peachy time is had by all. Only," Asey swung off on a side road, "I sized Tom up as not bein' anywhere near as bright as he thinks. Now either him an' Waddy is two fools, or both of 'em ain't, an' I am."

As they drew up in front of the Cummings's house, the doctor himself appeared on the front steps, assisting a young girl whose left ankle was bound up. Behind them was an incredibly good-looking young man whose incredibly perfect, white flannel suit brought forth a comment from Asey.

"My, my, is he real?"

"It's Blaisdell Morris, the manager and leading man of the Pochet Playhouse," Angelica whispered, "and the girl is that Lee Laurie who made such a hit on Broadway last winter. She's just an infant, but people went wild over her. She's quite good—"

"P'raps she is," Asey said, "but he b'longs under a glass case. Do they grow men like that in a hot-house, I wonder?"

"Ssh!" Angelica said. "Ssh! They'll hear you!"

Dr. Cummings saw the couple into their car and then walked over to the roadster.

"Well, Asey, what's news? Don't I have some pretty snappy patients? D'you know, ever since I first saw Morrie, I've been aching to know if those teeth were real. It didn't seem possible, but they are."

Asey wanted to know how the doctor had found out.

"Easy. Told him he seemed hoarse and gave him a tumbler of mouth wash to gargle. They're real, and he's undeniably the perfect male. Girl's got a nasty ankle. Sprain. Get out and come in, and tell me everything. What's happened?"

Asey gave a résumé of the night before, including their experience in the inlet.

"Laugh on," he said. "Anyway, the feller's still at

large, and the Lewis diamond's missin', an' someone planted the door key of Rosalie's room on Hilda, an' Waddy's writin' billy doos to Tom. Look it over, will you?"

"Secret messages aren't much in my line," the doctor said dubiously. "But if Waddy Barr wrote the letter, I don't think it'd be very complicated. We'll stick it in the oven and see what about lemon juice, and then I'll delve into a book I've got and see what might be done—"

At the end of half an hour, he handed the letter back to Asey.

"Nothing that I can find. Your fellows at the police barracks might do better, but I think it's a waste of time. You're endowing Waddy with brains he doesn't have. Now what?"

"Now," said Asey, "we go call on Waddy."

"Don't glow so," the doctor said. "Toying with that lump shouldn't be fun for you. I wouldn't even call it a workout. I think I can truthfully say that he's dumber than Blaisdell Morris, the perfect male. Morris is just a case of arrested development—probably would have been quite normal if he'd been ugly. But Waddy—why, the boy never had anything to develop, or arrest!"

As their interview with Waddy at the Barr house dragged along, Asey began to feel that possibly the doctor had been right about the mentality of the heir to the Barr millions.

Waddy insisted that he had never met Tom before, that he had never known Tom before, that Tom had never known or seen him before Saturday.

"I only saw him for the first time yesterday," he said for the twentieth time. "That's all."

"Then why in the name of common sense do you write him notes?" Asey asked with growing impatience.

"I tell you," Waddy said, "he looked like a nice fellow, that's all. Someone who'd do a good turn, that's all."

Asey looked at Miss Sage and sighed.

"Who was the girl you chased in the woods on Friday?"

"I don't know," Waddy said. "Honest, I don't know. I didn't get a good look at her. She just seemed to be any summer person. She wasn't a native."

"Huh," said Asey.

"Won't you take this cop away?" Waddy asked. "I'm tired of having him around. I can't see why he has to stay here. Neither does Mother."

"Just glance over your past," Asey said, "an' guess why he's here. Guess why he's goin' to stay here, too. So long. Try ponderin'."

"You sounded menacing," Angelica commented as they got into the car again. "D'you mean anything, or were you bluffing?"

"I still don't get this business," Asey said. "Waddy's a fool. We admit that, an' it's one fact all done and tied up in red ribbon. But he don't do the unexpected. Sure, he run liquor, an' he's been runnin' dope or somethin'. But you expect it of a punk like him. Letters— Well— Huh. We'll let it ride for the time bein' an' look into Tom."

He drove back to Skaket through a series of backroads framed with scrub oaks and scrub pines; Angelica winced as the branches and brambles scratched at the roadster's sparkling paint.

"I'm doin' it on purpose," Asey told her, "to show Bill it's a bum paint job. Who wears a beard near the station?"

Angelica stared at him.

"Tom pulled in on the freight and borrowed a flash from a man with a beard," Asey explained, "pr'sumably near the station. Said he tried a few houses. I guess we can figger it out."

He drew the car up by the Skaket station, and got out.

"Let's see. North-east storm. Walk away from the rain—I s'pose even Tom'd walk away from it, whether he knew what he was doin' or not. Tries five houses, I think he said. Prob'ly one or two. Huh. Who lives in the old Knowles place now?"

"The gingerbread? Oh, the white one. I've bought eggs and quohaugs there—the man *does* have a beard. Gould. That's it. Somebody Gould. Plump, red-faced man."

"Gould." Asey thought for a moment. "Must be Rufe. We'll go see."

"He'll probably turn out to be a cousin," Angelica remarked. "The world may not be your oyster, so to speak, but it certainly is your relative."

Asey shook his head. "Don't think. We don't connect with the Goulds that I know of."

But Mr. Gould greeted them, all the same, as though they were a pair of long lost friends.

"Asey Mayo—ain't seen you in years! R'member the last time? I was on the Daisy M—one of Thurber's tugs, and you was on a fruit boat. T-wharf, I think. Well, well. Come in!"

" 'Fraid we can't," Asey told him. "We come to r'turn a light you lent a guy Friday."

"Say, did that feller reach the Cole place? Honest, I didn't think the flash'd hold out. Didn't think he'd get there, for that matter."

Asey pressed the button. "Seems to of lasted, all right —whoa! there she goes! Used it up. Yes, he got there. I'm kind of int'rested in that feller, Rufe. Tell us about him."

"I ain't a light sleeper," Mr. Gould said, "but he banged loud enough to wake the dead. My wife got worried, so I come downstairs to see what was the matter, an' there was that feller, lookin' like a drowned rat. He said he wanted to get to the Damons, an' after I figgered out who they was, I drew him a map an' give him a flashlight. I'd of asked him to stay, but he seemed to want to go on. Funny feller."

"Know what time it was?"

"Yessir, I do. I asked him how he come, cause I couldn't see any car around, an' he laughed an' said he come on the freight. That gets in 'round three, usually."

"But did you hear it? Or look at a clock, or anything?" Asey persisted.

"Nope, but—say, you'll laugh at this. I got a rooster that crows every night at three-fifteen. Set a clock by him. After that feller left, I heard him—I mean the rooster—crowin' away, an' fore I got back to sleep, I heard the freight tootlin' at the South crossin'. So he must of come off the freight an' come over here an' gone b'fore three-fifteen. I tell you, that rooster don't never crow except at three-fifteen, an' the freight usually hits the South crossin' a little later."

"Well," Asey said, "that seems to settle that. Thanks."

"He—that feller ain't mixed up in this murder, is he?"

"It would sort of seem," Asey said, "that he wasn't. Okay. Come over some time an' see me, Rufe, an' we'll jaw over ole times. Bye!"

"It appears," Angelica said as they rolled down the main street, "that the group you have to work on is exceptionally truthful. Waddy liked Tom's face, and Tom came as he said—why did you check up on his arrival, anyway? I mean, would it matter what time he came to town? He was at the Coles' when the murder happened anyway."

"Yup," Asey said, "I had a kind of faint, feeble hope, though, that—oh, well. It don't work. You can't beat roosters an' train whistles. Trouble with this is, you got t' b'lieve everybody. I b'lieve Hilda's explanation of herself an' the key. I can't help b'lievin' Steve an' Betsey didn't have nothin' to do with killin' Ros'lie, for all they may have wanted to. I couldn't b'lieve Myles had anythin' to do with it. You could say he had a motive for the youngsters' sakes, but I don't see him wieldin' whale lances. Waddy's got his affidavits. Tom's told the truth, an' we prove it. I'd give a plugged nickel for a good lie."

"Who d'you think did it?" Angelica asked.

Asey shrugged. "My first guess is someone in the

house, or someone who'd been there. Outsider, like their burglar, wouldn't of known about that lance or where it was, or anythin'."

"What d'you make, though, of Waddy's lighter being there, and the key in Hilda's drawer? And this burglar? And the diamond?"

"Not to speak," Asey said, "of the lady who lost her white suede pump. Dunno. I'm goin' to run over to Barradio's now an' see if them boys ain't got somewheres about findin' who that girl is."

Ramon and Frank Barradio and Mike Mallon sat dejectedly on the front steps of the Barradio house. They greeted Asey without enthusiasm.

"No soap."

"Did you try?" Asey inquired in his best drawl.

"Try?" Ramon looked at him. "Say, we ain't been to bed last night, yet. We just got back. Tony won't let us in, an' we haven't any money, an' we ain't eaten since we left last night. Try!"

"Hm. Didn't you get nowhere at all?"

"We begun in Provincetown," Mike said. "We seen her picture somewheres, an' I thought it was there. Cop there tried to arrest us for lookin' into store windows with a flash. He thought we were burglars. I figgered, see, she might be an artist's model. She wasn't. Then we went over to Chatham an' looked at the movie signs, an' we looked on posters, an' then we come home an' went through a pile of magazines an' papers. We went through about a month of papers. We knew we seen her picture somewheres. These fellers wanted to stop, but I wouldn't. Oh—say, will you fix it with the cop in Hyannis that got us for speedin'?"

"I'll try. Go on."

"Well, then at last this morning I remembered where the picture was. In the—" he looked at Miss Sage, and then winked at Asey, "in the back part of Mopey's billiard parlor. Way back. Lots of pictures out there. We found her. We had to bust in, because we couldn't find Mopey anywhere. You'll have to square that, too."

"Who was she, you chumps?" Asey asked. "If you found the picture—"

"Sure we found it. We got it here. But it won't help none. There ain't no name to it."

"Let's see!"

Ramon handed him a frayed picture.

Asey looked at it, whistled and passed it to Angelica.

The face was that of the girl Dr. Cummings had assisted from his office, Lee Laurie.

CHAPTER ELEVEN

ANGELICA gasped.

"Lee Laurie! Asey, it can't be! Whatever would that child be doing around the Damons? It's just not reasonable!"

Asey told her drily that if she could name one reasonable thing that had happened around the Damons' house since Friday, he would personally present her with a medal.

"But *what* was she doing there?"

"Dunno. You boys is sure this is the girl you seen, the one you chased?"

The three nodded. "Say," Mike told him wearily, "by this time we know every eyelash. It's the girl all right. It's her."

"An' Waddy," Asey reminded Miss Sage, "might have guessed who she was. Even if he said otherwise. Well, we'll delve into this. First, what about Lem? Heard or seen anythin' about him?"

"We ain't had time," Ramon said, "but it wouldn't do much good to hunt right off for him. First day or so that he's on the loose, he's liable to wander most anywhere. Last time I found him out on the back shore, plowin' through the sand with an empty keg on his back. He thought he was in the Foreign Legion in the middle of a sandy desert, an' the rest of the comp'ny needed water. No tellin' where he'll turn up. But we'll start in on him now. Say, you wouldn't make Tony let us in, would you, or give us some money? We're starvin'."

"I'll speak to Tony. If I give you kids money, you'd prob'ly join Lem."

"Aw," Mike said, "aw, we wouldn't! We're reformed. We decided it last night. We think we'd like to be G-men. How do you get to begin to be one, Asey?"

"Not the way you fellers begun," Asey told him with a grin. "I'll see Tony, an' when this is over, you can come to me an' draw enough for a banquet, if you like."

When he returned from the house, Mike called to him as he stepped from the path into the car.

"Did Tony tell you about that guy, that Jap of Waddy's? Well, he's been here three times in Waddy's coupe, the one with all the chrome an' trick horns. He's tryin' to find out if we squealed, an' how much. Tony told him to get the hell out."

"Next time he comes," Asey said, "have Tony tell him that you give the whole business up, an' Waddy can crawl out of it as good as he's able. Don't forget, an' let me know about Lem as soon as you can."

He turned the roadster around and swung off in the direction of Pochet and the Pochet Playhouse.

"This is your home ground," he said to Angelica. "What about this cornfed theater an' its actors, anyway? Seems to me I heard it was a strugglin' prop'sition last year."

"It's picked up a hundred per cent so far this season, with Morris to lure the dowagers and Lee Laurie to draw in the young crowd. It's the old Nickerson place, you know. The widow, Talky Sal—"

"Chatty Sal," Asey corrected. "Oh, yes. I plum forgot about her. I think we'll let her chat to us first. She cooks for 'em, don't she, an' keeps 'em in order gen'rally. Huh. I should think it would be a sight easier to d'gest her cookin' than her words. She'll know everythin', an' what she don't know for sure, she'll guess at. Great guesser, Sal is. She," he added with a sidelong glance at Angelica, "she is a cousin, by the bye. Fourth a couple times r'moved, but still r'lated."

With his sublime disregard for main highways, Asey

turned off on another series of wooded, sand-rutted lanes. Angelica, who prided herself on her knowledge of Pochet and its vicinity, confessed that she was completely lost after the third apparently haphazard turn.

"We'll come in by the rear—oho." He slowed down the car. "Look ahead, with the basket. There's Sal now. This road c'nects with the cem'tery road. She's been up with flowers. F'heaven's sake, help me out an' don't let her get goin' on the late Benny B., will you? I liked Benny, but if I have to hear again how he slipped on that cussed clam shell an' died right off the bat, like a shot, I'll prob'ly have to hunt me up a clam shell an' try it myself."

Mrs. Nickerson, red-faced and perspiring, greeted them effusively. In one breathless sentence she commented on the weather, Asey's health, Miss Sage's shop, the murder, the possibility of rain, last year's drought, and the constant state of tension resulting from the care and feeding of twenty-two actors and actresses. Asey caught her just as she motioned to the empty flower basket, preparatory to launching forth on her trip to the cemetery and the grave of the late Benny B.

"That's what I want to know about, Sal. Your actin' bunch. What they do Friday night?"

"That was a ben'fit, an' they did another play from the reg'lar one this week. Then they sat up all night in the kitchen talkin' about what is art an' what is actin'. Y'know, art an' actin' is kind of like a drug to 'em. They talk an' talk, an' the more they talk about it, the less they seem to get anywhere. But I will say this for 'em they do more work an' less talkin' this year than they did last. That Laurie girl, she's put up the money, an' let me tell you, she makes 'em hustle, she does. She's got a powerful almighty temper, an' they're scared to death of it. Sometimes when she throws plates, she puts me in mind of Benny B. He always liked to throw things when he got good an' mad. He—"

"I r'member the time," Asey told her, "he tried to throw a plate of beans at my Uncle Seth. Yes—yes.

Seth caught 'em in mid air an' tossed 'em back. Say, Sal, what about this Laurie girl? Is she well off? Tell you, you sit down here on the seat an' give us the whole story on her. I'm kind of interested in her, I am."

Sal looked at him through narrowed eyes. "I cert'ny hope she ain't mixed up in this mess of yours at Damon's" she observed. "She's a nice girl, except when she's mad, an' then she just busts loose."

"Sound familiar?" Asey asked Angelica, thinking of Rosalie and her temper. "Huh. Go on, Sal. Didn't mean to interrupt."

"As it so happens," Sal settled her ample frame back against the leather seat, "I know quite a lot about her that she don't know I know, Asey, on account of Wheelbarrow Rich's sister's girl marryin' a foreigner out west. Shrewsfield, New York State, that's the place. That's where the Laurie girl come from. So I wrote Effie and asked her to tell me all about her."

According to Effie, Sal went on, the Laurie girl came from one of Shrewsfield's oldest and wealthiest families. After her parents had died in an automobile accident, a guardian had brought her up and looked out for her.

"Real good job he did, too, but when she was eighteen, she come into her money an' lit out for New York City. That was a year ago, or so. She got a part in a play in New York, an' in spite of everybody in Shrewsfield's sayin' she'd come to no good, 'pears like she fooled 'em, an' good instead. Just the samey, I don't think the stage's any place for a young girl. Why, the language they use, it's enough to make your blood run cold, Asey! They don't seem to mean nothin' by it, seemin'ly. Just sort of slips off their tongues easy an' unconcerned, but I often wonder what Benny B'd say if he could come back an' hear a r'hearsal in his barn!"

"How'd she hurt her foot?" Asey asked quickly.

"Sat'day aft'noon they have a kid's play, an' she wasn't in it, an' she went off in her car, an' when she come home, she had a bad feelin' ankle an' we sent for the doctor, an' he said she had a sprain. I want her to

let me rub it with skunk grease. Benny always said there
wasn't nothin' like skunk grease for a sprain, but she
wouldn't. I r'member the time Benny—"

"Skunk grease is good stuff," Asey said. "Tell you
what, Sal. We'll run you back. I want to see this girl an'
have a talk with her."

When they reached the old farmhouse, Sal hurried
out of the car.

"Miss Laurie, Miss Laurie—Asey Mayo the detective, he wants to see you! Miss Lau-rie!" Her voice
echoed back from the front hall.

Asey sighed. "If you was an actress, Miss Sage, an'
folks bellowed at you that a d'tective wanted to quiz
you, how long'd it take for you to be ready?"

"About two seconds," Angelica said. "Asey, I'm beginning to think that this afternoon isn't going to net
you very much."

"Seems," Asey agreed, "to have all the earmarks of a
blank. Well, let's go in. I wish I trusted actors more, but
the worst of 'em is so sort of vers'tile. My, my!"

The incredibly good-looking Blaisdell Morris met
them at the front door.

"Mayo? I'm Morris, manager of this company. Now
I want it clearly understood that Miss Laurie is ill with
an injured foot, and furthermore, she is not to be drawn
into this affair without—"

"What affair?" Asey asked silkily.

"Why, you're investigating the murder of Rosalie
Ray, aren't you? Now, no amateur detective has any
rights to—"

"I thought you was an actor," Asey said pleasantly.
"How come you happen to know about d'tectives,
am'teur or otherwise?"

"I played fifty-one weeks as the assistant district attorney in the 'Trial of Barbara Burch,'" Morris announced with dignity. "I know."

"You know a lot," Asey said. "I'll admit as much.
Now s'pose you step inside an' let us by, an' let me talk
with Miss Laurie."

"Miss Laurie is my fiancée," Morris said. "She does not—"

"That's fine," Asey said heartily. "Fine lookin' pair you'll make, too. Now you run along an' stop botherin' me. Or I'll start wavin' gold badges at you. I'm am'teur as a d'tective, but I'm hon'rary constable in seven towns an' I'm pretty sure this is one of 'em. If it ain't, an' you want to argue the point, I'm more or less certain I could get to be one without much effort. Or would you pr'fer that Lieutenant Leary of the state police come over with his fellers an' the newspaper boys?"

Morris backed away from the door.

"Just so," Asey said. "Run 'long. I see Miss Laurie's in here, an' I can talk to her 'thout havin' to take up your time."

Rather to his own surprise, Morris left without further comment, and Asey and Angelica entered the living room which ran along the entire south side of the house.

The long rose-colored drapes had been drawn at the windows, and the only light came from candles in pewter holders on the mantel, and a candelabra on the table. Before the fireplace on a chaise longue lay the Laurie girl, a Cashmere shawl thrown casually over her injured ankle.

To Angelica there was a vaguely familiar note about the whole scene. It puzzled her until a little spaniel jumped off the couch and was restrained by a warning "Flush!"

Angelica nodded to herself. Miss Laurie had been Elizabeth Barrett two weeks before. Asey had been quite correct, she thought, in his comment about actors and actresses. Miss Laurie was picturesquely pale. She not only looked pale, she seemed pale all over. It would have been more convincing had not Angelica and Asey, too, remembered her sparkling eyes and vivid cheeks as she left the doctor's.

"I only want to know a couple of things." Asey sounded disarming enough, but Angelica wondered if he didn't intend to match one act with another. "Was you at the Damons' house on Friday, an' is this," he pulled the white suede pump out of his pocket, "is this yours?"

"Friday? Oh, that *is* mine! How nice of you to bring it back! I'm so fond of those pumps. Did you guess it was mine? How clever you are! How did you figure it out?"

"Some of my men did the figurin' for me," Asey lied smoothly. "Very clever, the state p'lice."

He did not repeat his questions, and an uncomfortable silence ensued. Miss Laurie, Angelica decided, was digesting the comment about the state police, and she seemed very uncertain of her next speech.

"I—you asked me about Friday," she said at last. "I went to the Damons' early in the afternoon to see Tommy Fowler."

"So you know Tom, huh? Hilda was right. Go on."

"Well, it's hard to explain. He wrote me he was coming. You see, Tom thought he was engaged to me."

"What did you think?" Asey inquired.

"Oh, I did too, more or less, till I met Morrie. Then I knew that Tom and I would never be happy. So I went to tell him so and settle everything, but that place was so scary! There were men wandering around the woods, and that horrible Barr boy—"

"Know him, do you?"

"No," Lee said, "but he'd been pointed out to me and of course everyone knows his reputation. So I ran away before he and the others caught up. I went back later, after mail time, too. I wasn't playing that night, and another man chased me then. A perfectly dreadful place!"

"Must of been Lem," Asey thought out loud, "when him an' Steve was talkin'. Okay. What then?"

"I went home. Really, I didn't want to see Tom very much. He's such a talker, and so—well, such a trusting boy! So I thought I'd just settle it all in a letter. It would hurt less."

"Huh. What about Sat'day? Did you change your mind about the hurt?"

"Oh, no. Saturday morning I had a wire from darling Rosalie Ray. That is, it wasn't delivered until Saturday, although she'd sent it from New York Friday morning. She said she wanted to see me. So I went back, in spite of Tom and that scary place. That time two men chased me. Tw—were you one of them?"

" 'Fraid so. Why on earth did you run? Whyn't you stay put an' let us know who you was?"

"Why—why, when someone runs after you, you just naturally run," Lee said matter-of-factly. "I never for a moment thought of stopping! You know what a perfectly horrible place those woods are! And what with men chasing me every time I entered them! Anyway, I lost a pump and twisted an ankle, and the doctor says it's a very bad sprain. I don't know *what* I'll do if it doesn't get better by the end of the week!"

"How well did you know Rosalie?"

"Oh, quite well. When I first went to New York she happened to be on the train. Wasn't that a coincidence? She gave me all sorts of good advice and suggestions. She was simply dear to me. I—" she touched her eyes with a wisp of a handkerchief and for a moment her voice broke, "I can't tell you how awfully I feel about her, and everything. I cried and cried when I heard about it this morning."

The girl, Angelica admitted to herself, was clever. She didn't leap at her opportunity to wail and sob and carry on. She just stated her grief with what amounted to a childish simplicity that would appeal to and carry more weight with Asey than any violent emotional debauch ever could.

"Where'd you come from, Miss Laurie?"

"New York," she said promptly. "I've a dear little apartment in the—"

"I mean orig'nally."

"Oh," she laughed. "Shrewsfield, you mean! You know, I sometimes almost forget Shrewsfield! Tom came from there, too, did you know? He was the only person I knew in New York when I went there, except Rosalie. Our engagement was a sort of—well, a family arrangement. My guardian liked his people. Of course Tom's a dear, a perfect darling, and I don't mean to run him down, but after I got started and really began my career in earnest, I realized what a dilettante he was. Absolutely no ambition at all. Now Morrie—"

"I know," Asey said. "He's ambitious as anythin'. Oozes from him, as you might say. Tell me, are you Rosalie Ray's daughter, by any rare chance?"

Lee shook her head. "I wish I had been!"

"Are you quite sure? You see, we was told you was."

"How strange! But I'm not, truly. I can easily prove it, if you'd like. Will you call Morrie and ask him to bring my file from the safe? There's a birth certificate in it. Not the thing itself, but a—what d'you call it? A picture of it."

"Photostat. I'll tell him."

Morris produced the pasteboard file from the safe and presented it to Asey in his best assistant district attorney manner.

"You find the copy," Asey said. "I ain't got a bit of a desire to pry into the rest of it. Thanks."

He carried the paper over to the table.

"Mind snappin' on the lights? These candles flick."

"Oh, d'you mind awfully not?" Lee asked. "My eyes —the light hurts them so. I hurt them on the beach last week, going without sun glasses."

"Okay." Asey scrutinized the paper. "Say, I thought you was nineteen. 'Cordin' to this, you're twenty-three."

"Publicity," Lee said. "I went to New York when I was twenty-one."

"Thanks." Asey returned the photostat to Morris. "Thank you very kindly. Sorry to have bothered you. Okay, Miss Sage? We'll run along."

"Anything I can do for you," Lee said, "do let me know, won't you? Good night!"

Angelica noticed a look of relief and satisfaction in

the girl's eyes, and wondered why Asey didn't. Out in the car she brought the matter up.

"This," Asey said, "is only the b'ginnin'."

"What d'you mean?"

"I'll show you. Does it seem to you, as you let your mind wander back over the years, that they was callin' girls Lee as early as 1913? Up North, anyway?"

"Why, I don't know. I never thought. Where are you going?" she added as he swung the car around.

"Officially we've left. Now I'm goin' to hop back an' find out somethin' from Sal. Seems to me—you wait. Mind this drizzle, or can you stand the top down?"

"It's all right," Angelica said, and wondered what would have happened had she answered otherwise. Asey was already half way back to the house.

Within ten minutes he returned.

"There," he said with satisfaction as he slid behind the wheel, "that makes me feel better. One lie in this business has finally come to light. Somebody pr'ceedin' 'cordin' to rules."

"Will you," Angelica asked, "just elucidate a bit? All minds do not work with the same lightning rapidity as yours. I haven't the foggiest notion what you're talking about."

"Why, Lee Laurie's too good a name. Sal said her name was Laurie, all right. But like I said, I didn't think that Lee come in fashion till later. An' seems to me Sal called her somethin' else once today. So I asked her. Sal says Wheelbarrow Rich's sister's girl Effie, she said when this Laurie girl lived in Shrewsfield, her name was Fanny Laurie."

Angelica laughed. "No wonder she changed! You've got to admit 'Lee Laurie' is better, in these days, than 'Fanny Laurie.' After all!"

"Sure," Asey said. "Sure. Only why does her birth certificate have 'Lee' on it, if she wasn't ever known as Lee till after she come to New York?"

"Why—really, Asey? It must be a fake!"

"I sort of somehow feel," Asey agreed, "that maybe

p'raps it is. Even in that dim light, it looked fishy. Huh, she think candle light would gloss that over? I'm goin' to lay you a hundred to nothin' she's Ray's daughter. I'm goin' to call Lindsay an' have him get his fellers to work. An' then," he said, "we'll have fun. Nosiree, I ain't through with her, not by a long shot."

"Look," Angelica said excitedly, having the first bright thought about the murder she had yet felt worthy of utterance, "look. If Tom is engaged to her, or was, and if she's Rosalie's daughter, and if Rosalie had put her foot down, or Tom thought she had—well, doesn't that give Tom a motive for killing Rosalie?"

"Yup, but it wouldn't explain why Waddy Barr's lighter was on Rosalie's bed. Wasn't put there by anyone but the murderer, either, 'cause it'd been cleaned of fingerprints like the lance an' the door knob, remember. Tom come here Friday night on the freight, an' went to the Damons'. How'd he get any chance to lay hand on the lighter?"

Angelica thought a moment.

"Then the girl—why, she mentioned Waddy, and she didn't even seem to like the thought of him. She had every chance to find that lighter. I know she plays golf, for I've seen her at the club. Waddy claimed he lost it there. Perhaps she—why, she might have entered the house Friday night! After all, Sal wasn't sure of every individual member of that company on Friday, was she, even if they did chatter about art and acting?"

"I asked Sal just that. She went to bed at two. But someone told her they all stayed up till dawn. Maybe they all did, an' maybe not."

"Then—but it doesn't fit, Asey! No woman could kill another in any such horrible way!"

"Ever hear," Asey asked, "of Lizzie Borden an' her little axe? Or Madam Lafarge? Or the Borgias, or Adelaide Bartlett an' the Pimlico case? Or—say, I could keep on for an hour. Not meanin' to insult your sex, quite a lot of ladies has killed folks at one time or another, an' been just as horrid as anythin'. Well, one thing, the aft'noon ain't been such a blank as we thought. It's kind of b'ginnin' to jell."

"Jell? It's weaving around in the most insidious way. I confess to being a little scared. You can laugh if you want, Asey, but every now and then I have premonitions that come true. I don't have 'em very often, but they've never failed. I—all day long, I've felt that before this business is settled, there's going to be something perfectly awful happen. I feel it now more than ever."

Asey looked sideways at her and then laughed.

"I shouldn't worry. With all them troopers around, the people at Damons' is as safe as they can be. P'raps you'd like to go home to your own house?"

"In this pitch darkness? Margaret goes to her sister's at night. No, no, Asey. I can't explain it, but I don't want to go home. Friday night I was frightened stiff. I don't know why."

Asey slowed down the car and looked at her. "You sort of amaze me," he said.

"I'm amazing myself. Sorry. I'm not usually panicky but—oh, well, forget it. Aren't you going home by way of the speed boat?"

"Nope," Asey told her, "I'm goin' to trespass ruthlessly over Mrs. Wadsworth Barr's prop'ty, an' leave a feller to guard the car. Mind walkin' the rest of the way? One thing about this drizzle, it'll quench that bunch of curiosity seekers."

He chattered at random on various things as they walked along the strip of marshy land that divided the Barrs' property from the Damons'.

One of the troopers challenged them, then ran forward.

"Asey, I'm glad you're back! Say, there are three kids here that've been driving us nuts! And—"

"Asey," Ramon Barradio dashed up. "Asey! Listen, Asey! Somethin' awful's happened to Lem!"

CHAPTER TWELVE

"WHAT d'you mean?" Asey grabbed Ramon by the shoulder. "What's happened? Where is he?"

"That's just it!" Ramon said. "We went to the package store—Lem hadn't been there. Not at all!"

"And they hadn't seen him!" Frank said. "No one's seen him. They all thought he must of been off on a drunk, but we've asked and asked, an' not a soul's really seen him, or knows where he is."

"And we went to every other package store an' beer joint we knew," Ramon went on, "an' even to Harmon's—he sells corn. He just hasn't been anywhere! We—"

"We went to the gunnin' shack on the outer beach," Mike Mallon chimed in. "We went to the ole fish house on the bay—we been everywhere! Somethin's happened to him, Asey, for sure! If he'd got his liquor, we'd know he was all right, somewhere. But if he didn't get no liquor, he ain't drunk—where is he?"

"Where's that fool crow?" Asey asked.

"That's another thing. Lina says the crow's fussing around like sixty. Usually when Lem's drunk that bird just sits around and waits for him to get back. But he's fussing, an' he's nipped her ankles till they're raw. Everyone that comes near, he nips 'em an' then hops around. I bet that bird knows an' is tryin' to get somethin' acrost."

Asey looked at Angelica. "Out of the mouths of roosters an' crows—hmph. Seems to be a lot of livestock involved in this. Ham—who's this feller?"

A strange trooper strode up, stared at Asey, and then saluted smartly.

"I'm Glassford, Mr. Mayo. I—it's nothing very important. It's just the food."

"What's the matter with it?" Asey demanded.

"Well, it's gone. There were two hampers and a couple of gallon hot-jugs in the back of the car I drove down. One of the hampers is gone, sir. It's the one with the real food in it. The other's just crockery and tin plates and all."

Asey swung around and faced Hamilton.

"Who took it, Ham? This ain't much of a time to play tricks on new men. Roust it out."

"But Asey," Ham said, "none of us touched it! I give you my word!"

"I think, sir," Glassford said, "that it was that seedy looking guy in the pink shirt. I had to warn him off half a dozen times. He—"

"Pink shirt?" Asey asked.

"Well, pink striped, it was. He was an ugly looking customer, but gee, most of that bunch was a lot of hard-looking tickets."

Hamilton's lower jaw was sagging. Asey glanced at him and turned back to Glassford.

"When'd this guy come?"

"Oh, early. Just after I got here. He asked all sorts of questions and I finally told him to keep quiet, and then he pestered the newspaper men and Leary and everybody else. He tried to slip around the wire once or twice, but I kicked him out."

"Asey," Hamilton said, "I know you told me to tell 'em to watch out for a pink shirt, but honestly, I ask you—would it be sensible for a fellow who knew he was spotted to come roaming back? I didn't see him, but I've been on the other side and down at the landing taking Solly's place. Honest—it—the whole thing's crazy!"

Asey sat down on the Damons' chopping-block and laughed till the tears rolled down his cheeks.

"It's not funny one bit," Angelica protested. "After

our chasing that man, and his tying up Hilda, and swiping Betsey's food—"

"It's lovely," Asey wiped his eyes with a red bandana handkerchief, "he comes up and swipes the coppers' food an'—oh, Ham, did he talk with Leary?"

"For a long while," Glassford answered.

"Oh, the nerve of it! That feller must think he's a two-legged rabbit's foot himself. The nerve of it! Well, he's feedin' good, an' apparently he's aimin' on hangin' round a bit longer. I sort of wonder, now—"

"Ain't you goin' to hunt Lem?" Ramon Barradio asked. "I bet you he's hurt in the woods, or someone's killed him, or something. I don't think he ever left this part of town. Not a soul remembered seein' him Friday, an' he didn't drop in at Peases' on his way home like he almost always does."

"He wouldn't of," Asey said, "because after he left here he went straight to my house in Wellfleet—must of hitchhiked, cause he didn't use his own car. My idea is he'd of come right back here an' sort of stand guard himself. No one seen him around Wellfleet way. I asked after I found his note."

"Hey," Ramon said, "I bet I know how he got there —with that fellow that sells clotted cream—what's his name. Manuel's cousin, named Rosa. He goes over to Wellfleet every night, delivering. Lem often goes. He's one guy we missed out on."

"Take 'em to Rosa, Ham," Asey said, "an' find out. You kids come on back here."

"I suppose," Angelica remarked as they walked up to the house, "that this is the time for me to say I felt it in my bones all the time, but I don't seem to. I mean, this is something, but it isn't it. Couldn't you go through the woods with bloodhounds, Asey?"

"Yup, 'cept this is New England, an' I wouldn't know where to find one. People do funny things. Lem might of wandered off. Might of killed Rosalie an' beat it, for all we know. If they can find out from Manuel's cousin —hm."

While he and Angelica were eating a cold and belated supper, Hamilton returned with the three boys.

"Yessir, Rosa, he claims he took Lem to Wellfleet, an' left that note for you, an' brought Lem back an' dumped him by Barr's land. Lem said he was goin' back to Damons'. That sort of settles things, don't it?"

Asey drained his coffee cup and pushed back his chair.

"Ramon, what lodges does Lem b'long to?"

"Oh—" Ramon named three.

"Good. You—nope, I guess I'll go. Hamilton, where's Leary? Boston? For the love of God A'mighty, why? Well, no matter. No time to question blessin's. Ham, put your fellers in a close circle round this house. Locked up the oars an' fixed the motor boat? Okay. Put two men 'long the beach. Keep the lights on downstairs here, all night. Steve, you fix things so they don't go out. Now—have your p'lice cars locked, see? You folks in the house, stay put inside, an' don't one of you dare poke your noses out. Understand? Ham—well, I'll tell you the rest. No nonsense from any of you. I got a crazy idea brewin' in the back of my head an' I mean what I say! You—stay—put!"

"But—" Angelica was the only one who dared speak, "but—can I tell 'em about this afternoon?"

"Nope. You an' Myles take charge inside. See you later."

He stalked out, followed by Hamilton and the three boys.

"Asey," Hamilton said, "if we leave the barriers, the reporters and—"

"Let 'em come. More the merrier. But you put your lads in a circle, an' make it clear that the first one to step over gets more'n black magic."

"What—"

"Ham, my bright idea's too crazy insane to tell you. Carry on. Come on with me, kids. We're goin' to Paul R'vere."

All three of them had to run in order to keep up with

Asey's long strides. Ramon was the only one with sufficient breath left to talk when they reached the long
roadster.

"Gee—we goin' in that?"

"You be," Asey said briefly. "Pile in. Hang on. An'
keep quiet. I'm thinkin'—"

"But the Jap," Ramon said. "I forgot. He come back
an' Tony told him what you said, that we'd told everything. Tony said he turned green an' his eyes popped."

"Fine. That'd ought to bring Waddy round, if he's
holdin' out on anythin'. Now, who's the head of them
bison or elephants or whatever they was that Lem
b'longed to? Who? Okay."

The boys clutched each other in sheer delight as Asey
shot the car off.

"An' we thought," Mike whispered in Ramon's ear,
"we thought we was classy drivers! Wheee!"

It was after two in the morning when Asey parked his
car in Henderson's barn and crossed the inlet in his
boat.

Two wet and bedraggled troopers met him at the
landing.

"Okay, Asey. We've got your boat. What's up?"

"They's lots up. Nice weather for ducks, ain't it? No
matter what happens, tell your r'lief to stay put here.
Thanks. Night."

Three flashlights and two hardy reporters met him on
the path to the house.

"Nothin' now. Go to sleep till daybreak an' you'll get
some action. Night."

Reporters and policemen stared after him admiringly
as he strode into the house.

"I'd hate like hell," the Courier's ace man said to
Glassford, "to be on the other end of that action. That
man's a block of granite. What's he up to?"

"Ham knows, but he won't tell. What'd he have
under his coat? Looked like a bird."

Inside the house Asey presented a bewildered Myles

with a beady-eyed crow who nipped disconcertingly at his ankles.

"Bed him, will you? Don't let him get out. Where's Tom sleep?"

"Er—front." Myles eyed the bird. "Front, left. Does he always bite? I mean the crow?"

"Just excited," Asey said casually. "He'll stop when he gets used to you. Night. Got anythin' of Lem's around? Give him the sweater, then, an' he'll quiet down."

He marched up to Tom's room and flung open the door without bothering to knock.

"S'matter with this lamp? Bulb gone?"

"Twist it," Tom said sleepily. "I—wha—oh, Asey. My God, you look ruthless! What's wrong? More notes from Waddy? Got a cigarette?"

Asey tossed him a package.

"I ain't got a lot of time, so wake up. You engaged to Lee Laurie?"

Tom grinned. "Wa-el," he imitated Asey's drawl, "yes an' no, as you say. She calls me in and plays me up when she wants to get rid of some particularly sticky individual, and then promptly forgets me till the next time. I'm her official but lackadaisical fiancé. Neither of us puts much stock in it. Why? Is anything wrong about it?"

"Nope," Asey said. "It's somethin' I didn't have time to clear up before I left—"

"What *have* you been up to?" Tom demanded. "People are bursting."

"I have been giving the alarm to the elephants," Asey told him with a grin. "Me an' Tarzan, with a touch of Paul R'vere. You know Lee Laurie was engaged to Blaisdell Morris?"

Tom lay back on the bed and shouted.

"That's perfect! Every ingenue—every kid actress on Broadway, Asey, really doesn't consider herself a success till she's been engaged to Morrie. Know how old he is? Near forty. Laugh that off. Truly, Asey, I'm neither surprised nor hurt. Her guardian and my father figured this engagement out. They decided I wasn't much good, but she could do worse, and it would be nice to keep her money among white folks. They also figured that it would probably be the only way I'd ever become a millionaire. They were probably right."

"Is she Rosalie Ray's daughter?" Asey shot the question out.

"God, no! She's got a Ray temper, but that's just being spoiled. Whatever made you think so?"

"What's her real name?"

Tom laughed again. "Fanny. Don't ever let it out, or there'll be war. I've often held it over her head and promised to tell Howie or some of the columnists if she didn't behave herself."

"You're sure she's not Rosalie's daughter?"

"Asey, I'd swear it. I've known her since she was a baby. Look—call my mother, or better still, I'll give you a list of Shrewsfield's leading citizens. You can check up. My eye, if I thought she had anything to do with La Ray, I'd have broken the engagement myself! But why all this to-do about Lee?"

"Just fittin' loose ends," Asey said. "What's the time? Okay. Night."

Down in the kitchen he found Myles struggling with Lem's crow.

"Still at it? Ain't you exhausted?" he asked. "Want me—"

"Oh, no, no," Myles said hurriedly, "We're just getting used to each other. He's seen me before many times, of course, but he's just beginning to remember. Asey, you're not going to sleep in that chair?"

"I am, if you could guarantee to wake me in an hour. Or if you'd find an alarm—"

"I'll wake you," Myles said. "I'll be glad to; really, I've been feeling rather out of things. It would be a pleasure to do something—"

"Even playing alarm clock, huh? Thanks."

On the fifty-ninth minute of the hour, Myles coughed, and then shook Asey's arm.

"I—er—"

"Thanks. Now—glory, is it still drizzlin'? I don't s'pose it could be cleared off. Huh. Now, you can go to bed—only first, would you mind goin' from room to room an' tellin' folks not to mind what seems to be an unnecessary noise?"

"Certainly." At the door, Myles hesitated. "Er—I'd like to come with you. You know, I used to be quite a shot—did a lot of pistol shooting with the Bennett brothers in the old days. If that would help."

"Come on," Asey said. "Only—wake Steve an' tell him to tell the rest. Hustle."

As the first streaks of dawn came in the east, Asey pulled an old Colt forty-five from under his belt and fired three shots in quick succession into the air.

"Er—a signal?" Myles inquired. His own old Smith and Wesson was burning a hole in his pocket.

"Yup. At this point some hundred an' fifty of Lem's loyal lodge brethren ought to be filterin' through them woods, with a bunch along the outskirts in a circle an' their car lights on."

"Hunting Lem?"

"Lem," Asey said, "an' a crazy idea. Now, brother Crow—come 'long nice. Okay, Myles, you wield the lights. Nope, Ham. You an' your fellers stay put here. This p'ticular barn door is goin' to be locked b'forehand. An' for the love of Pete, if pink shirt bobs up an' asks for a cup of coffee, just p'litely nab him, will you?"

With Myles and the crow, and a handful of weary reporters, Asey strode off toward the woods.

By eight o'clock in the morning, every inch of the territory had been scoured without finding any trace of Lem Saddler.

"Why are you so sure," Betsey asked Asey, after he and Myles had returned to the house for a cup of coffee, "that Lem's around here? And that silly crow— why are you carting him around?"

"Nearest to a bloodhound we got," Asey observed, "only either he don't get the idea, just, or we don't seem to talk the same language."

"What are you going to do now?"

"Go through the woods once more. I intend," Asey smiled, "to find that guy if it takes all summer. Long as them fellers keeps up the fraternal spirit, why, we'll just hunt."

"Where's Leary?"

"Dunno. Ham says Boston. Maybe we'll have to rout out his lodges an' hunt him. Can't tell—s'matter, Hamilton?"

"That Barr woman," Hamilton said. "She's raging around and wants to see you. Something about that precious son of hers. You better see her."

"Tell her to run home an' b'have herself," Asey said. "I ain't got the time or the spirit to play with her now. All set, Myles? We'll try ole caw-caw again. I kind of wish he'd catch on to this bloodhound theory."

As they walked off toward the woods, Mrs. Barr thrust a trooper out of her way and rushed after them.

"Asey—Asey Mayo! Asey Mayo, d'you hear me?"

Asey spun around on his heel.

"Most anyone with eardrums from Provincetown to Yarmouth ought to be able to hear you, Mrs. Barr. Look here, can't you stop makin' a spectacle of yourself, an' go home, an' sort of tend to your own affairs? I'll grant you this business is a blot on Skaket's scutcheon, but it ain't your task to fiddle with ink eradicators. Now, scoot!"

"Waddy—"

"Look, Waddy had his chance to explain and tell us what we wanted to know. That's that. Now if you want to get into the headlines again as Local Matron Forc'bly R'moved from Damon Estate, just hang around an' bother me some more."

Asey rejoined Myles, and again they set off.

"Do you know," Myles said thoughtfully, "I think

we're underestimating this bird. It seems to me that when we walk east, he gets noisier—"

"Seems to me," Asey said, "that he don't hate one p'ticular point of the compass more'n any other. He seems to squawk with equal force at every one of 'em."

"Just the same," Myles said, "I think I'm right. He doesn't bite when we go east. He just gets noisier. When we go any other way, he bites. Er—you take it and see for yourself."

Asey tested the theory.

"By golly, you're right," he rubbed his ankle where the crow had nipped at it. "He does—but east leads us out to the clear, an' down to the shore. Say—I wonder—"

He blew his whistle and Hamilton appeared on a dead run.

"Mrs. Barr still there? Oh, she's gone, huh? Look, ain't there a sort of boat house on the Barrs' land? Ask one of the elephants about it for me, will you?"

One of the local men was brought up.

"Sure, there's a cabin there," he admitted. "Waddy used to have it as a playhouse when he was a kid. But we looked into it, Asey. It's empty, an' the door's padlocked, an' the windows is locked."

"Go in?"

"Why, no. It was padlocked."

"Well," Asey said, "this flyin' bloodhound wants to aim for it. Get some of the boys an' let's bust in. Let the critter go, Myles—you know, you seem to of picked up a lot about crows. Is it the bird fancier in you comin' out, or what?"

"I had ample opportunity last night," Myles spoke with a touch of bitterness, "to grasp a great deal about—Asey, look at him!"

The crow hopped on ahead, then darted back impatiently, flapped his wings, then hopped forward again.

"If that's not beckoning to us," Myles said, "I don't know what it is. He's stopped nipping, too. He—"

One of the troopers overtook them.

"Say, Asey, one of your local men just found the hamper someone swiped from Glassford, over on the other side near the swamp. Cleaned out."

"Okay. Come 'long an' play with us. New version of hare an' hounds. I'm thinkin' of callin' it crows an' elephants."

The rusty padlock on the boat house was easily forced, and the men piled in. Aside from a broken table and some dusty chairs, the place was empty.

"How about the floor boards?"

"Well," Asey said, "you might pry under 'em, but that dirt an' sand on 'em ain't been disturbed for some time—sure, go ahead."

With enthusiasm the men ripped up the floor boards, which revealed nothing but an abandoned rat's nest.

Myles touched Asey's sleeve.

"The crow—did you notice he didn't come in? I think this is half right, but not exactly."

"Warm, but not hot, huh? All right. We'll see if he has any other ideas. Look at him—I don't call that cooperatin' much. Takin' time off for a quick lunch—"

The bird was pecking away at a worm. After five minutes more of grubbing around, he scratched himself, blinked his beady eyes and let out a caw. Then he hopped toward the beach.

"He's crazy," Asey said in disgust as the crow stopped and looked back. "Listen, bird, we want Lem. We don't want a nice swim—say, ain't that a—by golly, bird, I take it all back! For your next meal," he started on a dead run toward the tall grass between them and the beach, "you get a quart of worms hand dug by me, personal!"

CHAPTER THIRTEEN

THE OTHERS stood there blinking as Asey followed the crow to the beach grass.

"Tch, tch," one of the men near Myles clucked his tongue in disparagement. "Loony."

"Cracked," another agreed. "Nuts."

"Nuts nothing," the trooper said. "I get it! Come on, you guys!"

Myles checked his impulse to dash after them, and instead adjusted his glasses and stared.

What the bird had been making for, and what Asey had apparently reacted to was a mound of salt hay and sea weed just barely visible above the beach grass. Asey, beside the mound, was tearing it apart while the crow fluttered about in low circles, cawing lustily. The outlines of an overturned dory came to light.

The other men had gathered around the dory and were starting to lift it. Myles removed his pince nez and trotted over to them.

Under the boat was Lem Saddler, tightly gagged, securely blindfolded, and bound hand and foot.

Myles thought the man was dead, but after the blindfold was removed, Lem's eyes opened and then closed wearily as though the effort had been too much.

"Alive," Asey said thankfully. "Get them hands an' feet free while I take off the gag. There—can you talk, feller?"

Lem nodded and tried to moisten his lips.

"Kind of dry."

Asey held one of the four proffered bottles to his lips.

"Not too much, feller. There. Okay?"

"Yup. My God, gimme a coat or somethin'! I'm freezin', or froze!"

Myles put on his glasses again. The man was clad only in a dingy shapeless suit of long underwear.

"I ache all over," Lem went on. "Whew, I thought you guys'd passed me up entirely. No, I don't need no help. I can get up." He lifted himself on one elbow and then fell back again. "Guess I do—wait'll I get loosened up. I'm stiff."

Finally much against his will he was carried to the Damon house by four of the men. Lying on a couch that had hastily been dragged out in front of the kitchen stove, he sipped coffee and asked Betsey shyly if he might have an egg.

"Egg? You—you poor man! You can have a dozen, if you want. You can have anything we've got!"

"Could I have a pair of pants, maybe?" Lem waved a hand toward the coat that covered his legs. "I never knew how ter'ble bad a man could want a pair of pants."

Steve produced a pair of flannels into which Lem gratefully climbed.

"There," he said. "Three—four eggs, an' I'll be all right. Fried, please."

Asey waited until Lem had disposed of more coffee and four eggs before he started in.

"Now, feller, what went on? This is Monday, in case you lost track. No one seems to of seen you since Friday, when Juan Rosa plumped you off on the road back of the swamp."

"Monday?" Lem said. "Only Monday? I figgered Wednesday, an' maybe Thursday. Well, it's kind of a long story."

After he left the note at Asey's house, he had driven back with Rosa to Skaket. The rain dispelled his fears that the Barradios and Mallon might start a fire in spite of Tony's lecture, but he was none the less anxious about the Damons. He knew there were plenty of other ways in which they might be annoyed. If Waddy Barr had started shooting, there was no telling what might happen, rain or no rain.

Only a few seconds after Rosa's truck went away, a man had stepped up to him from the side of the road.

"I couldn't tell you what he looked like, for the life of me." Lem's face was doleful as he answered Asey's question. "I been tryin' to think ever since. He asked if I knew a man named Smith around anywheres, an' I said I knew forty, an' which one? He said he was a medium-sized feller with nose glasses on a black ribbon an' a white moustache an' a Boston way of talkin'."

"Why," Myles said, "he—he might have been describing me! How amazing!"

"That's what I thought. I said, you don't want no one named Smith, you want Mr. Witherall, over to the Damons' house. He said no, it was Smith he wanted, an' he guessed he'd hit the wrong town. He wanted Pochet. I told him it was Skaket, an' he said thanks, and which way should he go, an' I showed him. Well, he went his way an' I went my way, an' next thing I knew, I was flat on my back chokin' to death. He must of slung his necktie 'round my throat from b'hind. I dunno. I was near out there, for a while, an' when I sort of got my breath again, he had my hands tied an' my mouth gagged an' my feet done up'n such a way I couldn't walk more'n a foot at a time. N'en he jammed a gun in my ribs an' said if I wanted to live, to tell him things, an' if I didn't, I would do no more tellin' to anyone."

"I get it," Asey said. "He used you as a sort of gen'ral d'rectory, huh?"

"All I done since is tell him things," Lem said, "an' show him places—say, where's Oliver?"

"The crow? He's in the shed. Bring him in, Steve," Asey ordered. "What about that bird, was he with you?"

"I had Oliver under my coat, Asey, an' let him loose just before that guy jumped me. H'yah, feller! C'mup an' see me! Yup, I could hear him around, an' I snapped my fingers at him like I do when I want him to go home. He didn't make no noise at all, an' the feller didn't see him, but I think he stuck around, even though I kept snappin' my fingers. I hoped he might go home an' worry Lina, an' maybe she'd get upset an' have someone try to find me. I was pretty scared by then. The guy'd covered all his face but his eyes with a handkerchief. Gee, he had nasty eyes! Pig eyes."

With the gun tickling his ribs, Lem had stumbled along somehow and led the man to the Damons'.

"Right out of the rim of your house lights, he stopped, an' tied me up, an' blindfolded me, an' dumped me under the trees. Honest, I never seen so much rain in all my life. I wiggled around and got the blindfold up so's I could see some, but it didn't do no good, much, 'cept I could tell your lights was still on. I figgered you'd be lookin' for trouble here, an' I sort of hoped the guy'd get caught if he tried anythin'. After about fifty years, the lights went off—"

"Between four-thirty an' quarter of five," Asey said.

"I wouldn't know. He come runnin' up to where I was an' waited, an' then he rolled me back more into the woods an' went off again. N'en he finally come back an' marched me off."

Friday night—what was left of it, and Saturday morning, had been spent in the middle of the woods.

"That was when he took my clothes off," Lem said. "Sat'day aft'noon he rolled me under some leaves an' went off, an' when he come back, I could tell by his voice he was pretty worked up. But he gimme some pie."

"My pie," Betsey observed. "Probably the only decent crust I ever made."

"Wasn't bad," Lem admitted. "Mite short, maybe. Anyway, he asked if Rosalie Ray was in that house, an' I said yes, an' he cussed for half an hour solid without repeatin' himself."

"Then he *must* have got into the house after he tied me up," Hilda said, "and overheard your conversation with Waddy, Asey, and learned about the murder—"

"Murder?" Lem turned white. "Murder? Who—"

"Rosalie," Asey said. "Catch you up with that later. Carry on."

The man finally asked the best way to get out of Skaket, and Lem had lied staunchly and told him by boat.

"I'd been peelin' my ears open, an' I thought I'd heard your craft, Asey. By then I was willin' to think anythin' hopeful, but it seemed a good chance to take. I said if he went to the landing, he'd find a speed boat, an' to head up the inlet an' turn right. I figgered if you was there, an' if you had a boat, an' if he didn't get caught pinchin' it, he'd ground, or get pinched for swipin' your boat, or get messed up in the harbor. Or—"

"Seemed," Asey suggested, "like somethin' ought to happen. Yup. It did."

"Well, that evenin' he dumped me under that dory an' left, an' then that night, I guess it was, seems to me I heard boats—"

"No question about it," Angelica said. "No question about it at all!"

After what seemed days and days to Lem, the man came back.

"Had a lot of food," Lem said. "He gimme some more."

"Say anythin' about his boat trip?"

"Nope, I asked him, an' he said there was too much fog."

"Then he must have roamed around Saturday night after bringing the boat back," Angelica said, "until yesterday, when he chatted with the police and stole their food. I don't get this—if he obviously doesn't want to get involved with the police and a murder, why does he stay?"

Asey shrugged. "Pr'sumably he finds out about Rosalie, an' d'cides to beat it, an' tried to, but somethin' brings him back. He d'cides to take a chance—an' you cert'ny got to hand it to him. He took his chance an' he got away with it. Talkin' to Leary! That pleases me a lot. See the feller again, Lem?"

"Not after he gimme some sandwiches. I kind of had to eat 'em dog fashion. How'd you find me?"

"Oliver done it," Asey said. "How, I dunno."

But it seemed perfectly comprehensible to Lem.

"He stayed around late Friday, I'm sure. He didn't make no noise, but I heard him hoppin'. Sat'day while I was in the woods, I heard him cawin' around, an' I rolled over on my face an' tried to snap my fingers loud enough to send him home again. He must of stuck around an' seen where the guy took me. Say, what's it all about, anyway? D'you s'pose he come to see Smith, like he claimed at first, or Mr. Witherall?"

"I ain't got no doubts," Asey told him, "but what he come to see Myles. Got any burglar kidnappers on your callin' list, Myles?"

"Asey!" Myles said.

"Don't look so upset," Asey told him. "I was just bein' funny. I wonder, is it that you look like someone? Maybe he was a wanderin' bum who spotted you an' thought you might be worth money." He shook his head. "But I don't think so."

"D'you mean you don't think the man was a wandering bum, or that Myles was worth money?" Betsey asked. "Because let me tell you Myles looks mighty prosperous when he's all dressed up. I'll bet that's it. And he didn't know who you were, Myles, so he pulled the Smith line on Lem to find out. I wonder—who *does* Myles look like, Steve? I never thought of it before, but he does look like someone."

"He looks," Steve said, "like half a dozen Republican governors—"

"He looks like a banker," Hilda said firmly. "The first time I saw him I thought of that banker, that Bostonian who was a Secretary of the Treasury or something, under someone. The one who kept a horse and buggy in Washington. You know."

"Turn around, Myles," Tom said, "and let's see the profile. Hilda, you and Steve are both crazy. He looks like Wally Farrodaile, the movie lad who plays heavy fathers. The one that got sued by so many girls."

"Really," Myles said, "really! This isn't the most flattering comparison I ever listened to. But I can think of an even better answer. Many times men have accosted me thinking I was Shane, the racetrack manager. I saw him once, and the resemblance was very marked. Outwardly, of course. I doubt if anyone would be mistaken after I spoke."

"Can't you," Angelica inquired, "possibly believe, any of you, that Myles was sought for his own sake, so to speak? This resemblance business seems awfully farfetched to me."

"Oh, no," Myles assured her hastily. "Why should anyone go to such lengths to find me? My, no. That's the answer, I feel sure."

They were still debating the question when one of Hamilton's men came in.

"Brady says no finger prints on that empty hamper we found, Asey. All rubbed off. Garrity says can't you break down and let 'em take a picture of Lem? Say, you got him ruled out of this?"

"Try to tie yourself up that way sometime," Asey suggested. "Lem's out, an' luckier than he knows. Say, want your picture in the paper, Lem?"

Lem hesitated. "Well, I s'pose if it was in, Lina might believe me when I tell her where I was. It's goin' to be awful hard explainin' to her that I spent since Friday bein' tied up in woods an' under boats. I'm 'fraid you got to help me out there, Asey."

Asey promised that he would. "What about you an' Oliver bein' took t'gether?"

Lem brightened. "Say, I'd like that. Nobody ever thinks this bird's any good. I'd like to show 'em dif'rent."

"I s'pose the crow d'serves all the credit," Asey agreed, "but I got a feelin' that the herd of el'phants is goin' to claim most of it. Can you walk all right?"

"Sure, now. But honest, Asey, I can't get my picture

took in these pants! See them puckers in the belt band. Pleats! An' I got an awful beard. Lina wouldn't ever believe it was me."

Asey sighed. "Get him a razor an' look into the pant problem, will you, Steve? I'll take you home after Garrity's through with you, Lem, an' tell Lina all. Last I seen of her she had knives an' rollin' pins ready. By now she's prob'ly rolled up a howitzer an' a couple Tommy guns."

It was nearly noon by the time Asey returned from delivering Lem safely into the hands of Lina, who had remained skeptical to the end concerning her husband's absence. She would not, she asserted, believe a hundred pictures in the paper, and only because Asey stood up for him would she refrain from giving him the beating he richly deserved.

Fencing off the thousand and one questions hurled at him by the press and the members of the household, Asey went into Steve's study and closed the door firmly behind him. He wanted to dally with some ideas. He wanted, if possible, to think.

This man who had biffed Lem over the head—Asey filled his pipe and leaned back in the chair. He had ideas about that man that were too silly almost to tell anyone about. Whatever it seemed, that fellow wasn't any common roadside bum, any wandering unemployed, any common tramp. He was a cold-blooded, purposeful guy who thought quick and took long chances, such brazen nervy chances that he got away with them. That was clear.

It didn't seem possible that such a man would go to such lengths to get at Myles. Going at it from the other side, Myles wasn't the sort of fellow to have guys like that after him. He couldn't—

Hamilton knocked on the door and came in.

"Don't mean to bother you, but those fellows from town want to know if you still want 'em to keep after the one that got Lem."

"D'scouraged, huh? Let 'em go. Make a speech to

'em for me, an' say we may need 'em again. Thanks for tellin' me."

But Hamilton didn't go.

"What about those three kids, Asey? They're still hopping around."

"If they're under your feet, send 'em home."

"They're not such bad kids, Asey. They want to stay here and—"

"Let 'em stay, then."

"Uh. About this fellow that made off with Lem, Asey. What d'you think of him?"

"I wish," Asey said wearily, "I could."

Hamilton melted out of the room, and Asey held a match to his pipe.

This fellow lurking around wasn't utterly vicious, apparently, for he hadn't killed Lem. He had removed Lem's gag at safe intervals, taken off the blindfold when he himself wore the handkerchief mask. Of course, Lem was valuable to him, but on the face of the thing, it seemed that the man wanted something. He sounded less like a killer than a hunter.

And that, Asey thought with a sigh, rooked his own ideas entirely, for he was after a killer. Why did the guy describe Myles? It was entirely possible he knew Myles would lead him to Steve and Betsey, but even granting that, what did those two have that anyone would go to such lengths to get? Neither money nor—no, that wasn't true. They had one thing that was exceedingly valuable, in one sense. They had the script of Rosalie's life, and all her notes.

He got up and strolled over to the desk as Tom came in.

"I know, big chief, but don't say it. Look, you didn't give me any chance this morning—and after all, a man ought to know about his fiancée. How does Lee Laurie fit into this picture? Or doesn't she?"

"Kind of an am'teur job on her part," Asey said. "That's all I can tell you, 'cause that's all I know right now."

"And something else. Did you check that couple of Rosalie's? Those servants?"

"Ham, or Leary, or someone did. They're okay. They was off on a terrible binge Friday night. The desk clerk and the chambermaid had a time with 'em."

"But this jewel business," Tom persisted. "They seem to be the only ones actually to know about the jewels. The rest here at the house simply took it for granted that diamond was a fake. Couldn't the couple have pulled a fast one?"

Asey nodded. "It's possible, but it don't hinge up. Nun-no."

"And those fellows that came Saturday night while you were careening around with the Sage—those photographers and all. Didn't they get anywhere?"

"You mean Lindsay's scientists? Nope. Got any more thoughts that's burnin' holes in your brain? I mean, if you got to get 'em out of your head an' off your chest, get along with it. Otherwise d'you mind leavin' this bush beatin' till later? What're you aimin' at?"

Tom laughed. "Asey, you're superb. Look, Hilda won't let me bum any more cigarettes till the trooper comes back with more, and Steve's out of tobacco."

Asey tossed him his pouch.

"Take it an' go elsewhere. D'part. Git."

"Thanks, pal." Tom left, grinning, and Asey locked the door after him.

Returning to the desk, he picked up Steve's manuscript and considered it.

Suppose the stranger wanted that. A scandal sheet or a tabloid would pay large sums for it, what with Steve's private wisecracks and Rosalie's notes in her own handwriting. But—Asey shook his head. That wouldn't do. It was all too complicated. Pink Shirt was a complicating factor himself, but he didn't go in for complicated businesses like that. Everything he had done thus far was marked by a smooth, startling simplicity. When he wanted food, he took it. When he wanted Lem, he took Lem. If he had yearned for that script and the notes, very likely he would have taken them without any shilly-shallying. About all he needed to do was to cut the window screen and reach in and grab.

"Mayo," he said to himself, "you're gettin' old. Crawl back to your first thought an' figger from there!"

Half an hour later he was still figuring, his cold pipe clamped between his teeth, when someone knocked on the door.

"Me," Angelica said. "I, and food. Sorry to bother, but no one else had the temerity to disturb you. I thought," she added as Asey opened the door, "it was about time for an interruption. That's an excuse I learned from one of my noisy adolescent nephews, who swears it's a psychological fact that people work harder after an interruption."

"Takes more energy for a hoss to start up with his load," Asey told her drily, "than a car. This p'ticular nag is takin' it on the chin. Come sit down. You might as well. Everyone else has."

"This hermit act," Angelica sat on the arm of the leather chair, "is not like you. Asey, how're you going to get him—don't ask who. I mean Pink Shirt, of course."

"Wa-el," Asey drawled, "I been broodin' about that. Pie an' sandwiches seems one of his weaknesses. We could always put rat poison on a piece of pie an' see if he dried up."

"This entire household," Angelica said, "is fast coming under the whimsey-pooh influence of Tom Fowler. He's off again, by the way, holding forth on the Republican party. He doesn't like it. Myles is getting pink around the collar. What are your plans?"

"If he's still 'round, he's got to be lured somehow. After all, fish bite sooner or later. Trouble is the v'riety of things they bite at. Like clams, or red flannel, or feathers, or salt pork—"

"Or your own specialty of soft soap. You could always dangle Myles around and see what happened."

"Except," Asey said, "that Myles is nicer intact than otherwise. Tell you what. Send Myles in here—"

Myles arrived with a rapidity which suggested that he had been waiting for the interview. His coat pocket, Asey noticed, still bulged with the old Smith and Wesson. Myles had obviously not given up the hope of shooting at something.

Before he had time to sit down, Hamilton returned.

"Stuff from Lindsay you phoned about last night."

"Thanks." Asey unwrapped the package and flipped through the papers inside. "You needn't wait, Hamilton."

"Is that the Bat McCracken poster? That—okay, Asey, I'm on my way!"

Asey shut the study door and then picked up the sheet which contained a smudge picture of McCracken, a few of his aliases, and a long drawn-out list of his various crimes.

"Bat McCracken, alias Barry Mack, alias Bat Mack, alias Bernard M'Cullom, alias Barney McCullough—"

Asey slapped his thigh. Barney McCullough—he was Rosalie's first husband!

Steve's comment flashed through his mind. "Longshoreman, bartender and general liability. Q: did she ever divorce him?"

Asey smiled. "Myles," he said, "did you ever think up an idea that was so crazy you didn't dare even say it out loud, an' then find out it was true? This guy roamin' around here ain't no am'teur. He's a pr'fessional who owned fingerprints he didn't want spotted. He—well, just you take a look at this, feller, an' see what I mean!"

Myles put on his pince nez and picked up the sheet of paper.

" 'Bat McCracken,' " he read aloud the caption under the picture, " 'Wanted for—' why, Asey, someone's made a terrible mistake about that photograph. That's not Bat McCracken."

CHAPTER FOURTEEN

ASEY sat down carefully and stared at Myles.

"Let's work this out," he said. "Why ain't this feller Bat McCracken?"

"Why really," Myles removed his pince nez and returned them to his pocket with an air of finality, "really, it isn't, Asey. That man was my bus driver!"

"Your—what?" Asey found it difficult to form his words.

"My bus driver," Myles explained. "You know. The man who took the place of the young fellow that was the first bus driver. The one who brought me down from Boston for nothing. You know, Asey. Angelica said she was going to tell you about it."

"She tried," Asey said. "I'll say that much for her. She tried. Ain't her fault I—you know, I'm speechless."

He strode over to the door, stuck his head out into the hall and bellowed for Miss Sage.

"D'you mind," he asked when she arrived, "steppin' in here an' tellin' me about Myles's bus trip? Yes, right now. An' will you be so kindly as to accept my 'pologies too?"

Angelica surveyed him with honest wonderment. It seemed to her an odd time to bring the matter up, and she remarked as much.

"Think of all the dull moments I've tried to brighten with that story, and now that things are practically popping left and right, you take time out to—"

"I've 'pologized," Asey said penitently. "You an' Myles spin your yarn."

He picked up his pipe and started to light it, but after

Myles's first few words, he put the match back into his pocket. As the recital progressed, he chewed on the pipe stem, occasionally removing it from his mouth long enough to whistle softly or to grunt in sheer amazement. He himself had been with Lindsay at the South Station on Friday afternoon and helped oversee the fifty picked men who formed the net that was to have landed Bat McCracken with neatness and dispatch. And two blocks away, just two short blocks away, Bat had commandeered the purple bus and chauffeured Myles out of Boston.

"I feel," Asey observed as Angelica wound up the story, "sort of weak like, as ole Tinny Rogers said the time he pitched out of the crow's nest of the 'Pride of Wellfleet' an' landed right side up on the bales of hay we carried for some livestock on board. Huh. Myles, whyn't you *tell* me this yarn b'fore? Whyn't you throttle me an' make me listen to you?"

"I quite forgot it," Myles said, "really. With Rosalie here when I returned, and Lem's excitement, and then the murder—it didn't seem important in view of what came afterwards. Asey, what d'you suppose happened to the first bus driver?"

"I've guessed," Angelica said. "He's the mechanic that was killed Friday. Don't you remember my telling you I'd heard about it on the car radio?"

"But he was a bus driver, not a mechanic!"

"All the samey," Asey said, "I think she's right, Myles. They found this fellow in an alley, dressed just in his underclothes. That seems to be a habit of Bat's. Anyway, later they found a pair of overalls an' in 'em a union card. That's the only way they identified him. Feller lived alone in a shanty near Boston. Had a p'lice record. Most likely had his drivin' license an' bus registered under a fake name. But he ain't important now—I'll sic Lindsay onto it. My golly, the chances Bat took!"

"And he drove me," Myles said. "Really, I can't get over that."

Asey told him it was a wonder he did. "Prob'ly you enjoy the d'stinction of bein' one of the handful of folks that went for a ride with Bat McCracken an' lived to tell the tale."

"But why did he ask for me when he accosted Lem?" Myles asked. "And did he know Rosalie was here?"

"I doubt it. Wait'll I tell Hamilton to roust out the el'phants an' bison an' red men again. I'll have someone look into the bus business too. If he dumped you, Myles, b'fore you got to the barracks, he most likely dumped the bus after you beat it. Stay here till I get back."

"My, my," Myles said reminiscently after Asey left. "My, my!"

"Is that," Angelica demanded, "the strongest language you can muster up to fit this situation? In the patois of my nephews, you slay me, Myles!"

He ignored her jibes, for he was too busy thinking. When Asey came back, he propounded his theory.

"Asey, if Bat wants me so badly he's gone through all this to get at me, don't you think it would be a good plan for me to go out into the woods with a flag of truce, or something, and—"

"Just you leave lion's dens to Daniel, an' Clyde Beatty," Asey told him firmly.

"But he wants me, doesn't he? I wonder," Myles toyed with the ribbon of his pince nez, "I wonder why he didn't kill me, if he killed that nice young bus driver —I mean, mechanic."

Angelica sighed. "If you feel you've missed something, Myles, doubtless Asey can fix it up for him to kill you now. Man alive, don't you see? You're a respectable-looking individual. You'd add to any bus. He couldn't hurt you in the streets of Boston, in the midst of traffic. He wanted to get away, and you were a nice blind. If he had been stopped, wouldn't you have sworn he was all right, had the police asked you?"

Myles hesitated and then nodded slowly. "I suppose I should have. I wonder—you say the first bus driver

wore no uniform when he was found. I wonder if that
was what Bat carried in that paper package?"

"What paper package?" Asey asked gently. "What
paper package do you mean, Myles?"

"The one he had under his arm when he got into the
bus. It was very much the size and shape of my own
package."

Asey opened his mouth to speak, and then closed it.
He had been on the verge of asking Myles if he had ever
bought Brooklyn Bridge or the Empire State Building
from a nice-looking man named John Smith, but he
couldn't bring himself to it. He met Angelica's eyes and
knew that she also had got the idea, but Myles seemed
entirely unaware that he had provided the explanation
of why Bat wanted him.

Asey looked at him quizzically. Myles had been a
business man, and Lindsay's reports said he was highly
thought of at Allingham's.

"I s'pose the answer is," Asey murmured, "they
couldn't bear to fox you. For sheer up'n down, out an'
out, gullible, credulous—Myles. Listen. Whatever package Bat carted with him at the point where your path
an' his crossed, that package c'ntained over fifty thousand in bearer bonds—what d'you want, Tom? If it's
tobacco," Asey reached into his pocket, "take this plug
Lem gimme, an' beat it! Yup, Myles. It also c'ntained
thirty thousand or so in large bills, some trinkets he
grabbed out of a jewelry store, an' other such like odds
an' ends. I—honest, I don't hardly dare ask, but
where's the package you brought home? Er—d'you
have it?"

Angelica gulped audibly.

"It's at my house, Asey. In the attic. Two blue cashmere sweaters for Betsey's birthday, resting there so she
wouldn't get at 'em beforehand. Two blue cashmere—
Myles, won't you have the common decency to get
down on your knees and give thanks? No wonder I felt
nervous Friday night!"

Asey chuckled. "I wonder what Bat said when he

found out. Ought to be sulphur lingerin' around the place even yet."

"D'you two mean," Myles began.

"We mean," Angelica might have been explaining the alphabet to a small and slightly fuddled child, "you took Bat's package for your own, in the dark. You made off with it. He had faked an accident to get you out of the way. You were still on a main travelled highway, and he couldn't bash you, and he undeniably thought you unworthy of a bash, anyway. He probably hesitated to take his package with him on his fake trip to a phone, feeling that you'd suspect something—though I must admit I can't see that he had any grounds for feeling it."

"An'," Asey went on, "when he found out, he come straight for you. Honest, Myles, even two of the best blue sweaters in the world ain't no fair exchange for a couple hundred thousand bucks worth of loot!"

Myles refused to accept their explanations.

"I admit it appears to be at least a reason for Bat's coming for me, and of course I'm near-sighted, but shouldn't we find out for sure?"

"We should an' we are," Asey said, "but *we* don't mean *you*. You're goin' to be hid away under guard, you are! An' to think you roamed the woods with me this mornin'! Bat's prob'ly ready to make mincemeat of you. Nosir, until we get Bat under lock an' key, or at least six feet of ground, you're goin' to get watched over like a quintuplet!"

"You know," Myles said, looking Asey straight in the eye, "I rather resent—I mean, you and Angelica appear to consider me definitely stupid. I was brought up to believe that if you accorded human beings a certain amount of politeness and decency, they returned it. Now I took this McCracken for a bus driver, treated him as one, and—"

"An' he bus drove," Asey said. "You're right. You took it for granted that one of the best bad men since Jesse James was a lamb, an' he baaed an' bleated. But—"

"But," Myles pointed out, "I'm alive. You yourself admit that the skeptics aren't. What I'm trying to make clear, Asey, is that you and Angelica don't give others the benefit of the doubt, I do. Thus far I've managed to get along quite nicely. Oh," he added as Asey started to protest, "I'm not going to question your motives or your wisdom in ordering me to stay cooped up here until Bat is caught, but I want most emphatically to have it understood that I consider it absolutely unnecessary. Do I—er—"

"You make yourself entirely clear," Angelica said. "I don't know when I've felt so small, and if Asey feels half as rebuked as he looks—"

"I do," Asey said. "Myles, I'm ter'ble sorry we made fun of the way you go at things. We didn't mean to wisecrack. It's just the—the plum enormity of what happened to you, an' you so unconscious of it all. Honest, though, I want you to stay put an' do as I ask. Your golden rulin' may of got the better of Bat for once, but that don't mean anythin' perm'nant."

Myles put on his pince nez, but said nothing. Asey watched him, and bit his lip. Myles wasn't offended, but it was plain that his dander was up.

"Will you be so kindly," Asey said, "to give me your word, Myles, that you won't try to hunt Bat on your own?"

"Of course he will," Angelica said, "won't you, Myles? You couldn't be so silly as to try to cope with Bat single handed! Can't you understand? The police of half the New England states and most of the Atlantic coast, for that matter, have all been up against this man without success. And with Lord knows how many casualties!"

But Myles would make no promises.

"Very well then," Asey said, "I hate to do it, but you get a guard over you till Miss Sage an' I get back from collectin' that package. We're goin' to have a guard, too, even if there don't seem to be a chance that Bat'd got wise to where his stuff was. Okay, Miss Sage?"

Out in front of the house, Asey spoke to Hamilton.

"I want two men, an' a fellow to watch Myles. An' the feller in the pink shirt is McCracken. Yup. Don't faint," he added as Hamilton turned a sickly green color. "Listen, line up the town boys along the woods by the road. Call 'em back. Along the woods, mind, an' not in 'em. Keep your own men out of the woods, too. Got that? If he's in there, let him stay there quiet an' peaceful. Your job's to see he don't get to the house, or out b'yond the line of men. An' r'member, Ham, he's got a nice brain."

Ham nodded. "Say, what about Lem?"

"He can take care of himself. 'Sides, he didn't know it was Bat, nor Bat don't know him. Now r'member, Bat's fooled Myles as a bus driver, an' your trooper as a tourist. He fooled the best guys in New York bein' a sewer worker. They hunted, an' he watched 'em hunt while he leaned on a pick. No fancy acts, no false beards, but he does a right good job. You hold this place till I look into his loot. Once I get that, I think I know how to nab him. Anyway I got a plan. Now, don't let Myles out of the house. Don't let no one around here you ain't seen b'fore, not even if he claims to be the s'lectmen's brothers. He knows we don't know who he is, or there'd of been more hue'n cry."

"But wouldn't he know? After hunting Lem—"

"He knows we hunted Lem an' no one else. We sure yelled Lem's name enough for the dead to know that."

"Mrs. Barr's here," Hamilton's color was slowly returning. "What'll we do about her? What about if Leary comes back?"

Asey sighed. "Just push 'em to one side. Now, don't go shootin' around, or let anyone else. If you get brother Bat, which ain't likely, don't let him know you recognize him. He's got a horrid nasty habit of shootin' folks that recognize him. Okay?"

Hamilton laughed mirthlessly "Okay? Oh, sure, Sure! Swell. But for God's sakes hurry back."

Followed by two troopers, Asey and Angelica went down to the landing.

"You look pretty upset," Angelica said as they raced across the inlet in the speed boat.

"I feel it," Asey told her. "Huntin' wild men ain't in my line. Huh. Henderson's barn doors is open. That's queer. I told him to keep my car shut up tight when I left it there last night."

Henderson, on the wharf, greeted Asey genially.

"Feller get the car to you all right, huh?"

"Feller—what? I don't get you," Asey said

"Why, feller come here couple hours ago an' took your car, an'—"

"Joe," Asey spoke quietly enough, but his eyes were like two chips of granite, "you r'member somethin' I explained to you last night, about anyone takin' that car but me?"

"Why, sure, Asey," Joe said, "but he had a note from you. He was a state cop. Ain't it all right?"

"State cop?" Asey repeated. "Joe, are you sober?"

"Asey, I don't—say, they's a row boat leavin' Cole's place, Asey. Headin' this way. Seems to be—"

Asey shaded his eyes, looked for a second, and then jumped back into the speed boat.

"It's Hamilton," he said. "I'll run over. You fellers stay here with Miss Sage."

The mahogany boat spurted out across the inlet and coasted up to Hamilton's row boat.

"Who?" he asked.

Hamilton didn't stop to question what appeared to be second sight.

"Glassford. He went out with the rest this morning, and told me he was leaving for the barracks at ten. He had a special detail. We thought he went with Larsen. But Larsen just came back and said he hadn't, and about then Vecchio found him out by the west end of the woods, on his way back to the house. I'd just called 'em all in."

"Glassford dead?"

"Pretty near. Unconscious. Fractured skull, I think. I sent for the doc and an ambulance. We didn't dare move him. Been bashed over the head. Lucky Bat didn't want us to hear his gun. He took—"

"I know," Asey said grimly. "He took Glassford's uniform. May please you to know he's got my car, too."

"The—My God! Well, it's the last we'll see of him, that's a cinch, if he's got the roadster. I'll go back and see to Glass, poor kid."

"Tell the doc I'll be back soon, an' not to mind how much money he spends on gettin' Glass fixed right," Asey said. "Tell him to call anyone he needs. An' don't kid yourself Bat may not come back. Pull all your men in from the woods, an' give 'em a password. Give it to the local men, too. They don't know the cops, an' with that car—he might wrap up the Skaket National Bank an' take the town with him! I'll be with you soon's I see if he got his package."

Back on the opposite shore, Asey went to Henderson's phone and kept the local operator in a dither for fifteen minutes.

"There," he said to Angelica when he came out, "I've warned the banks all 'round, an' the barracks, an' had the whole thing sent out over the radio an' teletype. Not that I think Paul R'verein'll ever get that guy, but it's the proper Em'ly Post notion of what to do. C'mon."

He appropriated the Henderson's old sedan and set out for Pochet.

"If he found out Myles was at my house!" Angelica said. "Oh, Asey, Margaret'll be there! Did you phone and warn her?"

"Yup, I thought of that, but there wasn't no answer. She's all right, though. Girl at the phone office said she went by to the Mond'y Aft'noon Club 'bout an hour an' a half ago. Seen her go in."

Angelica relaxed against the worn seat-cushions.

"Thank heavens! But the thought of Bat McCracken among my things—hurry, Asey!"

There was no sign of the long roadster in front of or near Angelica's house, but Asey took no chances. Before getting out of the car, he called to a neighbor.

"Say, seen a state cop here, Henry?"

"He was here 'bout half an hour or so ago," was the discouraging answer. "He got in all right, Asey. He said you sent him, and I told him Margaret always left the key under the third geranium from the left in the kitchen window-box. He went right in."

"I just bet he did," Angelica muttered. "I just bet— Asey, hurry and get out! I'll faint if I don't see what's happened to that Lowestoft and the Sandwich glass!"

"Wait a sec," Asey said. "Say, Henry, he have a package with him when he left?"

"Didn't notice."

"Thanks. Okay, Miss Sage. Don't take it too hard if there is damage, Miss Sage. Hope for the best."

"Little sunshine," Angelica said, looking under the third geranium from the left. "Pollyanna—Asey, he even put the key back! Here, unlock the door. My hand's shaking."

The kitchen was untouched, but Angelica pointed to an empty pie plate in the sink.

"Dabbling with the pie, the old pig! Margaret never went off and left a dirty dish. Oh—look!"

The three rooms on the east side of the house which served as her show rooms were in a horrible state of disorder. Apparently Bat had looked into, over, behind and through everything. Yet only one object was broken, and Angelica spotted it at once.

"See, that little mirror. The nail was loose. He must have joggled it. I could kiss him. I always hated that mirror. Never knew why I bought it. No one else wanted to buy it from me. Thank God, he barely bothered the china room except to yank out drawers—Asey, he certainly was thorough! See, he stirred up the ashes in the fireplace."

Upstairs the bedrooms had been completely overhauled, but there was no damage.

"Now," Angelica paused at the head of the attic stairs, "I left it beside the trunk, and you can see from here—yes. He got it. Now what."

"Now," Asey said, "put your key back under the geraniums, an' we'll give Bat sixty points an' game. I can't understand how he caught on. Say, what day's the 'Pochet Item' come out?"

"Monday. Today," Angelica said. "It used to arrive Saturdays, but now that Perkins works for the swamp project during the week, he has to print it Sunday. Worries his wife. She's a Methodist. Why do you ask?"

"Chatty little paper, as I r'call," Asey said. "You subscribe? Good. Ought to be out in your mail box. I noticed one of the el'phants had a copy this aft'noon. I'll hop out an' get it."

He scanned the front page of the 'Item' a few minutes later, and let out a whoop.

"Looky! Headlines. See! 'Miss Sage Entertains'."

"That's Margaret's work," Angelica said resignedly. "She likes to keep me and her cooking in the public eye. Myles, I suppose? Have I any reputation left?"

" 'Friday evening,' " Asey read, " 'Miss Angelica Sage, proprietress of our flourishing antique ship—I guess he means 'shop.' Anyway, 'entertained Mr. Myles Witherall to dinner. Mr. Witherall is the uncle of Mr. and Mrs. Stephen Damon who recently purchased the old Cole place on the inlet. Although they and Mr. Witherall have been in town since January, they have been pretty busy fixing up their new property and so have not gone out much in society.' "

"Pochet and Skaket," Angelica said, "ought to eat that up."

"An' this," Asey said, "is the crownin' touch. Listen. 'During investigations at the Cole place of the murder' —this is half way through the gen'ral ramblin's on Rosalie an' all, Miss Sage—'Asey Mayo is keeping his new car over to Joe Henderson's, by the inlet.' Well, well. 'Pochet Item' done itself proud. Bat prob'ly picked up a copy, an' done some mental 'rithmetic, an' I'll give him credit for gettin' four. Let's go."

At the Pochet four corners he pulled up and asked a small boy where the traffic cop was.

"He's beat it over to Cole's. He—"

"He—say, seen my car here? Seen it go by?"

The boy consulted with some of his friends.

"Yup. They seen it. 'Bout half an hour ago. Headed down towards Skaket way. He—"

Asey didn't wait for the rest of the sentence.

He pressed the accelerator of the Henderson car down to the floor boards and held his foot there while the sedan lurched forward. Within ten minutes they had crossed the inlet and were back at the Cole place.

Angelica remarked the lack of troopers at the landing.

"Odd. I thought they were supposed to be there. The whole place has a queer look."

"It looks," Asey said angrily, "like a d'serted village. I told that traffic cop to stay there! I told Hamilton— you know, Leary must of come back an' took charge. Hamilton! Hey, Hamilton!" he roared the name out in his quarterdeck voice, and the two troopers with them exchanged meaning glances.

At the third bellow Hamilton appeared on a dead run from the back of the house.

"Asey!"

"What's the meanin' of this—"

"Asey," Hamilton said breathlessly, rubbing a dirty hand over his steaming forehead, "I know. But hell's popping loose here, and I couldn't—"

"What happened?"

"First Pratt come along to say that Waddy Barr'd beat it in his car, and then Mrs. Barr come and had hysterics all over the place about the time the doc was getting Glass away. Doc says he's got a chance, Asey. Then after they got off and I got Mrs. Barr quieted down—gee, it took four men to do that, Asey! Then I looked around and the only one besides us in the house was that girl Betsey!"

"What!" Asey looked at Angelica and whistled. "The —the—where's Myles?"

"Myles beat it. Betsey said he beat it while we were busy with Mrs. Barr. Tom and Steve and Hilda all piled out after him. She was half crazy. Myles had told them about Bat, you see. She had some idea that Myles was going after Bat on his own, and the rest all went after him. That Hilda, she—"

"Is that all, Ham?" Asey asked. "Is that all that's happened? Sure you haven't had an earthquake or a fire or two?"

"The Grove girl had a Flit gun full of ammonia—"

"It's her favorite weapon. I know. Where are your men?"

"Why, I sent the boys out after 'em, Asey. I know you said not to, but I couldn't think of anything else to do! They couldn't be left running around—my God!"

A pistol shot broke through the stillness of the afternoon air, and echoed dully back across the inlet.

CHAPTER FIFTEEN

ANGELICA clutched at Asey's arm.

"Myles, oh, the poor—Asey, *do* something!"

"West," Hamilton said. "West end," and started off full tilt in that direction.

"South," Asey said judicially, making no effort to move.

Angelica, who had instinctively started after Hamilton, retraced her steps and waited for Asey.

"Do something, man! Anything! Oh, move! Get going! Oh, d'you suppose Bat found Myles?"

"Glory be, I don't know! What else'd he come back here for?"

"Asey!" Angelica was on the verge of hysterics, "Asey, do something! Don't just stand there!"

"Look," Asey said, "if Bat's r'sponsible for that shot, he ain't goin' to run into the arms of that mob linin' the road, 'cause he must be pretty certain by now that we're after him. He ain't dope enough to use my car now. Give him credit. If it's him, he'll be comin' back this way—oh, God A'mighty, what a chump I am! If he's been studyin' the papers, he's comin' back here for Rosalie's jewelry!"

He turned around and called to the two troopers who had accompanied them to Angelica's house.

"Hey, you. Stop edgin' after Ham. Get into my boat an' take her out to midstream an' anchor. Keep your eyes peeled 'long this shore. Pop away at Bat or anyone in a hurry. F'you see him an' he's out of range, blow my siren. Get a rifle—"

Hamilton came pounding back.

"What shall we do?"

"Keep your natives lined up in a circle on the out-skirts of the woods. Don't let them in! Put your own men in pairs an' set 'em beatin' through the south part. An' for the love of soup, see if you can grab them folks from the house! If Bat's at a point where he don't mind givin' himself away by lettin' us hear his shots—" Asey shook his head. "An' if he gets that girl, he'll just stick her in front of him an' march her along, an' down she'll go the first move we make. Where's Betsey?"

Hamilton sighed wearily. "I don't know. She's proba-bly out there too. I never saw anything like this! Asey, come along and—what about her?"

"Me? I'm going too," Angelica announced before Asey had a chance to speak.

"Nope," Asey said, "you're stayin' here in the house. Mrs. Barr in there, Ham? Well, Miss Sage, you go 'noint your en'my's feet with oil, or whatever 'tis. Put a man with 'em, Ham. Put a couple by the shed here. Get me a pair of binoculars, too. They's some in the livin' room. We'll go investigate."

Angelica, bursting with indignation, preceded the trooper into the house. If Asey had paid more attention to the look in her eyes, he would have known that she had no intention of staying put and soothing Mrs. Barr. At the very first opportunity, Angelica firmly intended to join in the general confusion.

"Asey," Hamilton said as they hurried toward the south end of the woods, "what about Bat? D'you think he killed Rosalie, or what?"

"Or what." Asey twirled his old Colt forty-five by the trigger guard. "He didn't know she was here, Ham. 'Member that maid said Rosalie come more or less on the spur of the minute, though she did seem to find time to wire that Laurie girl. If you ask me, Bat'd of been the last person she'd of let known. Nope, I don't think he killed Rosalie. All his fineglin' around was to get hold of his loot he thought Myles had. He might of been comin' back for Myles, or for what he could pick up of Rosalie's, but he's out as far as she's c'ncerned. But I have a sort of feelin' that whoever did kill Rosalie is goin' to try to profit by this."

"Profit? How, you mean, get Bat's stuff?"

"Nun—no. Just put the whole thing on Bat's shoulders. Ever since the b'ginnin' of this, Bat's messed things up at the crucial moment. If I was the one who'd killed Rosalie, I'd sort of play to that."

"Waddy's beat it," Hamilton said thoughtfully. "What do you make of it?"

"Waddy," Asey said, "ain't Bat. We can always get Waddy, even if he goes to Timbuctoo. Waddy ain't no mammoth int'lect. Leave him be till we clear up this. We ain't never goin' to get places till we clear up Bat."

"Maybe." Hamilton sounded dubious. "Asey, how in hell can we get him if the rest of the police in a dozen states can't?"

"Dunno," Asey returned, "but we got to. He busted a mirror at Angelica's. Maybe it means his luck's changin'. He's had enough luck so far to last a lifetime, anyway. He—hold up!"

The Colt stopped spinning as Hilda ran through the bushes toward them.

"That shot! Asey, have you found Myles? Was it Myles?"

"Nope. Go back to the house with Ham."

"I won't," Hilda said stubbornly. "I won't. Yes, I know all the things you're going to say, but I'm as safe with you as I'd be there, and I absolutely will not go back till I've found out about that shot!"

"Where's your ammonia gun?" Asey asked.

"I don't know and I don't care. I dropped it somewhere. It was too smelly to run with. Asey, I'm coming with you!"

Asey shrugged. "On your own head be it, then. I ain't got the time to argue. If you want to play with dynamite, go on an' play. Ham, I'm goin' to head for the end of Barr's land. They's an old town fire post there. I'm going to climb up an' take a peek around beyond the clearin'."

Before they reached the tower, they were joined by Betsey, Tom, and two troopers.

"Fall in," Asey ordered. "I could spank you kids till you howled for mercy—well, well, an' here's Steve! Ain't that nice! You fall in too!"

"Where's Myles?" the Damons demanded in unison. "Where is he? Who fired that shot? Have you found him? Have—"

"Nope. Just you string along an' keep still."

When they approached the rusty old framework of the abandoned tower, Hamilton laid a hand on Asey's shoulder.

"Listen, you can't climb that! The thing's falling apart, and besides, you'll make a swell target! Let me go, can't you?"

Asey grinned. "He wouldn't be fool enough to shoot now an' give himself away for sure," he said. "I'll only be a second."

With the ease and agility of a monkey, he swung himself up the framework, sat on the top bar and hooked his feet around the side piping. Then he raised the binoculars and began a methodical survey of the surrounding woods.

Some spots were completely blotted out by the tree tops, and others by the thick underbrush. But he could make out fragments of the line of local men stretched along the road in a semi-circle that began below Barr's land, close to the inlet, and extended almost to the end of the road in the other direction. There—yes. Off on Briar Lane was his car. Bill Porter, he thought, would get a piece of his mind about installing transmission locks that were picked like blind men's pockets!

He caught several glimpses of troopers as they moved through the woods, but they were all in pairs. Swinging around with a nonchalance that made Hamilton catch his breath, he looked back at the house and muttered under his breath as he saw Angelica slip out the side door. As he started to call Hamilton, a trooper dashed after her.

"Huh," Asey said. "Huh!"

It occurred to him, as he scanned the nearby clearings, that he'd rarely met up with such a self-willed bunch. Even Waddy Barr seemed to have picked up something from them. He couldn't understand Waddy's running away. The boy didn't have many brains, but he should have enough to know what was good for him. Beating it off wasn't, either.

Something glittered in a clearing perhaps a hundred yards away. Asey readjusted the lenses and sniffed his disappointment. Only a tin can. But beyond it, on the edge of the clearing, was something grey. Myles, he remembered, had been wearing a grey flannel coat.

The binoculars bobbed to and fro on the leather cord around his neck as he swung down the framework to the ground.

"See anything?" Hamilton demanded.

"Dunno. We'll take a look."

The group followed at his heels as he carved a bee line through the scrub oaks and blueberry bushes and the tangle of blackberry vines and poison ivy.

"Now," Asey said as they came to an overgrown wagon road, "you folks come to a halt here, an' stay put. Ham, we'll keep on."

"What's up?" Hamilton asked.

"I don't know, but I—stop. My God A'mighty, Ham, look there!"

Lying at the foot of a withered scrub pine was a figure in a grey jacket.

"Waddy!" Hamilton said in awed tones. "Waddy Barr!"

He walked over and knelt down beside him.

"Asey, that was the shot all right. Look—right between the eyes! Well, he never knew what hit him, though that's little consolation for him. Say, Asey, look at his head! That's McCracken's work. That's just the way Glass was. He must have bashed him first and then shot."

"Nope," Asey said, "I don't think so. Look beyond there. See that gun? That's Myles's old forty-four. He was shot first, Ham. He wasn't down when that bullet hit him. Look an' you'll see. I don't think it's Bat's work, either. He'd have climbed into Waddy's clothes. Well, I suppose the only bright spot in this is that he didn't get Myles. No, don't touch the gun. Pick it up in your hanky for Brady to play with. Go get him, an' that photographer, an' send one of them troopers here. Take that bunch back to the house, too. Wait up. Send Steve here first."

Steve looked at Waddy Barr and reached out a hand to steady himself against a tree.

"Asey! And that's Myles's gun! Asey, oh this is—this is the end! Asey, I took that gun from the house! I lost it when I raced over this way earlier. I thought I saw Myles, and I—oh, you won't believe it! No one will."

"Pull yourself t'gether," Asey said quietly, "an' tell me. What's the story?"

Myles, it seemed, had sneaked out of the house while Mrs. Barr's hysterics were being ministered to. Betsey was the first to discover his absence, and Steve and the rest had promptly set out after him.

"I was first," Steve said jerkily. "Asey, there had been three guns on the table. One belonged to the cop that Ham put over Myles. One was this old thing of Myles's, and the other was mine. As I dashed by and grabbed one, I noticed there were only two, Myles's and the trooper's. I took the forty-four, and the trooper grabbed his own. So—"

"What you mean is, Myles had taken your own gun, huh?"

"Yes. And Betsey had unloaded it, Asey! And I stuck Myles's into my belt and dashed out, and I lost it."

"You what?"

"I knew you wouldn't believe me! I lost it around

here. I hunted and hunted, and couldn't find it, so I went on without it. When I met you near the tower, I'd come back for another look. I—and Myles has mine, Asey, and it isn't loaded! And here's Barr, shot with this thing I took. And there's Myles, wandering around somewhere after Bat, with an empty gun!"

"I thought," Asey said in resigned tones, "that this business couldn't be more compl'cated. Once more I'm wrong. But it looks like we'd reached a peak. It ain't hum'nly pos'ble for it to get more muddled up. It couldn't—"

Three shots rang out in quick succession.

"What was that?" Steve demanded. "What—"

"Those come from near the house. Trooper—hey, feller! You stay right here, see?"

He set off with long easy strides toward the house. Steve panted along behind, and Betsey and Hilda and Tom followed at varying intervals.

Hamilton met them at the back door.

"Don't ask," he said weakly. "Go in and take a look! Go in and stare. Go in and pinch yourself. But it's real. I saw it. I saw it happen."

In the living room sat Bat McCracken, his wrists and ankles handcuffed. Angelica was bandaging his right hand, and Myles, his eyes gleaming behind his pince nez, applied a swab of cotton first to Bat's left ear and then to his right.

Asey walked in and gravely doffed his cap to Myles.

"Yours," he said, "on a silver platter. I hand it to you. I—what're you crying for, Bat? I didn't think you was the type."

"He's had rather an unhappy experience," Myles said. "Er—I found that Steve's gun was unloaded, and I had to use Hilda's ammonia gun that I'd picked up. I tried hard not to pump it directly into his eyes, but the ammonia was quite strong."

"Oh," Asey said. "My, my, to take the words out of your own mouth. Are these," he indicated Bat's wounds, "are these the three shots we just heard?"

"M'yes," Myles said, picking up a fresh piece of cotton. "He tried to get away."

"Bat grabbed at my gun," Hamilton said, "and damn near got it, too. Myles grabbed Pratt's, and went ping-ping-ping. Shot mine out of Bat's hand with the first, nipped the tip of either ear with the others. Asey, I've seen you shoot, but I never saw anything like that before in all my life!"

"Neither," McCracken spoke for the first time, "did I. Jesus!" He looked at Myles with something akin to admiration. "An' I picked you for a pushover!"

"You," Myles said with a meaning glance at Asey, "are not the only one. I always liked to shoot. I used to shoot quite a lot with the Bennetts. I kept telling you so, Asey."

"You could shoot it out with Annie Oakley," Hamilton said, "and make her look like thirty cents. You could—"

"Not meanin' to cut this d'served praise an' admiration," Asey sat down opposite Bat, "let's hear about it, Myles."

"Yes indeed. Have you any collodion, Steve? First, d'you know Waddy Barr's been shot? You do? Well, I heard the shot and knew it was my gun. I made for the sound, and went too far. I came back towards the house and saw a trooper—only of course it wasn't really a trooper, but Bat. He was standing with a club lifted to hit someone in front of him. Before I could do anything, he struck."

"Wait up," Asey said. "Bat, did you shoot the guy in the grey flannel coat? Let's get this straight."

"The guy," McCracken said, breathing heavily, "was back to me, leanin' forward against a dead tree, with branches that stuck out. I bashed him. I wanted his clothes. Christ, when he slid down and I took a peep at him, he'd been drilled! He was dead! I knew when that mirror busted, I was done for. When I seen him, I knew it again!"

"I s'pose," Asey said, "the sight of someone drilled was a great shock, huh?"

Bat shivered. "His eyes was open—he—say, I don't bash—"

"You mean," Asey said, "you confine your killin' to the livin'. Well, whoever shot Waddy either must of propped him against that tree, or else his clothes held him by stickin' on them branches. N'en what, Myles?"

Myles continued his story. After Bat had hit Waddy, he had stepped forward with Hilda's ammonia gun that he had previously picked up, and went for Bat before the man realized what was happening.

"Bat was really entirely unnerved," Myles said. "I see you have doubts, but let me assure you he was a jelly. I—er—doused him with the ammonia gun—"

"Didn't you see your own gun lyin' there?" Asey demanded.

"Not till later. Then—"

"Whyn't you take it?"

"I had Tom's gun," Myles told him simply. "Oh, it was empty, to be sure. I discovered that before I found Hilda's implement. But Bat didn't know."

"What took you so long gettin' back here?" Asey asked.

"Oh, Bat guessed. About the gun, I mean. He made a couple of breaks, and of course I didn't shoot because I couldn't. I had to overtake him and use the ammonia. Of course he was handicapped, too, because he'd received quite a dose of ammonia the first time. I—"

"Where was your gun, Bat?" Asey asked.

"Don't use 'em," Bat said. "Don't like 'em."

Hamilton laughed, but Asey nodded. "Come to think of it, you don't, only 'cept when you get real annoyed, like with armored cars. Go on, Myles."

"Finally I met a pair of Hamilton's men, and we came back to the house. Just as we entered, Bat tried to get away again, but then I could shoot."

"Why," Asey persisted, "didn't you pick up your gun when you seen it near Waddy?"

"I thought," Myles said, "there would be fingerprints on it which you would undeniably need, and I couldn't see any sense in spoiling them. I already had a gun, if not a loaded gun, and the ammonia seemed quite efficient.

"My, my," Asey mimicked Myles's tones. "My, my! Bat, b'fore we pack you off, why'd you come back here? Whyn't you beat it with your dough?"

Bat smiled.

"Feller," Asey said, "you're goin' to r'gret that smile. Myles, this Colt of mine's a nice gun. Play with him."

Myles looked blank until Angelica winked at him from behind Bat.

"Play—oh. May I?"

"Sure, why not? Pick them brass buttons off'm his coat. He ain't got no right wearin' 'em. Take him out on the lawn, Ham, an' let Myles blaze away. Bat don't care. He may pr'fer bashin', for he's heard a gun or two. When you get through, I'll b'gin." He pulled a jack knife with a six inch blade from his pocket and flicked it with a quick motion across the room. It thudded above a knot in the pine wainscoting and quivered there. Asey clucked his tongue.

"Pretty poor." Angelica rose to the occasion.

"Punk," Asey agreed. "Well, I'll get better with a bit of practice. After I get through, I'll hand you over to Hamilton, Bat. Pity Leary ain't here. He does that sort of thing better, but I guess Ham's men can handle you. They don't like what you done to Glassford. They also r'call other items. I shouldn't wonder if you didn't b'fore you're through, if you're still able to r'call anythin'."

"Listen, hick," Bat said, "don't kid me. I been places an'—"

Asey rose suddenly from his chair and towered over Bat.

"Move, Miss Sage. Out of the way, the rest of you. Hamilton, you'n Pratt pick up that chair an' carry him outside. That's it. That's right. 'Bout six feet more. Myles, want to pick them buttons off his coat?"

"Why," Myles put on his pince nez, "why, if you say so, Asey. Of course, I don't know your gun as I know my own—"

The rest of them stood in speechless amazement as the Colt barked three times and the top three buttons of the tunic Bat wore disappeared.

"Part his hair," Asey said.

The Colt roared again.

"Very nice. Sorry you already nicked his ears. Well, he's got a mole on his nose. Try that so—what's that? Wait, Myles. Mr. McCracken has a few words to say. Got enough, Bat?"

Bat nodded. His face was mottled and his mouth drooled horribly.

"Hideous!" Angelica said. "Oh, Asey, you—"

"R'member," Asey said quietly, "this guy has give plenty. So you really don't like guns, huh, Bat? Okay. What'd you come back for? Hurry up. I can't wait all night."

"Rosalie's stuff. Ice." Bat licked his lips.

"Thought you might as well get the works, huh? Did you kill her on Friday?"

Bat shook his head.

"You was here that night. An' she wasn't shot. Who did it? You know?"

"No."

"You lie," Asey said. "Myles, pick off—"

"I don't!" Bat's voice rose and then broke. "Honest to God I don't! All I know is her light went on and then off again a few minutes."

"How'd you know it was her room?"

"It was marked in a picture in the papers. I seen it."

"Didn't know it was her room Friday night?"

"No."

Asey considered. There was something queer there, for the bulb in Rosalie's lamp was dead.

"Was you ever divorced from her?"

"No."

"Has she a child?"

"Girl, by the Frenchman. She farmed it out. I don't know where."

"Sure about that?"

"Yeah."

"Why was you so nice to Rosalie?" Asey asked. "Like lettin' her have so many husbands, an' not goin' after her or her money?"

Bat smiled briefly. "She knew too much."

"She did, huh? Well, brother, where's your little package? The little package you took out of the attic just a while ago?"

"I put it down before I bashed that guy," Bat's voice had turned to a croak. "It's still there."

"You lie," Asey said. "Myles, did you see it?"

Myles shook his head. "Really, Asey, I didn't notice. I wasn't—er—noticing details just then. It might have been."

"Where'd you put that package?" Asey's words rang out as though Myles had shot them from the Colt.

"I tell you, I put it on the ground before I bashed that guy!"

Asey turned to Hamilton. "Go see."

Bat's head slumped down on his chest.

"Ponder, feller," Asey said, "on what'll happen to you if it ain't there. Rally round him, you guys. The rest of you come indoors. I think we've had enough of Bat. The wise an' mighty Bat! Say, one of you guys go get a couple photographers. Don't let 'em talk to him, just let 'em take his picture an' then shoo 'em off. Maybe it'll be an object lesson to the young. You're sure, Bat, you don't want to change your mind about where that package is?"

Bat opened his eyes and looked up at Asey.

"That's where it is. That's where I put it."

But after half an hour's search, neither Hamilton nor any of his men could find a trace of it.

CHAPTER SIXTEEN

"BAT'S holding out," Hamilton said. "We been over that place with a fine tooth comb for a hundred yards. Up trees, under leaves and everything, and there's not a trace. It wasn't there when you and I found Waddy. Myles doesn't remember it. I tell you, Bat's holding out. He's foxing. I bet you he still figures on beating it with his stuff."

Asey jerked his head toward the lawn, where Bat was surrounded by a ring of troopers.

"Does he look that way to you? 'F you ask me, them photographers was the last straw for him. He's wilted. Keeps muttering about that mirror he smashed at Miss Sage's."

"He's foxing," Hamilton insisted. "Don't tell me a guy like him would crack like this, after all he's done!"

"The bigger they are," Asey said, "the harder they fall. The mirror smashed his luck. Leastways, he thought so, so it did. Next he bashes Waddy an' finds the boy already dead. That ain't the sort of experience calc'lated to stiffen anyone's nerves, if you think your luck's turned. He ain't had much to eat, nothin' better'n the inlet to drink, an' you got to admit that Myles's shootin' was fancy. It'd of scared me to a pulp. An' b'sides all that, Bat wouldn't of hid that box. He'd of kept it with him, after the way he lost it to Myles. I b'lieve him."

"Then," Ham said, "where the hell is it?"

"You're the copper," Asey returned, "I'm just an am'teur."

"Do you think whoever killed Waddy was around,

and seen Bat and Myles, and then sneaked up and grabbed that package?"

"Most likely. You might see if any wanderin' el'phants or bison got hold of it. One thing, it's goin' to be nicer to hunt the package without Bat on the loose than otherwise."

"What's the doc think of Mrs. Barr?" Hamilton asked.

The doctor himself came downstairs at the moment and answered the question.

"I think she's worked herself into as dangerous and as violent a state as any woman can, Ham, without actually going crazy. Who let her know about Waddy?"

"None of us," Asey said. "She overheard a couple of the troopers, after Ham set out to hunt the package. I was sendin' someone for you when you come. How's Glassford?"

"I think Mason'll pull him through. He's a corker with that sort of thing. Asey, why was Waddy here? I know he ran away from Pratt, but why in the name of common sense did he run here?"

"You," Asey pointed out, "was the one who never give him credit for havin' any common sense to b'gin with. I don't know. Does his mother?"

"About the only rational statement she can make," the doctor said, "is that Waddy is a good boy and never meant harm to anyone, if you can call that rational. I'll have someone take her over to the hospital, Asey. She needs hospital care. Got a nasty heart, and this hasn't helped it any. Mind if I hang around, Asey? I've got to run over to Hyannis tonight to see Mason, and I don't want to bother going home. Ham, have your fellows make these phone calls for me, will you? It's all written down on this paper."

"Glad to have you," Asey said. "Maybe you'll have some perspective to c'ntribute to all this. With all this rippin' an' tearin' an' dashin', the rest of us has sort of reached a state of bubble an' squeak."

"Well," the doctor sat down, "I'll admit I have some

noble thoughts, Asey. I always do. Lord, what a pulp McCracken is! I never saw so many deflated egos around, what with him and Mrs. Barr. Yes, I have some ideas, Asey. Who killed Waddy, and who took Bat's loot, and why did Waddy come? Did you learn one single thing out of all this McCracken business that'll help with Rosalie?"

Asey nodded. "Yup. We know the light in her room went on an' then off again when the bulb was dead, an' we know she's got a daughter, an' probably if my wits wasn't so ossified, I'd find more things. Betsey upstairs, is she? I want her."

He found Betsey sitting in her room with Hilda. Both looked and sounded exhausted.

"Angelica's with the Barr," Betsey said. "I see in your eyes what you want. Give us five more minutes, Asey, and we'll provide some supper for you. I can't remember your having anything to eat all day long, though doubtless you may have picked up a crust of bread somewhere. Asey, just where are we?"

"I was just goin' to say," Asey told her, "that I'd p'vide your supper. Can I cook? Land alive, I cooked on more ships'n you could shake a stick at. Didn't you know I started my c'reer at the age of nine, cookin' on a Banks fisherman? Tell me where you hide your p'tatoes, an' I'll make you Cape Cod barefoot. An' spider bread, an' hasty puddin'."

"Barefoot? You're making it up," Betsey said.

"I ain't," Asey returned. "You may call it somethin' else, but it's real."

After a talk with Hamilton and another survey of Waddy Barr before his body was removed, Asey went into the kitchen and firmly refused to admit anyone. He wanted to think, and he was tired of answering questions.

He put the salt codfish to soak and peeled potatoes for his promised "barefoot"; he sniffed at the minute strip of salt pork he found in the ice chest. He wanted about three times as much, but that would do. A close examination of Betsey's closets disclosed no corn meal, so he abandoned the idea of hasty pudding and made instead three apple pies. One would never do, two might, but three should fill the bill.

After thrusting them into the oven, he sat down by the kitchen table and lighted his pipe.

He knew, although no one had brought the matter up, that everyone including Hamilton and his men thought he had been neglectful of the clews, such as they were, concerning Rosalie's death. They felt, and rather mistakenly according to his way of thinking, that the most important clews were tangible things, like the lighter and the missing door key that Hilda had found in her bureau drawer. They wanted more clews, like cuff-buttons and cigarette stubs and bits of cloth and handkerchiefs.

Leary had talked himself into a state of complete fuddlement on the lighter and the key, yet to Asey they were less significant than the things they stood for. They meant that whether or not the murder was the spur of the minute affair it appeared to be, the murderer had neatly planned to involve Waddy and Hilda.

Both, Asey admitted as he got up to open the front draft of the stove, were good choices. Waddy had his alibis for Friday night, and he believed Hilda was innocent, yet the very fact of their being involved indicated forethought and previous knowledge on the part of Rosalie's murderer. Whoever it was, he or she knew that Hilda's father had been one of Rosalie's husbands, and that Waddy was conducting a private war on the Damons. Waddy's lighter on the pink and blue basket quilt, and the door key in Hilda's bureau were not matters of luck or chance. One or the other might have been luck, but not both.

The whole business was something you could ponder on and reach half a dozen conclusions.

Steve was in a position to know most about Rosalie, and even if he had not mentioned it, he might well have known about Richard Grove being Hilda's father. Rosalie's outburst had put the Damons on the rocks for money. Certainly Steve had an ironclad motive. Certainly, Asey thought, even a writer should have got wise to the reason behind the prowlers, once he knew that the adjoining land belonged to the Barrs. Writers weren't supposed to have any business sense to speak of, but Steve was Humphrey Damon's son, and couldn't be utterly devoid of wit. He wasn't.

And McCracken said the light in Rosalie's room had gone on and off, so someone had been there after Steve got the lighting system working again. It wasn't likely that Rosalie had turned the light on, for the doctor said she'd taken some sleeping tablets. As far as the rest of the household knew, the lights were off.

The bulb was out, but Asey doubted if it had given out until after the murderer had finished cleaning off his fingerprints. That job had been too thorough.

Well, when you looked at it that way, it all pointed to Steve.

Then if you looked at it another way, all that went equally well for Betsey and Myles. Betsey had the temper, and you didn't have to watch her very closely to know that for her the sun rose and set in Steve. A girl like that would do things for others that she'd never do for herself. Hilda was a different sort, with a different disposition altogether. The things she had gone through and the life she had led all hadn't beaten her. They had tempered her, made her cautious. Betsey would have bluffed about the key, but Hilda came forward with the story, and with her own story too. She accepted things and went on, unperturbed, as she had during and after her experience with Bat.

Weighing the two girls, Betsey was the one who might goad herself to murder. Hilda, as she admitted, would have cold-bloodedly set about making Rosalie wish she were dead.

And Myles. Asey smiled and shook his head. Myles was in a class by himself. After that afternoon, he could believe anything of Myles. With a man like that there were no limits. You couldn't say, he'd do this, or he'd do that. By his performance with Bat, Myles had ruled himself into the lists as a likely, if not the leading candidate for suspect number one. He had seen Steve's notes, he had met Hilda, he might well have known about Waddy. And any man that had brought in Bat McCracken with a few drops of ammonia would hardly hesitate at a whale lance. Nor would he hesitate at using it for his family.

And there was Tom. Tom knew everyone and everyone admitted it. He probably knew about Hilda's father. But the joker there was that he didn't know Waddy. If he did, and was lying, he had no opportunity to get hold of the lighter or to know about Waddy's war with the Damons.

Then—he paused with the poker in his hand as someone knocked at the kitchen door.

He opened it and admitted the Barradio boys and Mike Mallon.

"You guys still here? Ain't you tired of playin' with the hounds yet?"

"Say, Asey," Mike said, "we've been tryin' to get in past them coppers an' see you for an hour. Listen. We seen Waddy when he come."

"We talked to him," Ramon added. "Gee, Asey, he was in a stew! We tried to tell him he couldn't go through the woods, and about Bat, and all, but he was crazy!"

"Did he say what he was comin' here for?"

"That's all he did say," Ramon told him. "He kept sayin' it over an' over again. That he got to see you. That's all he said, I got to see Asey, I got to tell him!"

"Why'n time didn't you get hold of a trooper an' bring him to me?"

"We tried to! We tried to hold on to him! Finally he pushed us away and got into his car and drove off! We—"

"Where was you then?"

"Up the north end of the woods. There wasn't many

of the town men there then, an' they wouldn't pay any attention to us nor give us a car to chase him with. They was too busy watchin' for Bat. Gil Chase—we tried to get him to grab Waddy an' take him to you, an' Gil said he could see Waddy any day an' so could you. Anyway, we couldn't hold on to Waddy, an' he left, an' we thought he went for good."

"Yup," Asey said, "he pulled up on the edge of his own land an' left his car in a thicket. One of the boys found it. Where you been since?"

"We waited here, an' then there was the shots an' all, an' then after we heard you'd got Bat, an' about Waddy, we went home. We ain't slept much since Thursday," Mike explained.

"An' we told Tony everything," Ramon said, "an' he told us we should tell you what Waddy said. Say, Bat ain't much, is he? Just a slobbery old dope like Crazy Pete over in East Pochet. He—"

"A week ago," Mike said scornfully, "you wanted to be like him! You thought he was swell!"

"I never! I said—"

Asey quieted them down.

"Did Waddy see anyone else, or anyone else see him?"

"I don't think."

"An' you're sure he wanted to get to me to tell me somethin'. Listen, have you guys got any idea what it was?"

"Not an idea," Ramon said. "Gee, Asey, he was off his nut! He hardly didn't seem to see us, or anyone, or anything, an' I don't think he even understood when we told him about Bat."

"We'll find out, though, if you want," Mike said.

"How?"

"Why, Asey, we'll go hang around Barr's. That Jap of his always knows everythin'. Shall we?"

Asey thought for a moment. "Y-yes," he said hesitantly. "Pry a bit. Maybe Waddy told someone. See what you can get, anyways."

The doctor entered as the boys were leaving.

"Don't try booting me out," he said, "if you can entertain the local spit and chatter club, you can bear up with me. Decided yet why Waddy was killed?"

"Yes," Asey said, "I have. He knew too much an' his conscience was smitin' him. He was comin' to me to blurt out the whole story. I'd sort of wondered if we couldn't melt him. I told Tony to tell his Jap we knew all, an' I guess it pulled him around. But he didn't get to me."

"Who killed him then?" the doctor demanded. "If that's the case, then he was killed by the same person who killed Rosalie, eh?"

Asey shrugged. "I was just doin' some figgerin' on her, an' that business when them kids come. How's this for a likely pie, huh?"

"Magnificent." Dr. Cummings didn't even glance at them. "Stupendous. But who? I'm not clear on this gun found near Waddy. What about it?"

"It was Myles's gun that Steve grabbed when he run after Myles," Asey said. "Claims he dropped it. Lost it."

"I hate to suggest that that yarn is similar to that mess on the table," the doctor said, "but you've got to admit to a general fishy odor. Of course truth is stranger than fiction and all that, and the boy was in a dither—should think everyone in this house was fit for a psychopathic ward by this time! But even so!"

"Uh-huh." Asey mashed potatoes vigorously. "It's pos'ble Steve picked it up again. Or Myles did. Or Tom. Or Betsey. Or Hilda. Or maybe a trooper or some stray elephant."

"And very possibly," the doctor's sarcasm rose to heights, "possibly a little birdling picked it up and bit the trigger. Yes. Well, I'll tell you what I think, after hearing about Myles's shooting. I think that Myles just took careful aim and squeezed. Asey, are you paying me the slightest bit of attention?"

"I," Asey told him, "am gettin' supper. Dinner to you."

"Well," the doctor retorted, "I can tell you one thing —salt fish, salt pork, boiled potatoes, fried bread, apple pie! I can tell you one thing, maestro, it's a hell of a balanced meal!"

"Ev'ryone to his own taste," Asey returned calmly, "as the feller said when he kissed his cow. Cape Codders have flourished on just such teeterin' fodder for some time, doc. An'—"

"And dammit," the doctor interrupted testily, "eight out of ten live to be ninety-five, and the other two put flowers on their graves for the next ten years! Did I tell you about Phrone Higgins? I put her to bed yesterday by main force, and I told my wife last night she couldn't last the week—"

"Phrone ain't old," Asey said. "Seventy-odd."

"Seventy-six. This morning I went to call, and she had her father out in the kitchen hulling wild strawberries while she poured paraffin on the first batch of jam!"

"Higginses," Asey remarked, "was always good cooks. My grandmother was a Higgins. She scalloped oysters in bed. Oh, not all the time. Not as a gen'ral thing, but once when grandfather was bringin' comp'ny home from Boston, an' she had a busted hip. She was a corker with oysters—"

"For the love of God!" the doctor said. "For—say, Asey, can't I have a piece of one of those pies? Now, I mean?"

It didn't occur to him until the middle of supper that his questions about Waddy's murder had not been answered. Asey could be very elusive when he chose.

While they were finishing the second of Asey's pies, Hamilton came in with Lindsay, the head of the state police. Angelica and the others stared at him interestedly, for he had been one of the youngest colonels to emerge from the world war, and his renovation of the police had occupied many columns in the newspapers.

He accepted a slab of Asey's third pie, and made polite conversation about the weather and the stock market and a current best seller. Angelica, helping Betsey clear the table, confessed in a whisper that she was disappointed in the man.

"Spitting image of a cousin of mine in the paint and varnish business, and just about as dull! Get Tom and Myles and the rest out of the way. He's burning to have a heart to heart talk with Asey."

When he and Asey were finally left alone in the dining room, Lindsay's cloak of polite inanities dropped off in a second.

"Asey, I didn't believe you'd got Bat until I saw him, and even then I had to pinch myself!"

Asey admitted drily that he had a few black and blue spots himself. "But don't," he added, "get the notion that I got Bat. I didn't have nothin' to do with it. That was Myles Witherall's job entirely."

"It doesn't seem quite possible," Lindsay said, "but on the other hand, I'm not surprised. I had an uncle who looked rather like him. Mild, polite, Bostonian to the core. Enlisted with me as a private. Machine-gun nests were his specialty. He liked to mop 'em up single-handed. Same thing entirely. Throwback to some pirate or witch burner, I suppose. Well, I'll see he gets his money. Stack of rewards for Bat, you know. Asey, has Leary come back, or have you heard from him?"

"Merc'fully, he's still off. I don't even know what he's up to."

Lindsay fitted his fingertips together and smiled.

"He's going to show you up, Asey. That's his plan, and I've got to admit his theory of this mess seems sane. You know what I feel about Leary. He's all right, but he doesn't belong in this outfit. But I needed a lot of new equipment."

Asey nodded. "An' he got thrown in. Huh. S'pose you need action on this too, don't you?"

"I do," Lindsay admitted. "In the past year I've trod on more toes than I like to think of, and I'm not a bit popular. I'd like to stick to this job until I've got things whipped into shape. This Ray business is considerably more than local, though."

"So what they call pressure," Asey said, "is bein' brought to bear, huh?"

"Exactly. Of course getting Bat has helped some, but that won't last. And from your messages and phone calls, I gather you need time."

"I do," Asey said. "This has sort of d'veloped into the Enough Rope Club. Today's goin's on has sort of changed my notions, too. Lindsay, I got a couple of funny ideas I been dwellin' on, but they ain't the sort of things you can force. They got to be led along easy an' let come to a head."

"What about this group?" Lindsay asked. "How far would they go to help?"

"You mean, when Leary comes in with his denouncin' act, would the goat be willin' to take it?"

"Yes. The papers would be happy, the lads who're mad at me would have to shut up, and then you could have time to do things in, and when you got ready— well, Leary might be squelched for good. I've got nothing against Leary, in one sense. He's not crooked, but he has so many friends he tells things to. Which is of course why he's been thrust on me. Asey, what about Wadsworth Barr? Get anything out of his mother?"

"She's gone off to the hosp'tal," Asey said. "She can't be got at for some time. B'sides, I don't honestly think she knows a thing. Little Waddy wasn't a pretty sort. Runnin' liquor, an' maybe dope."

"So you mentioned on the phone. I looked into that," Lindsay said. "Seems Martin, the Federal lad, knew about him. His stuff never got anywhere, or hasn't lately. Martin was after the higher-ups. Asey, Leary's got a case, I think. He got hold of a reporter, and they've been—"

"Ah!" Asey said. "Hilda Grove, huh? I know. All about her father an' Rosalie. An' someone planted that door key on her. But offhand, Lindsay, she's the one I'd give a clean slate to. B'sides, she didn't know Waddy.

Couldn't of got that lighter. Only came Friday night. Hadn't any reason to kill him."

He got up and paced back and forth in front of the fireplace. If it were Tom or Myles or Steve that Leary intended to land on, he shouldn't have minded asking them to fall in and sacrifice themselves to Lindsay's plans. But Hilda had had enough.

He said as much to Lindsay. "Honest, I know how you feel. If Leary could land on someone, it would help hurry my ideas up, too. But I sort of hate to see that kid take any more of a beatin'. She's had enough."

"We might ask her," Lindsay said. "I think it's sort of a rotten thing to do, too. It's a rotten idea anyway. But Leary's got a lot of stuff. That reporter's helped him, and don't think I could kill that story, because I couldn't. What about fingerprints on that gun near Barr, anyway?"

"Blank. Wiped clean, like the lance an' the stuff in Rosalie's room. Myles's prints on the cartridges. There you are. There ain't a thing right now where I could counter Hilda with someone else. Y'know, I had a feelin' Leary'd get this angle, an' I was all set to toss Waddy at him. Well, we'll go talk with Hilda."

But he made no move to go, nor did Lindsay.

"I hate politics!" Lindsay said vehemently. "I hate red tape! If I had my way, I'd let you handle this as you wanted, and at your own leisure. But if Leary bursts out with that stuff he's dug up, and that pen pusher!" He sighed. "If you think the girl innocent, I believe you. If we stick up for her, I'll have to leave this outfit with my tail between my legs. Oh, damn it, let's go tell her. I feel like a mug!"

"It won't s'prise her a lot," Asey said. "She thought of this herself the other day."

The rest of the household, except Hilda, were in the living room, trying hard to appear at ease and unconcerned and disinterested.

"Well," Dr. Cummings couldn't hold in any longer, "Well, what's up?"

"Nothin' much. Where's Hilda?"

"In my study," Steve told him. "She wanted to write a letter and I told her to use my typewriter. She always cleans it beautifully and oils it. Wonderful mechanic. She can put wicks in cigarette lighters, even."

"That ain't bein' a m'chanic," Asey said, "that's sheer genius. Okay, Lindsay."

In the hall outside the study door, Asey paused.

"Say, ain't there no way this can be figgered out without usin' a scapegoat?"

Lindsay shrugged.

"What about that Lee girl, Lee Laurie?" Asey asked. "I almost forgot her. You do the lookin' up I wanted?"

"The photostat she has may be a fake, but the original's all right. Fanny Laurie. I've got it and some other stuff with me. By George, Asey, maybe we could—let's prepare this girl for Leary, and then get together. We might be able to bluff Leary."

Asey tapped on the door and opened it.

He started to enter, then seemed to change his mind.

"What's the matter?" Lindsay demanded, trying to peer into the room over Asey's shoulder. "What's the matter?"

"Take a look," Asey said in a harsh voice. "Just take a look! Scapegoat, huh? What a nice couple of old peace-on-earth-good-will-to menners you an' me turned out to be! Scapegoat, nothin'!"

CHAPTER SEVENTEEN

WITH a maddening deliberation that drove Lindsay to exasperated mutterings, Asey sauntered into the study and closed the door.

Hilda stood beside the desk, staring down at its cluttered surface. There was a spot of color high on either cheek, her nostrils were dilated, and her lips were pressed tightly together.

When his wife looked like that, Lindsay thought, it meant she wanted to scream. But this girl made no sound. It was impossible for her not to have heard Asey's scornfully spoken words, but she did not raise her head when the two men entered. She might have been carved out of marble; Lindsay had an odd, uncomfortable feeling that she was miles and miles away, entirely unaware of their presence.

He followed Asey's eyes to the desk top, trying to pick from its confused disorder the particular object that seemed to be holding her attention. Typewriter, oil can, erasers, ash trays, untidy little heaps of index cards, a bottle of iodine, an ivory elephant, a putty knife—none of those, certainly, could make a woman look like that!

Lindsay moved nearer the desk and a shiver ran up and down his spine. A pile of papers had hidden from him the object that Asey had so quickly spotted. No wonder Asey had spoken as he had!

Beside Hilda's fingers on the table was a diamond. Rosalie Ray's diamond. The Lewis diamond. There wasn't any mistaking that.

Hilda continued to stare at it.

"Amazing." She raised her head and looked at Asey, "Amazing, isn't it? This thing represents to me virtually everything unpleasant in this world. When Rosalie wore it and I thought it was a common paste brooch, it meant absolutely nothing at all. Now it means unhappiness and—oh, well, why go into it? How utterly, incredibly stupid that a chunk of glass could do what that has done, don't you think?"

She flicked it with her finger and turned away from the desk. Lindsay, completely bewildered, watched the gleaming stone hit the iodine bottle, carom off and come to rest beside the ivory elephant.

"Ugh!" Hilda walked over to the leather chair, sat down and lighted a cigarette. "Ugh! Horrid thing! I can croon over the polished leather of a first edition, or tooled morocco by Zahnesdorf. I can get lyrical over illuminated manuscripts and vellum bindings. But how women can rave over diamonds!" she shuddered. "Diamonds! The fat levantine I work for wears dirty diamonds. So do all her friends. I don't know which is worse, dirty diamonds on their greasy fingers, or glittering diamonds on things like Rosalie!"

Lindsay looked at her and then turned to Asey. It gave him a certain amount of negative satisfaction to note that Asey looked nearly as flabbergasted as he himself felt.

"They make soft people softer, and hard people harder." Hilda crushed out her cigarette and lighted another. "When people speak of diamonds in the rough, I invariably think of horrid—"

"Look," Asey found his voice, "for the—say, how can you sit there, Hilda, an' d'liver an oration on diamonds at this point?"

"I'm sure," Hilda retorted, "that under the circumstances you can hardly expect me to pass the thing off without comment! It's the first time I ever knowingly laid eye on the beastly thing that made my childhood a nightmare and haunted me all my life! For the love of soup yourself! When a ghost confronts you in the flesh, d'you just giggle girlishly and let it pass? Maybe you could ignore it, but I can't! Asey, I'm terrifically disappointed in you!"

"Not half as dis'pointed," Asey said, "as I am about you. Oh, Hilda, you've gone an' let yourself in for it now, for sure!"

Hilda stared at him uncomprehendingly.

"Let myself in for what? Why, I thought you and I had this situation in hand, Asey!"

"We did," Asey said, "but we come in here, an' find you with that diamond. Listen, just explain, will you? If you can explain?"

Hilda paused with her cigarette half way to her lips.

"Dear God! Asey, you don't think *I* had that foul thing, do you, all the time? I just found it!"

"Where?" Lindsay asked.

"In the typewriter, of course. The machine was simply filthy. I always have to clean it for Steve every time I visit. I'd forgotten to write my family. Poor things, they probably have been reading the papers and having apoplexy about me. Anyway, I thought I wouldn't bother to clean the type, but the carriage stuck. The diamond had dropped down inside and gummed things up."

"I could do better than that," Asey said.

Hilda drew a long breath. "Really, I'm so mad with you I can hardly talk, Asey Mayo! Listen, Rosalie was in here with Steve Friday evening. He typed off some notes. That was before they had their difference of opinion. She probably leaned over the machine when he was through and the diamond dropped into it. It's a cinch to lose things in typewriters. Particularly an old dirty thing like this one. Look at that pile of green fernery dripping from the key shafts! Steve won't use an eraser brush. Look at the fringe from the type shafts! Whiskers, no less. No one's used this machine since Friday. The diamond's just been here. I've thought all along it was odd that Myles didn't notice it when he peered in the window. And," Hilda stubbed out a ciga-

rette with vigor, "far be it from me to crack, my lad, but
you've spent a lot of time in here. Even an amateur
ought to have sniffed around some."

Asey turned to Lindsay and grinned.

"She's got me there. I never looked at the machine.
Let's see, now, Hilda. Pop it in where it was."

"I'll show you, but you do the popping. I won't touch
the thing. It was way under, Asey, mixed up in the in-
nards of the thing. Drop it."

Lindsay, accustomed to the business-like and scien-
tific methods of his office, was a little shaken at the in-
formal manner in which Asey casually tossed the Lewis
diamond around to see how it had become hidden. Obviously the value of the stone meant nothing to Hilda,
and apparently Asey felt much the same way. He handled it as he might have handled a pebble from the
beach.

"Well," Asey said at last, "it could of fallen in all
right, but to of got back there, someone must of give it a
little push. An' a fat lot of good that does us, because
every one's dribbled in an' out of here. Too bad."

"Will I have to pick oakum," Hilda asked, "or don't
they do that any more?"

She addressed her inquiry to Lindsay, who didn't
begin to grasp what she meant.

"They give up oakum," Asey assured her. "I think
you scrub, but I ain't sure. Hilda, you won't go to jail,
but—"

"But I'll get a chance to flirt with a turnkey," Hilda
said. "I know. Don't try to break it to me gently. I know
you believe me, Asey, but I'm sure the boss here
doesn't, and I felt from the first that brother Leary and
I would cross swords. It's just the curse of the Groves,
this stone. If I'd had the wit to think out what my finding it would mean, I'd jolly well have stuck it back
among the eraser drippings. Do I get handcuffs, like
Bat?"

"You do not!" Lindsay said. Like Asey, his admiration for the girl was mounting. "Asey, we can't let this

go on. Why not stick the stone back? You can find it later. We can't let her go through with this. Leary—no!"

Hilda smiled. "I get it. So Leary went trailing off to get the lowdown on me, did he? And he's got you in a spot, hasn't he?"

"I'll tell you," Lindsay sat down and lighted a cigar, "just what a spot it is, too." He launched into a monologue which would have whitened the hair of a taxpayer. "There, that's it. That's—"

"Wait up," Asey said, "I got an idea. We'll pull one on Leary. Look, Hilda, this story about your father is bound to crop up. We can't stop it, but we can get ahead of it. Look, can you bear the thought of this? Lindsay'll take you to Boston right now, before Leary gets here. I'll hold him off long's I can, an' when he tries to spill the beans, Lindsay, you get that female with the syndicate column—what's her name? She interviewed me once, an' I felt like maple syrup for a week after."

"Mirabelle Hicks. I know her. I get it—"

"Sure. Make a good yarn out of it. Girl finds missin' stone that ruined father—no. Ruined mother's life. Fathers don't count with Mirabelle. Have her take the story an' dose it, an' spread it over the front pages b'fore Leary gets a chance."

"It's good," Hilda said. "I mean it, don't look at me that way! I mean it. It *is* a good story. I ought to know. Lovely Suspect Has Borne Much, Now Comes Final Blow. Really, that might work."

"Will work," Asey said. "If you get to be a heroine that people cry over, Leary can't touch you. All d'pends on Mirabelle. She can do anythin'."

"Don't tell me," Lindsay said. "She got women's clubs and church clubs all over the state weeping for Mrs. Smur. Remember Mrs. Smur, the one that fed her husband arsenic? By the time Mirabelle got through, I think even the judge forgot she was on trial for murder. All he and everyone else could remember was Mrs. Smur's twins."

Asey chuckled. "Hilda, what a pity you ain't got trip-lets! Lindsay, don't let it go at that. Get hold of Steve Crump. He's a friend of mine. He ain't so expensive. Get him ready. N'en if Leary pulls anythin', Steve can fix him. He knows every trick of law. You keep Hilda at your house. An' let it be known that b'fore t'morrow noon, we'll get this all cleared up."

Hilda and Lindsay looked at him.

"You can't," Hilda said flatly. "You couldn't."

"Wonderful what you can do," Asey said, "when you set a time limit. Uncle of mine once brought the 'Flyin' Cloud' round the Horn to 'Frisco in eighty-nine days b'cause he decided it could be done. Hilda, you're a sport. Chances is we'll stave Leary off an' nothin'll come of it, but we're settled for everythin'. Lindsay, look after her. Both of you beat it, quick!"

"My clothes!" Hilda said. "I've got to have a tooth brush, at least—"

"No time. Tell Mirabelle, an' t'morrow you'll have an avalanche of 'em. I told her I had a hard time gettin' handknit wool socks, an' she said so in the paper, an' I got sent upwards of three hundred pair in a week. Lindsay, leave me all the dope you got on Lee Laurie, an' take care of Hilda!"

The entire household tramped across the Barr's land to the road where Lindsay's car was parked. Angelica shook her head as the car roared off, preceded by two troopers on motorcycles.

"You may know what you're doing, Asey Mayo, but I think it's a crime! The poor child! And she was actu-ally laughing! I think she's brave, even if that's an old-fashioned adjective you're not supposed to use these days."

"I'm really awfully afraid she's not putting it on," Betsey said. "She's really getting a kick out of it. After all, Asey's right. She's going to get the publicity anyway, and it might as well be used to save her. You know," Betsey added wistfully, "I wish I could have gone, too. I always wanted to ride with a police escort. Oh, look!"

Another car came tearing along the road from the opposite direction.

"Leary," Asey chuckled. "Hustle off, all of you but Myles. Scamper back to the house! Myles, they'll stop along here. Go up an' say h'lo to Leary, an' sort of lead him away from the car while he's givin' you blazes for roamin' off from the house. I'll see to the rest."

While Myles vainly attempted to insert a word into Leary's outburst, Asey strolled up.

"Leary—gee, I wish you'd of got here a mite sooner! Lindsay's been here, an' he's just started back with Hilda. He wanted you. He—"

"*He's* got her?" Leary turned and ran for his car.

"Wait!" Asey called. "Better take the short cut to Pochet if you want to catch him. By the woods. Swing back."

"Okay!"

Leary's car roared off.

"An' in the middle of the Pochet short cut," Asey said, "I'm awful 'fraid he'll get to hate life. In fact, even if he gets that carb'reter fixed up, I have doubts about his gettin' to Boston t'night."

Myles did not question the statement.

"Er—what are you going to do now?" he asked.

"I'm goin' to give time a run for its money," Asey said.

"You know," Myles said thoughtfully, "I don't see how you can possibly unravel anything where there's so little to unravel. There seem to be so few clews."

"Clews," Asey told him, "is primar'ly a state of mind. For the one that leaves 'em an' the one that finds 'em an' the one that tries to hitch 'em together."

"Oh, yes, yes indeed," Myles said, hoping that he had made an adequate reply.

"An' also," Asey went on, "I'm goin' to look into a red herrin' named Laurie."

Back in the house he retired to Steve's study and picked up the papers Lindsay had left for him.

There were half a dozen sheets concerning the Laurie

girl. Asey grinned as he read a note attached to the first page. It was from the chief of police of the town of Shrewsfield, who announced that he also acted as town clerk, notary public and mortician, that he had known Fanny Laurie since she was born, and there wasn't a soul in town who wouldn't and couldn't vouch for her.

"A nice, bright girl except for her temper," the note concluded, "fraternally yours, colonel, P. Snyder."

The photostat of the birth certificate he enclosed was similar to the one Asey had been shown, except that the girl's name was given as Fanny, and the year of her birth—Asey whistled. If there wasn't any mistake in his arithmetic, Lee Laurie was over twenty-seven.

He called Tom Fowler in.

"How old's the Laurie girl?"

"Officially, or for publication? She's really twenty-seven. She came into her money when she was twenty-five. Look, what's this fascination that little Leesie-Weesie holds for you, anyway? D'you like the type, or is it something more specific?"

"I want to prove she's Rosalie's daughter," Asey said, "an' it's comin' hard."

"It ought to, Asey, you're miles off. Look, I wasn't an eye witness, but she was practically born on our front door steps." Tom filled his pipe and borrowed a match from Asey. "Phone mother and have her tell you the story. She tells it beautifully. You see, mother'd had a musicale, and Mrs. Laurie insisted on coming. When it became obvious that she'd made an error of judgment, mother took charge. And the electric brougham wouldn't start, and mother didn't think it was delicate to have the negro coachman take her to the hospital, so mother drove. She met the fire horses out for a run on Chestnut Street, was neck and neck with 'em on Oak, and passed 'em on Maple. Father used to call her Fire-Horse Annie after that. Mother thought it was very indelicate."

"Huh," Asey said. "What's a faked certificate or two

when you can practically trace someone's entry into this world? Where was the hospital, Willow Street?"

Tom laughed. "Around the corner of Maple, on Eucalyptus, believe it or not. My, the fun I'm going to have with Lee when I get back to New York. I shan't feel bound to contain myself now I'm no longer a fiancé. I can live at the Ritz for months on the proceeds of 'Why Lee Laurie Bit the Spelling Teacher's Thumb in Two.' And her first appearance on the stage! She was the spirit of Christmas at a children's festival at the church, Asey, and she had one god-awful cold. 'Ib de spiddit ub Grizbuz.' And then—"

It took Asey fifteen minutes to stem the flood of reminiscences about Lee Laurie and her youth. Tom was wound up.

"All right," he said at last, "if you don't want to hear any more, you don't, but I thought I was doing you a favor. Very few people knew her home life as I did. I was just trying to help."

After he left, Asey smiled. Tom had helped, in a way. His nervous volubility had proved one thing Asey had felt all along, that Lee meant more to him than Tom wished people to think.

He went through the papers once more. They all bore out what Tom said, that Lee Laurie was a genuine, bona fide daughter of the Alfred Lauries of Shrewsfield. Still Asey wasn't satisfied.

The fake certificate she had tried to fool him with in that dim light—that was a silly move and apparently without reason. After all, if Fanny Laurie, aged twenty-seven, chose to have people believe she had been born Lee Laurie, and was only twenty-three, she could do so without resorting to faked birth certificates.

Of course Fanny was a name better hidden, and it was always nice for an actress to be able to shear a few years off her age. You could call it vanity.

"But," Asey said to himself, "it would take an awful *lot* of vanity!"

He went back to Steve's notes again and plowed through them until he came to a page of dates.

Rosalie had married La Roc in 1906. If their daughter were still alive, she could very easily be around twenty-seven.

Asey thumped his fist on the edge of the felt mat under the typewriter. He was reasonably sure that the Laurie girl didn't kill Rosalie, and he was certain she hadn't shot Waddy. But there was something fishy about her and her visits to the Damon house, and her relationship with Rosalie, and this easy, casual, off-and-on engagement with Tom.

He went back again to Lindsay's papers, and then to the items from the Shrewsfield chief of police. Somewhere there should be something to tie up, if he could only find it.

"This girl looks like Rosalie," he muttered to himself. "She's got a Ray temper. Rosalie. Huh. Rosa-lie. Lee. Dum it, it's here somewhere!"

He pored over the page that concerned Lee Laurie's family. Both her mother and father were natives of Shrewsfield, and not a single detail about either even remotely suggested Rosalie or the stage. They were just well-to-do small town people who might have come from Skaket or Pochet or any nearby village.

Angelica came in with a cup of coffee on a tray.

"Sustenance," she said. "Soon I shall demand tips. You look mad."

"I ain't mad," Asey said, "I just feel thwarted. If you want to cheer me up, tell me that Elida Bolton was on the stage and a bosom pal of Rosalie's. Otherwise I'll just get more thwarted."

"Elida Bolton," Angelica said. "Hm. She went to Miss Marble's with my sister. The only time I ever saw her was in a Cue Club play. Perfectly hideous thing, on the order of 'Charley's Aunt.' As a matter of fact, I think she did go on the stage afterwards. Constance would know. Why, in the midst of all this turmoil, d'you pick on dear Con's school friends?"

"Elida Bolton," Asey told her in a strangled sort of voice, "is Lee Laurie's mother. Or was. How does that hit you?"

"Well, it's literally hit my coffee on the rug," Angelica said, stooping to dab at the spot with a handkerchief. "What odd contributions I make to this! Harboring stolen goods, and picking Elida Bolton out of my memory! Truly, Asey, it's absurd. I should never have known her as Mrs. Someone-or-other. Con always speaks of her friends by their maiden names. She calls Van Druten Adam's wife 'dear Beansey Pease.' Well, now that I've solved your little problem, what are you going to do about it?"

"Prod," Asey said, "with a couple of what I quaintly like to consider ideas. So long. Keep this crowd in hand, will you?"

"They don't need me," Angelica aid. "Myles is sound asleep with the 'Transcript' propped up in front of him. The 'Transcript' thinks Myles is a good citizen for landing Bat, Asey. It says so right out. Mr. Witherall Apprehends Bad Man with Unique Implement. I told Myles to write the editor at once and sue him for libel. It should be, Mr. Witherall, Comma, with Unique Implement. Anyway, they mention Myles's clubs and trace his ancestry as far as it seems refined. Asey, can't I go? Betsey's gone to bed, and Steve and Tom are playing Russian banque for matches. I do so want to go with you."

Asey shook his head. "Not tonight. Ham's comin' with me. You stay put."

"It's a gyp," Angelica told him. "I un-thwart you, and what thanks do I get for it? Stay home and take care of the children, forsooth!"

Asey chuckled, but he didn't relent. Taking Hamilton, he walked through the woods to where one of the troopers had brought his car.

"An' Bat forced the lock with a piece of wire!" Asey said. "Wait'll I see Bill Porter on that! I'm goin' to talk with Lem first, Ham. You needn't bother to come."

Lina said that Lem was out in the barn.

"That is, he's s'posed to be there," she observed. "S'posed to be findin' mason jars for me. But I wouldn't swear to it. I expect 'most anything from him now."

Lem greeted Asey sadly.

"Hear you got that guy. That's good."

"S'matter?" Asey asked. "You an' Lina fightin'?"

"She still don't b'lieve me," Lem said, scrubbing at a dusty preserve jar with a piece of dustier rag. "She says if the feller I say kept me bound up was Bat, I'd be dead. If you ask me, I'd say she was disappointed I ain't. What can I do for you, Asey?"

"I'm toyin' with ideas, Lem. You happen to hear a boat Friday night while Bat had you outside the Damons'? 'Course it was pourin' cats an' dogs, an' the wind was heavy, an' for all I know there wasn't no boat. But you mentioned hearin' mine Sat'day aft'noon an' night."

Lem remarked that after he had been tied up an hour, he heard grass growing.

"Sure, Asey, I heard a boat Friday, for all the rain an' water an' wind. I heard you come."

"You mean Sat'day aft'noon. That's when I come," Asey explained. "What I mean is the *first* night Bat had you. Friday, an' on into Sat'day mornin'."

"That's what I mean too," Lem said. "Friday night late, or Sat'day mornin' early. Say, you got a flashlight there in your pocket? Come round to the hen house a sec, will you? Some rat, two legged or four legged, is after my hens, an' I thought I just heard somethin'."

Asey obligingly walked with him out to the hen house and swung his flash around.

"Now what about this boat business," he went on as Lem moved a trap, "Friday? I think we sort of got c'nfused there. I come Sat'day aft'noon, Lem. You couldn't of heard me the night b'fore."

"But it was a speed boat," Lem insisted. " 'Course, I was hopin' for someone to come, so I s'pose I just naturally thought it was you. But I'd swear in court I heard a speed boat Friday night, or Sat'day mornin', rather, just b'fore daylight."

"Let's see," Asey said, "who owns speed boats like mine around here?"

"That's just it," Lem said. "Only one is Waddy Barr's, though you couldn't rightly say his was anywhere near the boat that yours is. Then," he added as an afterthought, "there's that new one that feller's got. That actor, Morris. He—"

"What?" Asey demanded. "Say that again!"

"Yup, Morris's got one," Lem said. "But it don't seem hardly possible that either him or Waddy Barr'd any call to be streakin' out around the inlet on a night like that, does it, now?"

CHAPTER EIGHTEEN

"Course," Lem continued as he turned back into the barn, "Waddy an' Morris do crazy things, but honest to goodness, Asey, it never entered my head there might be any pleasure boats out in that rain. D'you think it was Waddy, up to some mischief?"

He looked over his shoulder and found that he was talking to empty air. Asey had gone.

Lem grunted, went to the door, and picked up the lights of the Porter roadster as it sped down hill.

"Waddy an' Morris," he muttered as he went back to the mason jars, "ain't the only ones that do crazy things hereabouts! Not by a long shot!"

Asey swung the roadster off on the Pochet road.

"I'm goin' to see that Laurie girl," he said to Hamilton. "You come in with me, an' look menacin'. Keep one hand on your gun—that's always good, an' back me up. This business is b'ginnin' to take on the proportions of a dead whale."

He told Hamilton about the boat that Lem had heard.

"Whyn't we think of boats before, Asey? How'd you think of 'em now?"

"Dunno, 'cept if anyone but Bat had been roamin' around, Lem'd of known it, I think. If they come through the swamp, that is, or cut through Barr's land. So if there was anyone else, it seemed a good chance they might of come by boat. I asked him just to make certain. Didn't expect to get anywhere."

He pushed the car at terrific speed along the back lanes, and Hamilton, after trying his hardest to appear nonchalant, finally gripped the door handle and hung on for dear life. He had ridden with Asey often before, but never expected to get used to it.

"Ham," Asey said in a tone of mild protest, "I drove cars thirty-nine years, an' I ain't never had an ac'dent 'cept when someone bumped into me once. I was parked in a Boston g'rage, an' was pers'nly two miles away at the time. Say, d'you suppose this show'll be over now?"

"Ought to be. After eleven."

The old Nickerson barn which served as a theater was dark as they drove by, but the farmhouse itself was blazing with lights.

Asey walked into the long living room where he and Angelica had interviewed Lee Laurie, and surveyed the crowd that milled around.

"What is art," he murmured under his breath. "What is actin'. Huh. Evenin', Miss Laurie," he added as Lee came over to him. "I see your eyes is better."

"My eyes? What d'you mean?"

"Wa-el," Asey drawled, looking at the glare of lights, "last time I seen you, you was usin' candles for sunburned eyes. I want to see you. First," he took off his yachting cap and strolled to the center of the room, "will you ladies an' gentlemen," he asked in a quiet voice that somehow penetrated the babble of conversation, "be good enough to go elsewhere? The p'lice have need of this room."

The chattering stopped at once. "Just like a radio program snapped off in the middle," Hamilton told Angelica later. "Honest, you could hear the dust move!"

Not everyone in the group knew who Asey was, but even the handful who didn't raised no protest and asked no questions. Hamilton, with his hand on his gun, looking as menacing as he could, added the necessary weight to Asey's request.

"Now," Asey said to the girl when only the three of

them were left, "now, sit down, please. I've some things to settle up."

"I want Blaisdell," Lee said. "I want him! I won't be bullied!"

"No," Asey told her, "you won't. You won't have him around, either."

"I will not say a word or answer a question," Lee said, "unless I have someone here!"

"Very well. Ham, go out an' get that little red-head with the freckles, an' bring her in. Miss Laurie, I'd like that phony birth certificate you showed me."

"I've lost it," Lee said defiantly.

Asey picked out a comfortable chair, sat down and crossed his legs.

"Miss Laurie, I'm tired tonight. I don't feel like makin' the effort of bein' unpleasant. I ain't goin' to bully you. Nor rant or yell or put on a show. But I want to make one thing clear—okay, Ham. Come in an' bring her. They's goin' to be no more ad libbin' on your part, Miss Laurie, nor more gallery playin', nor rehearsin'. The play's on, right now. I'd strongly s'gest," he ignored the almost inaudible chuckle of the good-looking girl Hamilton escorted in, "that you act yourself, for once. I want that birth certificate, an' I want it now."

Lee walked over to his chair and stared at him.

"Never in my life have I—"

"Youngster," Asey said with a smile, "don't try that insolent subway look on me. I once helped with the big cats in a side show when I was a kid, an' I promise you I'll stare you down."

The red-headed girl held her handkerchief to her face. Her shoulders were beginning to shake.

Lee looked at her, looked at Asey's grin of amusement, and at Hamilton, with his hand still on his gun. For a moment she hesitated, and then she proceeded to display the Laurie temper.

The seven-branch candlestick crashed through the closed window. Three books followed it. A bridge lamp landed in the fireplace, where its shade caught and burned merrily.

Asey continued to grin, Hamilton kept on scowling, and the red-headed girl shook with quiet laughter.

Lee tugged at the cover on the long trestle table, and the miscellaneous assortment of objects on it swept off on the floor. Flowers, peanuts, ash trays, magazines, bric-a-brac and a dozen empty highball glasses all mingled together and took on a slimy likeness as the water from the flower bowls trickled along the wide cracks. Two violent pushes, and the table itself banged down on the mess.

Her audience made no comment nor did they change their expressions. Gravely, Hamilton presented the red-headed girl with a clean, dry handkerchief. She smiled her thanks and wiped her cheeks.

Lee stalked around the room, overturning chairs, hurling glasses and china at the hearth, pulling lamps out from their sockets. Finally she lay down on the floor and yelled steadily for five minutes.

"Fine!" Asey said approvingly when she finally ceased. "Great! I don't think I ever seen a more thorough job, 'cept for that little ash tray on the pie-crust table. You forgot that. Want me to bring it to you?"

Lee started to scream again.

"If that's Morris bangin'," Asey made a megaphone of his hands and called to Hamilton, "just tell him to go 'way, will you? An' bolt the door."

Lee got up from the floor. She was more bewildered now than angry. It was long past the time when people gave in and gave her her own way. It was the time when people usually brought her smelling salts and an ice bag and led her away to bed. These three not only didn't seem to care a rap, but they were ignoring her, talking to themselves in low tones.

"Bristow, is it?" Asey said. "Well, Miss Bristow, I agree with you. She's got all the makin's of a mighty fine shrew. Miss Laurie, I shan't rest happy till I see you in that shrew thing. An' say, won't you smash that ash tray? It's disturbin' me. Don't seem right, somehow, for that to be settin' there d'mure like an' whole. Look, gimme that birth certificate, will you?"

To her complete amazement, Lee found herself picking her pocketbook up from the mess on the floor. She extracted the photostat and presented it to Asey.

"Thanks." He walked over to a wall bracket and held it to the light. "I see. You got a photostat of the original, an' fiddled with it, an' had this took from that. Now, why did you change your—"

"I shan't need her." Lee pointed to the red-headed girl. "She can go."

"But she's enjoyin' this!" Asey protested. "She says she loves to see you in action. She an' I agree you got Attila sewed in a sack. No grass grows where you land, either. Oh, well, I guess you'll have to run along, Miss Bristow. Sorry."

"So'm I," the girl said. "Lee darling, since last autumn I've hoped that someone like Asey would let you ride it out, and that I'd be on hand to see it. I won't tell, my sweet, but God, it's been grand! 'Bye."

"You would pick her, wouldn't you?" Lee asked. "The—"

"She appealed to me when I come in," Asey returned, "an' she still does. Am I to understand you're ready an' willin' to talk? That's nice. Why'd you fake this thing?"

"That name!"

"Oh, come now," Asey said. "Why?"

"The name, and my age. It's always good to be as young as you can decently appear."

"They told me first," Asey said, "you was under twenty. You tried to make me think you was twenty-three an' now it seems you're twenty-seven. Much more, an' you'll be Fanny Ward or Edna Wallace Hopper. Nope, it ain't good enough. Aimin' to travel?"

Lee sat down on the arm of the chair which the Bristow girl had vacated. "No, why?"

"Offhand, I can't think of no one cartin' around birth certificates 'less they're after passports. Why'd you?"

Lee sighed. Under the harsh light of the wall bracket she looked almost double her age.

"Maybe for p'rtection," Asey suggested. "Got your fingerprints listed in the files, too? Whose idea was the certificate, an' why's it faked?"

The girl looked so miserable that Hamilton began to feel sorry for her.

"Rosalie thought of it," Lee said at last. "She—say, you trooper there. Does he always go at people like this?"

Hamilton said that Asey usually found out what the circumstances required him to find out.

"Well, it's nice to know someone else has felt the way I do. Like something wriggling on a pin under a microscope. Rosalie thought of it, Asey. She was my mother."

"I know. An' Elida Bolton met her—let's have your side of it." Asey rejoiced inwardly that he hadn't been forced to bluff the story out of the girl. Theatrical details weren't things you could conjure up on the spur of the moment, at least with any degree of accuracy.

"Mother, I mean Elida Laurie, ran away with a road show and Rosalie was in it. After a while they yanked mother back home. She—"

"Meanin' Mrs. Laurie when you say mother?"

Lee nodded. "I'd like to have seen Rosalie erupt," she said bitterly, "if I ever called her that! Anyway, they yanked her home and she married dad, and they had a daughter in due time. The child was sickly, and when it was only a few weeks old, they took it to New York to some specialist or other. They did all they could, but the child died. Then one of those crazy things happened. As they left the hospital they met Rosalie leaving with her baby. Me. My father, La Roc, had died six months before, and Rosalie was broke, and didn't want me much, I guess. To sum it up, mother and dad and Rosalie got together, and mother and dad took me home, and Rosalie went off with a fistful of money. No one in Shrewsfield ever knew. The Lauries had gone away with a sick baby and they came home with a healthy one, and after all, all babies look alike."

"Did you know?" Asey asked.

"Not till I inherited this money a couple of years ago. I think mother and dad felt that the less I knew about Rosalie, the better. I had some of Rosalie's characteristics, and they didn't want them accented. But dad left a note with this money. I was mad at first, and then I was thrilled. I'd always been crazy about acting and the stage, and Rosalie Ray, too."

"Did she know that you knew?"

Lee nodded. "I wrote her. Our meeting in the train wasn't any accident. She arranged it."

"Did you—seems odd to ask, but did you get along?"

Lee lighted a cigarette and blew a cloud of smoke at the wall light.

"Like a shot, at first. After a while, she became jealous of me. You couldn't blame her. I got along so easily, and her start had been so rocky."

"Huh. Does Tom know about you an' her?"

"Not a thing. He and Rosalie hated each other. He'd known her a long time, and he laughed at her, which was simply fatal. Rosalie nearly ruined my apartment when she discovered I was engaged to him. Last winter he found out somehow, probably from Steve, that she had a daughter, and started prying. That set Rosalie off like a rocket."

"Why didn't she want you known as her daughter, anyway?" Asey asked. "You was a success. You—"

Lee looked at him and smiled. "There were times, Asey, when she looked younger than I do. An adult daughter would have killed too many illusions. That's why that birth certificate. So that if anyone guessed, I was all set. It was her idea about changing the name and the age."

"What about Tom, now?" Asey asked.

"I loved him," Lee said honestly. "I adored him. Before I left Shrewsfield he seemed the most wonderful thing! He just knew everyone you read about, and—"

"An' how!" Asey murmured.

"And he'd been everywhere, and he was so nice looking, and his clothes were so good. Then after I got to New York and began to get places myself, I began to realize he was a liability. I'd have thrown him over then, if Rosalie hadn't wanted me to. I kept on with him just to annoy her. He served a purpose, too. But when you get so far in this business, you begin to think of people in terms of assets."

"An' I take it that Morris is the asset now?"

"More than Tom, certainly. Oh, Tom's a good egg, but we were on the point of breaking everything off before I came down here. I promised to tell him one way or the other on Friday. Actually, Asey, I don't think he ever cared much for me."

"You don't, huh? Now I think dif'rent."

"Oh, he protested breaking our engagement, but that was a matter of form, that's all. He never really loved me. I think he intended to come home and marry me when he got tired of playing around. His family were great friends of the Lauries', and my guardian. I think they hoped I'd make him settle down, and after I went on the stage, they boosted the engagement, hoping he'd make me come home and settle down."

"You're sure he didn't know about Rosalie?"

"I don't see how he could."

"Okay. Now I got a couple more things to clear up. What was you doin', runnin' around the inlet in Morris's speed boat on Friday?"

He asked the question more or less as a matter of course, expecting instant denial. But Lee laughed merrily.

"How'd you find out about that silly trip?"

"Silly!" Hamilton appealed to Asey. "She thinks it's silly!"

"It was," Lee said. "I wanted to cool off. I'd been scrambling eggs for hours, and I was dead! The kitchen was purple with smoke, and hot! So we went all the way up the inlet and back, in all the rain. It was glorious. Don't you simply adore rain, Asey? When I was little I used to think the sound of rain on a tin roof was the most glorious thing in all the world."

"Rain has its points," Asey admitted. "What time was this jaunt of yours? Would you know?"

"Of course not. Oh, yes. Yes, I do. We got back around half-past five. I asked Morrie and he looked at his watch. We were gone over an hour."

Asey put his cap on the back of his head and surveyed the girl.

Her temperament act had been entirely convincing, but he honestly thought she had been telling him the truth afterwards. It occurred to him that he had been pretty foolish. If she could turn on an energetic, passionate mad like that, she was pliable enough to switch to another rôle without literally stopping for breath. Her frankness had disarmed him, as she had probably intended it should.

"I s'pose," Asey said thoughtfully, "it's hard to let a cue go by if actin's your business. Honest, though, even a duffer like me gets an occasional whiff of common sense. Ever been inside the Damons' house?"

"My dear man, I don't even know them."

"Does Morris know about Rosalie?"

"He does, but I told him only after we heard of the murder. He thought I ought to tell the papers right away, because it would be such marvelous publicity, and then I thought I'd better wait until the worst had blown over. We decided to wait until we put on 'Rehearsal.' That was my play I starred in last winter, you know. You see," Lee lighted a cigarette and let it dangle from her lower lip as she talked, "we knew that would be a hit, and if we told about Rosalie then, we'd probably have to shoehorn the crowd in for the rest of the summer."

Asey wondered how he ever thought he needed proof of her relationship with Rosalie.

"Active anger, d'mure honesty an' cold-blooded business inside of half an hour. That's—what say? Oh, I said you was as hard b—I mean, as businesslike as your mother, ain't you?"

"Oh, I'm better than she ever was," Lee told him casually. "She always let her feelings ball her up."

"I know, an' you just use yours to ball others. My, yes. Yes, indeed. Ham, bring Morris in, will you?"

Morris didn't seem at all disturbed by the débris in the room. Probably, Asey thought, the man was used to that sort of scene.

"I've told him everything, Morrie," Lee said. "Now what d'you think, can we put 'Rehearsal' on next week? If you think we can, then we'll get the full force of everything. Asey, and Rosalie and the works. Asey, you'll simply have to come to the opening. Just as you are now. It's a pity you don't wear a beard."

"We could fix that up," Morris said, looking critically at Asey. "We'll put him in the box. Oilskins, I think, too. At least an oilskin cap—what d'you call 'em. South-westers or north-easters or something. That cap won't do. And—"

"An' a bucket of quohaugs in one hand," Asey said with withering sarcasm, "an' a baybr'y candle in the other. Maybe I'd better dance a hornpipe an' sing a chanty or two! Are you two people crazy?"

"It'll be just simply wonderful for you," Lee told him firmly. "Probably get you jobs and things, and you'll meet everyone. You know, Morrie, I've felt all along that we needed more Cape atmosphere, if you know what I mean. Asey'll be too, too marvelous! Not—"

"Not," Asey said, "to bust this idea of yours or drop bombs into your little dream world, let's get back to business."

But Lee and Morris were too busy with their plans to pay any attention to him.

"We shouldn't have waited," Morris said. "I told you so. There's going to be trouble, even if Rosalie made that will. She—"

"What will?" Asey inquired.

Hamilton noticed the purr in Asey's voice, and began to feel sorry for the couple. He had learned long ago that people who were the target of that purr required sympathy.

"Rosalie's," Lee told him matter-of-factly. "Of course I couldn't say how much it should amount to. She spent a lot, but she simply coined money on the radio. And she'd been nowhere near as extravagant as she used to be. She simply used to hurl money around for her jewels. But she stopped that."

"Prob'ly," Asey said, thinking of the jewel case he had seen, "she just run out of 'em to buy. So you knew you was goin' to have them an' her money, did you? An' you was out in the inlet Friday at five-thirty in the mornin', or so, was you? An' she was jealous of you, an' you most likely treated her with this beautiful an' kindly consideration of yours. Well, well, Hilda Grove'll thank you. What a *lot* of publicity you're goin' to get, sister!"

"Of course," Lee said smugly. "Why not? It's all good."

"That's what you think. But it won't squeeze no cash out of your public, on 'count of what your public will be limited an' unfeelin'."

"What's the man mean?" Lee asked Morris, who shrugged helplessly.

"Local involution plus local dialect," he said. "The same thing that happens to Mrs. Nickerson when she gets so unintelligible over her Benny B. The—"

"Make him say it!" Lee interrupted excitedly. "He probably does it beautifully, that thing about clams not being quohaugs, or something. Say it, Asey! Your dialect's really quite good when you drawl."

"Thanks," Asey said. "I shall treasure that compl'ment. What I mean, Miss Laurie, is that you won't play to no capacity houses, b'cause you're goin' to be languishin' away in jail for killin' Rosalie. Is that dialect plain enough to you?"

"It's the most absurd thing I ever heard!" Lee said

coldly. "Morrie, I tell him we went up the inlet and back, and he accuses me of being a murderer!"

"What time," Asey asked Morris, "did you get back from this boatin' epic?"

"Four-thirty," Morris said promptly.

"She told me five-thirty."

"She's wrong," Morris said. "I looked at my watch. I know. Anyone can prove it. Ask Bab Bristow."

The red-headed girl was brought back by Hamilton.

"Yes, they came back into the kitchen around four-thirty," she said. "They got an awful beating for going."

"Then why this seemin' dif'rence b'tween your idea of time," Asey asked Lee, "an' Morris's? You said he told you it was five-thirty."

"Oh, I did tell her that," Morris said impatiently, "but it was four-thirty, don't you see? It was standard time. So it was an hour wrong."

"Will you," Asey asked Bab Bristow, "explain in words of one syl'ble, please?"

"Morrie," she told him with a chuckle, "hasn't a mathematical mind. He also has to travel around a lot, usually by train. This time business got him down. He kept going for trains and either found them gone an hour before, or not due for an hour. He gave in entirely. He keeps his watch on standard time. If he said it was four-thirty, in other words, it was—"

"Five-thirty." Asey finished for her. "I see, I get it. It percolates. Hamilton, let us arise an' go—"

"You can't go!" Lee told him. "We've got next week to plan about, and about the reporters and all. Wait till we get this settled. First we'll have to work out a statement, and then you can—"

Asey shook the red-headed girl by the hand.

"I don't like to d'scourage you," he remarked, "but you won't never be a success in this line of business."

"Why not? I'm supposed to be pretty good."

"Maybe, but you're laborin' under two awful handicaps. One's a normal, lucid sort of mind, an' the other's a sense of humor. Let's go, Hamilton!"

But before they reached the roadster, Asey turned back to the house. In the living room he walked over to the pie-crust table, picked up the unbroken ash tray and hurled it with devastating results at the hearth bricks.

"Not temp'rament," he explained pleasantly. "It just kept preyin' on my mind. 'Night."

Hamilton sighed as they sped away.

"That was going pretty good there for a time, wasn't it? I guess they're out of it, but she's kind of put Tom in a spot, hasn't she? Going home to see him?"

"I don't think Tom's in any more or less of a spot than he was b'fore," Asey said, "nor any of the others either. No, I ain't goin' home yet a while. But I'm goin' to stop toyin' with shoe strings an' tree barkin'." He punched at the roadster's fancy horn buttons as he slowed up before crossing the main road. "I'm goin' back to facts, Ham. I'm goin' back to see Lem."

CHAPTER NINETEEN

IN THE study at the old Cole place, Angelica bit the end of Steve's battered pen, made a wry face at the taste, and bent again over the papers on the desk in front of her.

"Myles," she said after several moments spent in contemplating the pages, "it's absolutely no use at all. This mess might be the diagram of a forward pass, or Chinese, or a letter from my nephew Timmy."

"You mean," Myles asked, "you can't read the writing?"

"Of course not! I can read it beautifully, but it doesn't make any sense. How'd you get along?"

Myles picked up a single sheet of note paper.

"Mine's rather monosyllabic," he said apologetically. "It just says, 'Rosalie killed. No prints. Waddy's lighter there. Key in Hilda's bureau. Bat did it.' "

Angelica moved her chair to see him better.

"Two hours, and that's all you managed? Myles, why on earth d'you harp back to Bat?"

Myles started to remind her that Bat had happened only that afternoon, but forbore. It did rather seem a long time ago.

"Why not Bat?"

"Myles, he'd never been inside the house, didn't know about the lance, or that Rosalie was even here! Why should he suddenly decide to kill her after all these years? Besides, he didn't kill Waddy."

"I don't see why he couldn't kill her after all these years as well as during them," Myles said. "Those whale lances are the first things anyone would notice on

221

entering or even peeking into the window of the living room. And," he was a little defiant about it, "anyone could have killed Waddy. Everyone in the woods had an equal chance of finding and using that forty-four of mine. I could have found it myself."

"Well, did you? Did you kill them both, Rosalie and Waddy Barr?"

"Of course I didn't!" Myles bristled with indignation. "Bat—"

"Look," Angelica said, "Bat couldn't have killed Waddy. He didn't like to shoot. Remember? Well, don't let's go into it. He didn't kill Rosalie, and he didn't kill Waddy. Is that absolutely all you thought out? Is that all you've written down?"

"Every bit. The more I thought, the less I could write. What do you have?"

Angelica shuffled through her pages of manila paper.

"Only about one-third of this is pondering," she confessed. "I found myself playing tit-tat-toe. Whenever I'm faced with lots of clean paper, I always play tit-tat-toe on it. And I draw pigs. It's probably Freudian. Well, anyway, I find I've got excellent motives for Steve and Betsey and you and Hilda and Tom—Tom only if Asey's ideas about the Laurie girl pan out. Myles, did Steve and Bets know he was engaged to her?"

Myles nodded. "Yes, but they never took it very seriously. He always referred to her as 'My affianced bride,' and they thought he was fooling. Anyway, Angelica, I've decided on Bat, in spite of all the motives. It's *got* to be Bat, don't you see? The rest of us are nice people. Nice people don't rush around stabbing and bashing and—"

"Some nice people," Angelica interrupted, "seem to rush around shooting!"

"Oh, go on with your guesses," Myles said. "It's not as though I hadn't kept telling you and telling you all that I could shoot!"

"Hm. Well, all of you have motives. Hilda's out because Asey says so, and because she had no chance to get Waddy's lighter anyway. Bat's out. Tom's out. He didn't know Waddy and couldn't have found the lighter. You—well, personally I count you out—"

"Thank you!"

"But in the unpleasant light of reason, you're capable of anything. After the way you carried on today. Now it certainly can't be Steve," she nodded in the direction of the living room, where Steve and Tom were still playing cards, "nor Betsey. None of 'em ever saw Waddy till Asey dragged him here. It doesn't make sense!"

"Betsey did," Myles said, and then wished he could take the words back. "Oh, I promised her I wouldn't tell! She told me only after Asey talked with Waddy. She went to boarding school in Ohio one year, and Waddy was at a boys' school in the same town. They went to dances together."

"And you say—Myles, didn't she recognize the name when she came here? Didn't she know?"

Myles shook his head. "Betsey's met a lot of people since she was fourteen. Think of her jobs, alone! She didn't recognize the name, or him, until the other afternoon when he was here. She wanted to tell Asey, but I begged her not to. A boy and girl episode sounds so— well, under the circumstances I thought it wiser to keep the story out of print. She wondered if his note to Tom wasn't a sort of reassurance to her that he had nothing to do with Rosalie's death, and all."

"You mean, he'd been annoying the Stephen Damons without knowing Mrs. Damon was a childhood girl? But those tobacco pictures! He should have known, Myles!"

"Betsey," Myles observed, "was rather a thin scraggly girl with freckles at that age. Much as I love her, I'll have to admit she wore bands on her teeth. No, she thinks he didn't recognize her any more than she recognized him, until the other afternoon. Besides, she says he was John Barr, then. Apparently the Wadsworth part came later. D'you think we should tell Asey?"

"I have a feeling," Angelica said, "that there's no sense in bringing up any more complications. And I also feel that if it's a part of Asey's plans to ferret it out, he will whether we tell him or not. He——"

"Aw, no," Asey said, opening the door. "That ain't like you, Miss Sage. Tell Asey all."

With obvious reluctance, Myles told. He couldn't make out from Asey's expression if the story impressed him or not.

"Huh," Asey said. "Where's Betsey, in bed?"

Myles and Angelica said she was, but Steve and Tom, coming in to the study, said she was in the kitchen, making coffee.

"Couldn't sleep," Steve explained, "so she's making herself some, and I shouldn't wonder if she wouldn't make us some too, if we asked nicely."

"Double order," Asey said. "While it's brewin', I'm goin' to do some rec'noiterin' upstairs. An' you needn't," he added parenthetically as he paused on the threshold, "come up to help, any of you. I might go so far's to say I'll chase you down if you try."

Steve commented on his cat-like tread as he left.

"Uncanny. Listen—he's reached the landing, and you'd never know except for that flapping floor board. Hamilton, what's he up to? What's he been doing?"

"He went to see Lem," Hamilton said, "and Lee Laurie, and then back to Lem again. He helped Lem catch a rat in the hen house. He waked up the hens and the roosters and all the livestock. We had a pretty noisy time."

"That's a good functional description," Steve said, "but you'd never make any money in the writing business. Let's go at it step by step."

They pumped Hamilton at length. He answered their questions cheerfully enough, but little information was forthcoming.

"Is it true," Myles finally asked, "that a part of your training consists of court procedure? I mean, are you taught—"

"Of course he is!" Steve said. "Dope that I am not to

get it! Ham, you're a skunk. Playing expert witness with us, huh? Come on, didn't he get anywhere?"

Hamilton smiled and relented some. "After we left Lem's the second time," he said, "he thought he had it. I thought so too. But we went to call on the brakeman of Friday's freight, and it didn't work. Then—"

"Brakeman of Friday's freight?" Tom asked. "That sounds uncommonly as though Asey was after me. Well, I hope you found out that the brakeman is a potential murderer, did you?"

"We were after you, not the brakeman," Hamilton said with a grin.

"I know and that's what I mean. That fellow nearly blotted me out of existence with a hunk of coal. Whizzed by my ear. He wasn't the most amiable brakeman I ever set eye on. No gentleman, either. No sporting instincts."

"You ought to be glad he wasn't," Hamilton said. "It's lucky for you he remembered kicking you off the freight at the Skaket station. He—"

Betsey came in with a pot of coffee.

"Someone get cups, please. What's Asey doing? He's marched around from room to room as though he was playing musical chairs or Going to Jerusalem or something."

"Making pie beds for us," Tom told her. "Old Cape Cod custom. How'd you hear him, Bets?"

"By the floor boards." Betsey sat down and pulled her dressing-gown up around her throat. "I always put on Steve's breakfast egg when ours squeak in the morning. Means he's in front of the mirror brushing his hair and staring fascinatedly at himself. Myles is harder. Some days he does his daily dozen and sometimes he cheats. Anyway, Asey's been in our room for hours, though I doubt if he's admiring his rugged profile."

Angelica and Myles exchanged glances.

Directly overhead a floor board cracked, and then cracked a second time. There was something slightly ominous in the sound. Everyone in the study felt it.

Betsey shivered and pulled her robe closer.

"Cold," she said briefly. "Is it raining some more?"

It was a safe topic, but even Angelica didn't feel able to summon up any adequate reply. The uncomfortable silence grew to such proportions that succeeding noises from the floor boards above were almost deafening.

Suddenly Tom began to sing. He was half way through the "Drunkard's Song" before Steve forcibly silenced him.

"I can't help it," Tom said. "When I get to a point where I can hear watches ticking, I have to take steps. Help me out, Stevie, with your little tenor. We might just as well sing as to sit and cringe."

In Myles's room Asey sat on the spool bed and listened to the jaunty chorus filter up. On the floor in front of him were six lamps. He stared at them for several minutes before going to the head of the stairs and calling Betsey.

"C'mere a sec. See these—"

"What on earth," Betsey said, "have you—"

Asey put a finger to his lips. "Quiet like. Tell me which goes where."

Bewildered, Betsey indicated the lamps belonging to the various rooms.

"And that's Rosalie's, and that's ours. Why?"

"Sure?"

"Didn't I pick 'em out? Don't you suppose I know the lamps in my own house? What in the world has seized you, Asey? Why are you tiptoeing around like—like," Betsey searched for a simile and ended up feebly, "like a hen with her head cut off."

"Wrong gender," Asey said. "My, my, how livestock does crop up! Put the lamps back, will you? An' go to bed. 'Night."

He ran lightly downstairs and called Hamilton.

"What are you—" Steve began.

"What have you—" Angelica said at the same time.

"I ain't," Asey told them, "an' I haven't. Come 'long, Hamilton."

Hamilton picked up his cap and obediently followed.

"An' for goodness sakes," Asey said, "don't ask me why or what or anythin' else. How many men you got here?"

"Three, and they're dead on their feet. D'you want 'em to—"

"I want 'em around the house. Call 'em, an' I'll talk to 'em myself."

A few crisp words on the importance of keeping those in the house there, and others elsewhere, and Asey made for his car.

It was beginning to rain, but Hamilton didn't dare offer any suggestions about putting the top up. When Asey's jaw set like a steel trap, it was no time to quibble about rain drops. Hamilton didn't even murmur when his visored cap flew off into the blackness. At that speed, there was no use.

Asey chuckled suddenly and passed over his yachting cap.

"Take this, Ham, an' fish around in the compartment back of you for my Stetson, will you? Couple trench coats there too, that you might haul out."

Hamilton wriggled into one coat and draped the other around Asey's shoulders.

"This the golf club road, Asey?"

"Yup, I want the pro. Oh, don't worry, Ham, I don't want a lesson. I want him."

McNabb, once awakened, pointed a finger at Asey and prodded him.

"Man, it's second sight. I was coming for you first thing in the morning!"

"Got some dope on that lighter?"

"I have. Just after I got into bed, a lad from Orleans telephoned me. He's been away and just got back, and heard from his brother I was asking around about it. He says he found the lighter last week before he left. I tried to get you by phone, but they said—"

"An' he give the lighter to Waddy?"

"He did. Mr. Barr promised him a dollar, and forgot

to give it to him before he left. That's why he didn't tell the others, because he thought they'd laugh at him."

Asey's grin broadened into a beaming smile.

"Mack, can we borrow your car? Good. Ham, take it, an' go back to Damons'. I'll be there soon's I can."

He raced out of the club's rear entrance, jumped into the roadster and sped away.

"I don't think he's crazy," Hamilton said. "It's just that he tries to keep up with the way he thinks. I don't know what he's after, but—"

"But he's got it," McNabb said, watching the roadster's lights tear along the road. "Man, he's got it!"

Asey drove to the Barrs' house, swung along the drive to the garage. There was a light in the house, but he wasn't going to waste time with the servants. What he wanted to see could be seen without—he stumbled over a figure and nearly fell.

"Who—Barradio? What're you lyin' out here for? My God A'mighty, don't you kids know enough to go home when it rains? What're you doin'?"

"Tony won't let us come home," Ramon explained. "He said you told us to stay here, an' we had to. Asey, we can't find a thing. Not a thing. Waddy come home Friday an' went to bed, like he told you an' everyone else. Honest, we can't find out anythin'—what're you goin' to do? Hey, don't bother jimmyin' that window. We already done it."

He lifted up the rear garage window easily, and Asey threw one leg over the sill and went inside.

The beam of his flashlight disclosed five cars. Two of them, large imposing black sedans that might have belonged to an undertaker, obviously belonged to Mrs. Barr, and Asey ignored them. He passed over the station-wagon and focused his attention on a rakish roadster without a top, and a powerful two passenger all-weather coupé.

"Which did Waddy drive most, the roadster?" Asey flashed his light around the dash and floor boards, and then slid underneath the car and waved his light around some more.

"Usually. What—"

"But probably the coupé Friday, considerin' the rain." Aséy stood up. "We'll see—"

"You're wrong, Asey," Ramon said. "Waddy used the roadster to go to the show an' Hyannis with. That's one thing we know."

But Asey continued his examination of the coupé.

"Okay," he said as he rolled out from under and got to his feet. "You guys told me once, now I come to think of it, only I wasn't in a catchin' on mood. I want you all to stay here an' forc'bly r'sist any efforts to dislodge you. Understand? Stay here till some cops come, an' say I said so. 'Bye."

He slid in behind the wheel of his own car again, just about the time that McNabb and Hamilton managed to get Mack's old sedan going.

"One more stop," Asey said to himself, "an'—nope, I don't even need to make it. Angelica settled that. I guess—yessireebob, I guess this settles it!"

A sand train was rumbling by the Skaket crossing, and he had to jam on his brakes and wait for it to get by. He smiled to himself. The delay would have irritated him earlier, but he didn't care what held him up now. It was all cut and dried and settled.

Leaning forward on the wheel, he watched the cars bump by, and lifted a hand to tilt his hat brim and let the rain drip away from his face. The hat rather surprised him. He had almost forgotten giving his yachting cap to Hamilton. It had fitted him well, surprisingly enough, and so had the coat. Hamilton was taller than he thought.

The rain beat down harder, and Asey reached into the compartment behind the seat for an old slicker to cover the seat beside him. As he pulled it out, something fell. He took his flashlight and turned around and peered in.

Then he slammed down the lid of the hatch and snapped the lock.

It was crazy. It was impossible.

"But I'd do it myself," Asey thought. "I'd do it myself. An' Hamilton's just about gettin' there, an'—"

The roadster's engine raced as he bore his foot down on the accelerator, watching all the while the swaying lights of the sand train's caboose. A few minutes before it seemed to be going at a reasonable speed, and now the confounded thing covered an inch an hour. Time! He kidded himself he had time! Unless he'd made a grave error in judgment, there was going to be another murder at the Cole place if time didn't stand still and wait for him!

He shot the roadster over the tracks finally, so close to the caboose grating that a man inside screamed and reached for the emergency cord.

The boat, Asey decided in a flash, was quicker and safer. Thank the Lord it was still at Henderson's!

Remembering a short cut, he swerved off through a lane, pushed the car straight through Henderson's strawberry patch down to the wharf. The mahogany finish of the speed boat took a beating as he sliced the moorings with his jack knife and slashed at the canvas cockpit-cover that Joe Henderson had spent half an hour putting on.

The starter groaned, and then the engine purred. Asey offered hasty thanks to heaven and set out across the inlet. Coasting in to the Damons' landing, he jumped ashore and left the boat drifting. Providence, he thought as he raced up the path, had been kind so far. She'd probably see to the boat.

At first he thought there were no lights at all in the house—perhaps he was ahead of Hamilton after all. Then the hall light flashed on, and the study light.

Asey reached the front door, tried it quietly, and gritted his teeth. Locked, of course, as the back one would be. He edged around to the study window and looked in.

Hamilton, still wearing Asey's cap and trench coat, shut the study door behind him and walked over to the leather chair. He sat down, tilted the cap to the back of his head, and yawned.

Reaching into the pocket of his own coat, Asey pulled out the old Colt forty-five. He would have given all his shirts to get inside, indoors. But he couldn't without making a lot of noise.

Footsteps sounded near him, and a sleepy trooper hove in sight. Asey clamped a hand on his mouth, shook his head and pointed to the window.

The trooper nodded and yawned, without bothering to look inside. After the three days he had just spent, nothing surprised him. Nothing mattered.

"Back door locked?" Asey formed the words with his lips.

"Uh-huh."

"Stay here. Keep still!"

He looked into the study again. Hamilton was already sound asleep, his cap tilted over one eye.

Slowly, very slowly, the door behind him began to open. Asey nodded to himself. He was right.

"Hey—look—"

Without turning his head, Asey put his left hand over the trooper's mouth and let it stay there for a second.

The crack in the doorway widened. Asey moved out of the light and gripped his gun.

He waited until the crack disclosed a man, waited until the man closed the door behind him.

"What he's *got!*" The trooper's agonized whisper showed that he had waked up.

Asey nodded.

He waited until the whale lance, the twin of the one that had killed Rosalie, was poised over Hamilton, and then Asey raised the Colt and fired.

CHAPTER TWENTY

BY THE time Asey and the trooper smashed their way in through the back door, the whole household was milling excitedly around the hall in front of the study.

Asey pushed through them to where Hamilton stood, gaping foolishly from Tom Fowler, who lay on the floor, to the ugly whale lance beside him.

"Is he dead?" Steve demanded. "Who shot him? Who fired that shot?"

"Handcuffs, Ham," Asey said. "Got any bracelets? Well, come to, man, an' put 'em on him. I shot him, Steve. He ain't hurt. Only his shoulder. He's faking."

"He came for me," Hamilton snapped on the handcuffs as though he weren't quite sure what he was doing. "He kept coming after you shot, Asey. I knocked him out. Asey, how'd you—did you know he—I mean, what—"

"It may charm all of you to know," Asey said, "that he planted Bat's package of loot in the hatch of my car. Don't ask me how he done it. Must of snatched it an' stuck it there somehow this afternoon. I just found it, an' b'lieve me, I ain't got my breath yet!"

Angelica found her voice. "But he tried to—you mean, he was going to kill Hamilton with that—that thing, there? Why did he want to kill Hamilton?"

Asey pointed to the yachting cap still drunkenly perched on Ham's head, and the trench coat.

"Thought he was me. Looked it, from b'hind, an' he had on my things. When I found that package in the car, I knew he put it there so's he could beat it when he got the chance, an' have the stuff with him. N'en I r'membered Ham had on my things. 'F I'd been Tom, right now was the time to scram elsewhere, when everyone was dead beat, an' he was apparently okay. I kind of figgered he'd like a lick at me, too. Put him on the couch, Ham. Help him, Steve. He's bleedin' some. That's the heck of this sort of thing. Plug a man an' then have to patch him up."

"I—" Betsey bit her lip. "Shall I get bandages and things?"

"Yup. We'll take him on to the doc's in a few minutes. Way I feel about that guy," Asey looked down at the lance, "I guess he can wait a bit. Hey, Ham! Watch it!"

He grabbed at Tom's left wrist and removed Hamilton's gun from its holster.

"What—"

"Just," Asey told Angelica, "I'm weary of shootin', an' Tom was inchin' for Ham's gun. Tom, snap out of it, will you? Very well, don't. But you ain't got half the chance Bat had while Myles was pottin' at him. Just brood on that. I guess, Ham, if he's goin' to play games, we'll get the doc over here. Have someone fetch him, will you?"

Deftly Asey set to work with the cotton and bandages.

"Rough job, but it'll keep your suit nice an' clean. Now I think—"

"Asey," Myles put on his pince nez, "won't you just clear this matter up for us? We can't talk!"

"I'll tell you," Asey said, "an' Tom can help, only they really ain't much for him to help with. It's all cut an' dried. Tom come Friday, only not on the train, see?"

"Hamilton distinctly said that a brakeman or someone said he did," Angelica told him. "A lot of to-do about flinging him off the freight."

"He flung someone, but not Tom. Tom just colored his chance a little. Local color'll make any lie seem truthful. I don't know just how he come, but it don't matter if it was by ridin' rails or hitch hikin'. Point is, somewhere on his way to see Lee, he met up with Waddy."

"Asey," Steve said, "you're cracked! This isn't true!"

"Sorry. Anyway, Tom was c'mbinin' you an' Lee, an' on his way to her, he met Waddy—"

"But that won't work out about the lighter!" Angelica interrupted triumphantly. "Waddy didn't have it!"

"Waddy did. I found that out just now. An' Tom borrowed it. That ain't hard to b'lieve. He's borrowed cigars an' cig'rettes an' pipe tobacco an' matches ever since I set eyes on him. Once you get Waddy's lighter back to Waddy, connectin' it with Tom don't r'quire no master mind. Well, he told Waddy he was comin' here, an' Waddy says, my, my, do a job on them Damons for me, an' get 'em out of the place an' I'll help feather your nest, I will."

"You don't mean," Betsey said flatly, "any such thing. Tom wouldn't do a thing like that."

"Tom," Asey said, "loves money. An' up in your room b'hind the mirror was a roll of ten hundred-dollar bills, like the one on the note Ham was s'posed to give Tom from Waddy. I took 'em, an' that was a mistake I realized after I found that package. Tom—didn't he come to your room t'night, Steve?"

Steve drew a long breath. "He came to get a cigarette, and he straightened out the mirror. But—but if it's so, couldn't he just naturally have had the money?"

"Would he of bummed his way here if he had? Would he be like to keep his change b'hind your mirror? Would he of had bills with the same serial number as the one Ham had on that letter?"

"Now see here," Angelica said, "Rufe Gould told us—why, he proved that Tom came on that freight! He heard the train, and his rooster crowed, and all. He definitely proved it was train time, three-fifteen or so!"

"An' it was most likely six or eight minutes to four. That so, Tom? Golly, I wish you'd enter into the spirit of this thing more! Tom went to Gould's, all right, an' got a map an' d'rections. In leavin', the beam of light from his flash hit the hen house, an' the rooster crowed. Just like Lem's did for me t'night. Some livestock we got around here, I tell you! Y'see, after Waddy an' Tom fixed up whatever their plans was, they realized he couldn't stay at Barr's or be seen with Waddy. They faked the freight idea. The rooster was a stroke of luck for Tom. They did it then so's Tom could pretend arrivin' on the freight, an' to all outsiders, they'd be total strangers. It worked real nice for Tom later."

"Fiddlesticks!" Angelica refused to be convinced. "What about the train tooting? And how could Waddy get Tom here in such a short time? Tom came at four."

Asey grinned. "Waddy used his open roadster when he set out that night. It rained. He parked Tom somewheres, went home, dallied around an' pretended to go to bed. N'en he got up an' took his coupé, an' they come up to Gould's an' put on their act. The real reason for all of Waddy's alibis was to cut out his bein' hitched up with Tom, see? Well, anyway, that coupé's got a locomotive whistle on the exhaust. That's the train Gould heard."

"What?"

"Yup. Then Waddy took Tom to the inlet, ferried him over here in his speed boat. Lem heard it. Sure, I know what you're goin' to say, Betsey. Tom was wet an' muddy. Wasn't hard to get that way that night, was it? I'd ought to of known about the exhaust whistle. Them kids said somethin' about his trick horn. An' that light Gould give him would never of lasted. He said himself it was awful weak. No one outside of a native with a lantern could of got here from town Friday night with that rain. Couldn't of been done with that dinky flash, an' a drawin'."

Myles wanted to know if Tom had known that Rosalie was going to be there.

"Nope, but she was here. Didn't he ask why?"

Betsey admitted it. "I said, or maybe it was Hilda

who told him Rosalie just came about the script—wait. Rosalie said she had an errand. We told him that."

"An' he thought the errand was seein' Lee about him."

"You know," Myles said, "I've just remembered. About the first thing he asked was if there'd been any message for him. I—"

"Sure. Lee was supposed to settle this engagement of theirs. She promised to settle it Friday."

Tom chuckled, and the others stared at him. A faint smile played around his lips, but he didn't open his eyes.

"An' Lee hadn't," Asey went on. "Least, she come here to bust it off with him, but you folks didn't know. So Tom figgered Rosalie'd won her fight to cut him out. Cause an' effect. No Lee, no message of any kind, an' Rosalie here on an errand. If Lee wasn't through with him, she would be, 'cause Rosalie'd make her. Nice time to do away with Rosalie for good, with all that was goin' on that night, an' all you folks in a dither. Do away with Rosalie, an' he'd a chance, he thought, of gettin' Lee back. An'—he knew Lee'd get her mother's money. Rosalie was her mother. Knew that too, didn't you, Tom?"

Tom was laughing softly. He didn't deny Asey's story. Angelica turned her head from the couch. There was something horrible in that soft laughter.

"Tom," Asey quoted, "knows everyone an' everythin'. Feller, you talked too much about money. Well, so much for that part. This aft'noon, it was him that picked up Myles's gun, an' got Waddy b'fore Waddy got me. He was there when Bat come, seen Myles do his stuff, an' then went an' picked up the package. Seemed to me Tom looked awful hearty tonight for a man that dallied with his supper an' ain't et much of anythin'. Kind of voluble an' nervous, he was. Rest of you looked worn, but t'night he looked awful plump an' flourishin'. He ought to. He's got half Bat's bank notes plastered on him. I felt 'em when I stuck that cotton on his shoulder. See?"

He walked over and pulled back Tom's sweater.

Steve whistled feebly.

"And we," he said, "have been playing Russian banque for matches!"

Asey smiled. "Money seems to of done for him. He prob'ly could't bear to see his comft'ble old age on Lee's inheritance go bust b'fore his eyes. Feller, you prob'ly still love Lee, an' think you may of got her with Ros'lie gone, but deary me, you wouldn't of. You're cold-blooded, but at that she's got you beat—"

Dr. Cummings bustled in with his inevitable little black bag.

He looked at Tom without the slightest indication of surprise and nodded professionally.

"I didn't think," he said critically, "you were it, but I expected Asey'd clear this up tonight. Get me some hot water, someone. Asey, that's a nice clean wound, and—"

Angelica looked at him and rose.

"Let's," she said, "go into the living room before I scream!"

"Okay," Asey said. "Go easy there, doc. They's around fifty thousand on his chest. Ham, stay here, an' don't go snoozin' off again!"

In the living room, Betsey began to sob.

"I can't help it, but we've known him and—"

"Remember," Steve said sharply, pretending hard that he didn't feel the same way, "he planted that key on Hilda—did he know about her, Asey?"

"He knew everyone," Asey said, "an' everythin'. Prob'ly had that diamond marked to go, too."

"He used the typewriter yesterday," Myles said. "Probably he—"

"Did he leave Waddy's lighter behind on purpose?" Betsey asked.

"Prob'ly seemed a nice ironic little joke," Asey said. "He hired himself out to Waddy to cause trouble, an' he did just that. He also had Waddy in a spot. He could

say Waddy paid him to do it, an' Waddy'd of had some
time tryin' to prove he knew nothin' about Ros'lie,
under the circumstances."

"What on earth was all that to-do about the lamps?"
Betsey demanded.

"T'night in Ros'lie's room I tried the light, an' it
worked. Now Leary an' the doc both said the bulb was
dead, but it'd just been twisted up out of its socket
some, see, an' turned off that way. Tom's lamp in his
room was like that when I asked him some questions
the other night. I thought the bulb was gone, an' he said
to twist it. Just his way of turnin' off lamps, I gather. So
t'night to make sure I went into his room. Bulb there
wasn't twisted, but the lamp in Hilda's room had its
bulb twisted off. Lampshades was the wrong color to fit
the rooms, so it seemed to me they'd been switched.
You said that lamp b'longed to Tom's room, Betsey.
That was all."

"But why all that elaborate—" Angelica began.

"Didn't you hear Bat say the light in Ros'lie's room
had gone on an' then off? Well, Tom thought he'd do
some mixin'."

"It's odd," Myles said, "but tonight earlier, I found
that my bedroom light wouldn't go on, and changed the
bulb. I wonder if—"

"He was trying to work you in, too!" Betsey said.
"He—he had it out for all of us, didn't he? And think
what would have happened if you hadn't come back,
Asey! Think!"

They were still talking about it fifteen minutes later
when Asey heard the doctor call him.

"I got to go. See you pret' soon. Nope, I wouldn't
come if I was you. I'll run up to Boston with Ham an'
the rest, an' I'll bring Hilda back, too. Safe an' unpubli-
cized. I got to get over to Henderson's b'fore I start, an'
grab Bat's ole package, too. It's locked in my hatch—
speakin' of loot, Myles, you got some comin' to you."

"I—what?"

"R'wards for catchin' Bat. 'Bout fifteen thousand I know of."

He hoped the news would take their thoughts off Tom's departure, and Angelica saw to it that it did.

"Fifteen thousand! Myles, what are you going to *do* with it? How are you going to spend it?"

Myles polished his pince nez casually.

"I think," he said calmly, "I shall buy Betsey two new sweaters for a birthday present."

Angelica hooted. "With fifteen thousand staring you in the face, all you can think of is two sweaters?"

"Well," Myles said, "well—"

"You can go to England," Betsey said, "with your friend Amory Thatcher, and you can just roam around London to your heart's content. And buy books, and— Myles, for Pete's sakes, don't you want to travel?"

"P'raps," Asey suggested with a chuckle, "p'raps he'd like to take another bus trip."

Steve and Betsey hooted, but Myles's eyes gleamed as he put on his pince nez and looked thoughtfully at Angelica.

"Perhaps," he said, "perhaps."